Shadow of the Noose

Magnus DeWitt studied the prisoner, at once infuriated by him yet admiring his audacity and agility under interrogation.

"Perhaps you'd be more cooperative if we put you to the torture," DeWitt suggested.

"I would immediately tell you anything that you wish to know, Major," said Laidlow. "For I am extremely faint-hearted and cannot stand pain."

"Such as your status as one of Washington's trusted spies?"

"If you wish, sir."

"And the names of your fellow spies? Bell and Hunter, for instance?"

"As you desire, sir."

"You have bedded your cousin?" DeWitt frowned.

"Under torture I'd admit that, but no other way," said Laidlow. "Who is there who would not like to make love to the charming Molly?"

Major DeWitt reddened guiltily and turned away to leave. "We will no doubt hang you, you know."

"Really? For what? There is no proof!"

"Sir Henry Clinton needs an example to deter other Rebel spies. And you, sir, are *it!*"

The FREEDOM FIGHTERS *Series*

TOMAHAWKS AND LONG RIFLES

MUSKETS OF '76

THE KING'S CANNON

THE
KING'S
CANNON

Jonathan Scofield

A DELL/BRYANS BOOK

Published by
Dell Publishing Co., Inc.
1 Dag Hammarskjold Plaza
New York, New York 10017

Dell ® TM 681510, Del Publishing Co., Inc.

ISBN: 0-440-04292-5

Printed in the United States of America

First printing—May 1981

PART ONE

1

"So you say Washington's rebel rabble have gone into hiberation at Valley Forge, Magnus? And the traitors of the Continental Congress ply their treason in Baltimore?" There was both rage and pleasure in the light blue eyes of aging Tory Alastair DeWitt as he discussed the progress of the American war with his red-coated visitor, his eldest son Magnus.

They sat before the fireplace of Alastair's study in the manor house overlooking the Hudson River. The weather was even worse than the usual icy mid-January day in New York, and Magnus was grateful for the warmth of the blazing fire before him. He had just arrived from New York City, where he served as adjutant to General Sir Henry Clinton.

Now Magnus drained the tankard of ale his father's pretty bond servant, Joanna Blake, had just delivered. He sighed and wiped his mouth on a fine linen napkin. "It's good to be home, Father," he said. "I prefer home to either New York City or Philadelphia, especially since I need not worry about spies here." Magnus's main task for Clinton was handling intelligence matters.

"Spies?" Alastair growled. "We have them even here in Hastings!" He leaned back in his chair and ran his fingers through his thinning hair. "The rebels would take away all the DeWitt business interests if they had their way—if Clinton and Howe hadn't driven them out of New York last year. When will the King's cannon put a stop to this nonsense? Two years and still the rebels hang on! And without the means to pay for a war! And against the might of the King! Ridiculous!"

Magnus nodded. "The word is that Mr. Washington isn't having an easy time of it, Father," he said, following what had become a British tradition in ignoring the rebels' military ranks. "Valley Forge is no paradise and provisions are scarce."

"Let us hope that they starve," Alastair declared. "That's no less than they deserve for their disloyalty to the Crown."

"It's taken a number of miracles to keep the rebels in the game, Father. Not the least of them was Howe's failure to press his advantage in Jersey in the end of '76. Sir Henry believes—and I agree with him—that we could have avoided the defeats at Trenton and Princeton and instead routed Washington and finished the war. All we had to do was chase the rebels across the Delaware."

"And now," Alastair said unhappily, "Howe has

fumbled once more, it would seem. We have both Philadelphia and New York, yet have traded Burgoyne and his army for them—a dear price, indeed. We still far outnumber the rebels. Why can't we put an end to them?"

"It's only a question of time," Magnus told his father. "Sir Henry is certain of it. Our spies say the rebels are freezing at Valley Forge. Desertions are soaring—and no one can know that better than I, for I interview deserters from the rebel ranks each day. Even if Washington's army survives the winter, it will be so depleted that we can easily wipe it out if we take the offensive this summer."

Alastair nodded, gazing at the glowing logs in the fireplace as he thought how costly the war had already been to the DeWitt business interests. "If the rebellion isn't put down soon," he declared, "a large part of your legacy will have been wiped out by the rebel privateers. We lost another boatload of dry goods last month, and our ship as well."

"In spite of the escort I arranged? Incredible, Father! Outrageous! Where?"

"Off the Virginia coast, I'm told. There were three of the pirate privateers against three of our ships, yet they put us to rout. And now it's said that the French are serious about becoming full partners with the rebels. If it comes about, if the French send ships into American waters, our trade may well be a thing of the past. Even now I must pay dearly for crews to sail our vessels."

The DeWitt merchantmen had been sailing the Atlantic ever since the 1760s and not one ship had been lost to squall or pirate—until now.

"Virginia," Magnus echoed musingly. "Sir Henry feels we ought to mount a campaign against the

South. We have a lot of friends down there. If we were to take Georgia, the Carolinas and Virginia, perhaps we could put a stop to the rebel's piracy once and for all. As for the French, I'm told there is precious little chance they'll do more than lend the rebels a few francs. Should they decide to send their fleet over here, they'll pay dearly for it, I should say, for their sailors simply do not measure up to the British forces."

"Let us hope that you're right," Alastair murmured, then picked up the bell to summon his bond servant. Joanna appeared a few moments later with fresh tankards of ale for both men.

Magnus noticed his father's openly admiring look at the girl, but he said nothing of it. He had known for some time that the slim, black-haired servant spent more nights in his father's bed than did his mother, Trientje DeWitt. But Magnus cared little about his father's keeping a mistress. Once Magnus himself had sampled Joanna's charms. He had found the girl willing, and for a time he had been hard-pressed to put her out of his mind. But he had, because it had been necessary.

"What about Schuyler, Father?" Magnus asked when the girl had left them alone. "He's twenty-two and finished with college. He ought to be getting on with his life. I've already arranged a spot for him with Sir Henry's personal guard and I have a good friend who'll shepherd him. All he need do is say the word."

Alastair shot his eldest son a sour look. "I fear he would rather paint or write poetry. Or perhaps play the confounded pianoforte! He won't listen

to me, won't even respond when I ask him why
he avoids the future as he does."

"I'll talk to him," Magnus said. "We've never
been close, perhaps because of the large difference
in our ages. But he's always listened to what I had
to say. Perhaps I can make him realize his responsibilities and bring him to his senses. If so, maybe
he'll go back to New York with me."

Alastair's lined face showed the conflict he felt.
There had long been a tradition in his family of
professional soldiering. He wanted Schuyler to
share it, and yet the boy seemed to him to be so
soft and artistically inclined, so different from
every other DeWitt. Alastair wondered if the boy
could make a soldier at all, if he wanted the youth
to even try to follow the family tradition.

Suddenly the sound of his wife's pianoforte
drifted to his ears. Since Trientje was away, visiting
a sister in Connecticut, it could only mean that . . .
"Your brother seems to have returned from the
Golden Hawk, Magnus," he said.

Magnus listened for a moment, then grinned
wryly. "Well, at least he's not playing a rebel
marching song."

Alastair heaved his not-inconsiderable girth
from his easy chair and made his way to the door.
"Thank God," he said, "that the boy has better
sense than that—although he spends a great
amount of time at the tavern with its rabble-rous-
ing elements."

The Golden Hawk stood on the stagecoach trail
overlooking the Hudson. It had long been a meeting place for the revolutionaries, though its proprietor, Benjamin Ballis, had somehow managed

to keep it open to trade from Loyalists and Patriots alike. He had taken no sides publicly, although Alastair suspected that Ben leaned toward the Patriot side. Alastair forgave the man mainly because the DeWitts had supplied Ballis with imported whiskey and other goods for some years, both before the colonials' trouble-making "non-importation policy" and since.

Before the outbreak of hostilities, Alastair had spent many a night sitting before the Hawk's huge fireplace, eating, drinking and arguing politics with Ben. But not since—mainly because of Alastair's reputation as a dyed-in-the-wool Tory. His mere appearance in the tavern sparked the immediate hostility of any rebel-sympathizer and even that of some of the fence-straddlers. Things had been far worse in 1776, of course, when the rebels held New York. But ever since Howe had taken the rebel forts surrounding Manhattan, Long Island and Staten Island, local hostility toward loyalists had been restricted to little more than an occasional exchange of words. A red-coated batallion from the city could easily be summoned to retaliate if the rebels around Hastings should cause trouble. And there was also the regiment of Tory dragoons formed by Magnus in the aftermath of Howe's New York victories. Though it was now in the city with Clinton, it too was available in the event of trouble. . . .

"How goes your war, Magnus?" Schuyler asked with a slightly mocking grin. He had left the piano and came to the study when his father called him, and now he stood shaking his brother's hand in greeting. There was a startling difference in their heights, Magnus a good six inches shorter than his younger brother, although they shared the blond good looks of the DeWitts. "Has Sir Henry arranged to send Howe back to London yet so he can take over the war? And are you in New York or Philadelphia? I've heard Philadelphia's a beautiful city, with a gaggle of comely wenches on every streetcorner."

Magnus made a face as he threw an arm about Schuyler's shoulders. "Philadelphia may be beautiful," he said, "but you can have it. As for what you call 'my war,' it ought to be your war as well, Schuyler. Isn't it about time you begin to repay our father and our King for our prosperity? Were it not for them, you should have no pianoforte to play," he said jokingly.

Schuyler shook his head smiling at the remark. "And what of our mother, Magnus? It's my understanding that the pianoforte came to her from our Dutch grandfather. Must I not also repay her? And him? And what about the Dutch King?"

Alastair shot his younger son an unhappy look. "What Magnus says is true enough, boy," he said. "Your commission in the King's army is waiting for you. Your brother was kind enough to arrange it, and he'd like you to go back with him to take it up."

"As would you, Father?"

"As would I."

Schuyler was about to say something more when Joanna knocked on the door and entered the room. She brought Schuyler an ale, delivering it with a faint smile that made him look at her in surprise. There had been more than a few times when he had envied his father this pretty girl's attentions, but she had conscientiously maintained an impassive attitude toward him. He wondered if her strange smile portended a change in her feelings, but then he shrugged off the thought. After all, she belonged to his father, he reminded himself.

"Can't the army make do without me for another few months, Father?" Schuyler asked. "I have little thought of—"

"We would have no Army at all," his brother scolded, "if all of us thought and acted as you do."

"I daresay King George has quite enough regulars to do his bidding without me, Magnus. He managed to defeat Washington up and down the Delaware last fall. Even occupied Philadelphia and sent Congress scurrying for cover."

"And lost Burgoyne's army at Saratoga," Magnus broke in.

"One loss against a great many victories," Schuyler observed. "I fail to see that my presence is necessary."

"Are you telling us you won't serve His Majesty?" Alastair demanded, his cheeks growing flushed.

"Of course not, Father," Schuyler said, rising from his chair. He looked at his father, noticing the redness of his face. He had seen the old man seem to approach apoplexy before and knew he'd better calm him down. "I only mean that I've just ended my studies and need some time to myself. Since I left Yale I've been without responsibilities for the first time in my life, and must admit I'm rather enjoying it."

"With the war raging around you?" Magnus exclaimed. "With rebel spies everywhere? With the future of the colonies in doubt because of the irresponsible thinking of a few so-called patriots?

How can you ignore all that? Don't you have any pride? Don't you care about the turmoil around us?"

Schuyler shrugged. "The war is not mine," he said mildly. "I talk about it with those who wish to. And I listen to what they have to say of it. I do not agree with all of the rebels' contentions, although I think they do have a point here and there which is well taken. Perhaps our King *has* been a trifle unfair with us. Who knows? Not that I favor the revolution," he added. "If the war continues, we shan't have much of an economy, from what I hear. It's said that the Continental Congress is wearing out the printing presses printing new, nearly worthless money to pay the army."

In the end, Schuyler agreed that he would take up his commission in June and "do my best" to continue the family tradition "by serving brilliantly." No one noticed the slight edge of self-deprecating irony in his voice.

"I'll drink to that," his father said, smiling for the first time. The three male DeWitts raised their tankards and downed what was left of their drinks.

2

MAGNUS DEWITT was refreshed after his two
weeks at home with his father and brother,
and only a little disappointed that Schuyler
could not be convinced to come to New York until
he accepted his commission in June.

Once he returned to his desk in Sir Henry Clinton's headquarters, Magnus had little time to dwell
upon anything but work. As Sir Henry's adjutant
and one of his most important advisers, Major
Magnus DeWitt performed a number of vital func-
tions for his superior.

It was Clinton's plans which Howe had used to
accomplish the brilliant British victory over Long
Island and New York less than eighteen months
ago, and everyone knew it was only a matter of

time before Clinton would replace Sir William Howe as commander in chief of the British forces in America. Howe had had a less than smashing record in 1777, and he had been grumbling for months that he was going to resign.

And so, Sir Henry had ordered Magnus to prepare to become the working head of British intelligence in the colonies by heading up a special effort designed to turn up the identities of rebel spies in British territory.

It was not, Magnus soon discovered, an easy task. Not a day passed without interviewing a number of deserters from Washington's Valley Forge forces, yet none either could or would sell out any of the spies operating on the Continental Army's behalf in and around New York and Philadelphia. What the deserters did tell Magnus was that Washington had so many spies "he knows when Howe will attack before Howe does."

If it were true, Magnus could do little about it. Not until late in April did he come up with something of real interest—a sealed note from "A Friend of the King" that was delivered by a tall, spindly-legged man who claimed to be a rebel deserter and asked for Magnus by name. The note had fantastic implications and excited even such a veteran of intelligence work as Magnus:

> Sir: I am in a position to deliver a high command (of the Continentals) to the King—if the right terms can be agreed upon. I will contact you again through the courier who delivered this to learn what you will offer.
>
> A Friend of the King

Magnus tried to pump the courier for information, but without success. He was not surprised, for none but an idiot would pick a messenger with a loose tongue for such an important mission.

For hours Magnus puzzled over the identity of the mysterious "Friend of the King," but in the end had not a clue. Clinton was delighted to learn of the contact and speculated freely. He and Magnus reviewed the entire list of known Patriot generals before reaching the conclusion that they had no idea which one it was. Sir Henry instructed Magnus that he wanted to be kept personally informed about any future messages arriving from the turncoat rebel general.

Now events began to accelerate. First came the report from London that the French had indeed signed a treaty with the rebels to play an active part in the American Revolution. Then, not long afterward, came other news—more important news in Clinton's headquarters—the news that Sir William Howe's resignation had been accepted and Sir Henry was the new commander in chief.

Magnus was with Sir Henry when he received the news from the captain of a British merchantman. After the captain left, Sir Henry was strangely subdued. When Magnus commented upon it, the British general shook his head sadly and dropped his round body into the chair behind his desk.

"What you fail to perceive, Magnus old boy, is that aside from the fact that in addition to the rebels I must also face the French—and their fleet—being given command places me in a difficult position. It means there is no one above me."

Magnus, dumbfounded, stared silently at his superior.

Sir Henry paid him no heed, beginning to drum on the desk with the fingers of his right hand. "In the past," the new commander in chief continued, "there has always been someone above me to approve or disapprove the plans I've drawn, or order changes in them which resulted in their betterment. But now . . ." For a moment Clinton looked absolutely desolate. Then his expression changed, his eyes brightening. "By George!" he declared. "Magnus, my boy, I shall create my own superior—in my mind, of course. I will call him 'Perfection.' No, make that Lord Perfection. Or perhaps General Perfection. Hereafter, I will let the general assess my plans against his own standards. What think ye of that, Major DeWitt?"

Magnus wasn't certain what he thought, or that Sir Henry could actually be serious. He smiled uncertainly and nodded in approval. To commit himself more than that was to court disaster; the general was both clever and, at times, very eccentric.

"Done!" cried Sir Henry, striding forward to embrace his aide, then taking Magnus's hand for a firm handshake. "I gratefully accept your earnest congratulations, my good Major DeWitt, and do hereby appoint you as my adjutant. Together, you and I—and General Perfection, of course—will grind the rebels under our heels. Sir William was much too soft on them. He would rather have licked their boots than their army!"

If Clinton's odd behavior left Magnus wondering about the new commander in chief, it had no adverse effect on the zeal with which he attacked his duties. Soon after the general's new appointment, Magnus uncovered two Patriot double agents, but left them free to continue their spying so that Clinton could use them.

Then came a second message from the turncoat rebel general.

> *What say your superiors to my proposal, Major DeWitt? I await your reply by my personal courier.*
>
> A Friend of the King

Apprised of the message, Sir Henry was undecided what to do. "I simply can't promise the blighter anything, Magnus, until I have an idea what he can deliver," he said.

"I'll tell him that," Magnus said. "Shall I mention that he'll have to contact me in Philadelphia hereafter?"

Clinton shook his head. "If he's anybody at all, he'll probably already know about our change in command."

Magnus gave a great deal of thought to his response to the would-be turncoat and finally wrote:

> *We should look favorably upon your proposal, sir, if only we had an idea of your importance in your army's scheme of things. Send us something to show you are privy to important information and command so that we may negotiate with you in earnest.*

A week later, Clinton and his staff boarded a ship for the short voyage to Philadelphia. Magnus was even more excited than Clinton as his superior officially relieved Sir William Howe, who would soon be sailing for England.

Several days later, however, the excitement that

permeated Clinton's staff turned to trepidation as word came that the French fleet had set sail for America some time ago, possibly to support a rebel attempt to retake Philadelphia.

Sir Henry was beside himself, and the knowing smirk on Howe's face when the new commander in chief began sounding him out on his ideas about the French fleet's destination did not help Clinton's tortured mind. Clinton was not amused when Howe said, "I'm sure, dear fellow, that Lord Germain will shortly inform you of France's intentions." Lord Germain was Secretary of State for the colonies in Lord North's cabinet, and his incessant meddling in the war was only one of several reasons he was thoroughly despised by British officers.

Magnus spent the early days of his stay in Philadelphia questioning Howe's agents as discreetly as he could about the possible identity of the turncoat general he was corresponding with. Only one would venture a guess as to the man's identity. His guess startled Magnus: General Charles Lee.

"Lee?" Magnus repeated, rising from the chair he occupied behind his desk in Clinton's headquarters. "We just exchanged him!" The agent shrugged. But when he had gone, Magnus reconsidered the suggestion and came to the conclusion that it might be correct.

Lee had been captured by the British in December of '76 while foolishly attempting to meet his mistress in a tavern three miles into territory held by the British in New Jersey. It was a tip from a British double agent which had led to Lee's capture, and he was taken by troops or a regiment he had at one time commanded in Portugal. There had been much laughter in the British ranks when word got around about Lee's blunder.

Magnus had met Lee on several occasions and had always come away wondering why he was a prisoner; Lee's sympathies seemed to lie more with his captors than with his former confederates of the Revolutionary Army. Until early in April, little more than a month ago, Lee had been confined in New York. At that time he was exchanged for a British officer and now was reported to be back in Valley Forge with Washington.

Lee? Yes, Magnus thought, he could be the one. The question was: Had he been given back the number two position he had formerly held in Washington's command? Magnus had no intelligence reports indicating more than Lee's mere presence on the Valley Forge scene.

He hurried in to tell Clinton and the new commander was jubilant. Clinton agreed with Magnus's conclusion, telling him that he, too, had "chatted" with Lee back in New York. His evaluation was that Lee would rather serve with the British than with the rebels. "He once even came right out and asked me if I could get him a generalship in the British army, Magnus!"

"What did you say to that, General?"

"At the time I was in no position to arrange it, even had I wished to. But I wouldn't even have tried, for I don't like the man. He's a pompous ass. Believes he's the world's most knowledgeable strategist. He criticized Washington constantly, so much so that even I could only partly agree with him."

"We can't use him, then?" Magnus said, his expression showing his disappointment.

Clinton rose from his chair to wrap an arm around his aide's shoulder. "Of course we can, Magnus, don't get the wrong impression. However, a lot depends on whether or not Washington is insane enough to give the fool important responsibilities. Your job is to find out what Lee's status is."

That night Magnus attended a ball given by Mrs. Lottie Mayer, wife of a prominent Philadelphia Tory, but his mind was far away from the festivities. He was jogged back to the present only when Captain John Andre, a tall, handsome youth on Howe's staff, approached him and asked for a moment.

Magnus was startled by what Andre had to say. The man wanted a slot on Clinton's staff! Incredible cheek, Magnus thought.

Before Magnus could reply, the brash young officer was swept away by not one but two beautiful Loyalist belles. Watching Andre dancing with the beautiful Peggy Shippen, who was taking Philadelphia by storm in spite of the tenseness of the times, Magnus shook his head. Andre was merely a dandy wearing a British officer's uniform, he thought sourly.

Nonetheless, Magnus could not help but admire Andre's success with the ladies. He half-wished that he had been born tall and aristocratic-looking instead of short and stocky. Though only in his thirties, Magnus was already fighting the heritage which had made his father portly at an early age. Only Schuyler of the male DeWitts in the past hundred years had escaped the family's trademark, he growing tall and remaining trim in spite of his inactivity since graduating from Yale.

Schuyler. The thought of his brother brought

Magnus back to the problem of Captain Andre.
If Howe's aide were successful in joining Clinton's
staff, Magnus might have difficulty in ultimately
getting Schuyler on the staff. Well, Magnus would
see about that. He had been with Sir Henry since
Breed's Hill in Boston and knew his general's every
thought. That Magnus had Clinton's respect was
attested to by his promotion to major last year,
when an opening had come up with the death of
another major during the fighting at Brandywine.
There were other captains whose seniority entitled
them to the promotion, but Sir Henry had given it
to Magnus.

Not that Magnus needed the extra pay. Even in
the rebel-ravaged economy of the 1770s, the De-
Witt fortune was solid and immense. Magnus
could secure whatever cash he needed simply by
asking for it. But the prestige was important, and
Magnus knew that the higher up he advanced, the
more he could count on as a reward when the war
was history and rebel land holdings were distributed.

Seeing Andre bow to his partner as his dance
ended, and then turn from the beautiful Miss Shippen to look for him, Magnus slipped out of the
ballroom and was soon walking toward his own
quarters a few blocks away. He would avoid Andre
for the time being. Clinton's new staff would be
little different from his old one. And it certainly did
not need a dandy on it.

The next day Sir Henry announced that he
would evacuate Philadelphia. Stores would be
shipped up the Delaware and thence to New York,

while the troops would be ferried across the river, and would then march through Jersey to Perth Amboy, where they would be ferried across to Staten Island, then to New York. The troops would have gone by sea, he told his staff in response to a question, but for the "uncertain whereabouts" of the French fleet.

"With the rebels little more than twenty miles away," Clinton told his staff, "our withdrawal must be as quiet as possible. I'd suggest that for your own safety all of you keep absolutely secret what I have told you. If Washington's sharp-shooters attend our crossing of the Delaware, they might well cut us all down. They have no respect for officers."

Sir Henry ordered that the army's engineers be set to work improving the city's fortifications in hopes of concealing British intentions "as long as possible." Magnus suggested that they could, with the proper use of letters, trick the enemy into believing the British would move their troops by sea.

"How?" Clinton asked.

"Letters must be written by every staff member to someone in New York. Each should drop a subtle hint that the writer will soon be on a sea voyage. I'll see that the best of the letters are intercepted by the rebels."

"Brilliant," Sir Henry exclaimed.

So it was that Magnus arranged with several of his double agents to deliver the bogus mail to Washington's espionage people at Valley Forge at the proper time.

Two days later, as British engineers were busily engaged in improving Philadelphia's fortifications, Magnus received a visitor—the messenger of the rebel turncoat. The man produced a wax-sealed message from a shirt pocket and handed it to Magnus.

The moment he had unsealed and read it, Magnus became more excited than he had been in a very long time.

> *Lafayette has been ordered to Barren Hill to reconnoiter. He will be in place by the twentieth of May. If you move fast, you can take him.*
>
> *Give my messenger a thousand dollars cash to show your good faith and appreciation. I trust this will prove to you that I am privy to important information. If this is clear, perhaps you will feel free to make me an offer I cannot refuse. Respond earliest.*
>
> A Friend of the King

Barren Hill? Magnus knew where it was, but nonetheless checked the map of the Philadelphia area that was on the wall of his office. It was ten miles or so north of the city, along the Schuylkill River halfway between Philadelphia and Valley Forge. Ideal for the operation the traitor described.

Perhaps, Magnus exulted, they really could take Lafayette with one swift stroke. He had the messenger wait while he arranged for the cash requested. When he gave it to the man he told him to return in a week. "I shall have something 'hard' to pass along to your friend."

Clinton was overjoyed at Magnus's news. "What a stroke of good fortune," he exclaimed. "We must make good use of it, Magnus, my boy. Barren Hill, eh? Good show!"

"I would urge that we tell as few people about this as possible, General," Magnus cautioned. "And perhaps wait until just before we strike to tell anyone at all. The rebel spies in the city have their ears open for just such news as this, I fear."

"Well said, Magnus," Clinton responded. "I heartily agree. This is much too important a prize to allow anything to interfere with its taking. I shall consult with General Perfection and lay my plans immediately. Taking Lafayette at the very beginning of my command will be a bright feather in my cap! It will make Lord North very happy, I should think."

Magnus nodded. "It will not please Washington," he said. "And perhaps the French might rethink their treaty with the rebels after the marquis is ours."

"Let us hope so, Magnus. Now I must make plans for two great events: the capture of the Marquis de Lafayette and his introduction to my inept predecessor and Philadelphia society at a little party on the twenty-first."

Magnus prayed General Perfection would caution Clinton not to be overly optimistic. Not even the best-laid plans were proof against failure.

3

"HAVE YOU LOST your senses, girl?" Schuyler DeWitt whispered to Joanna Blake, who stood before his bed clothed only in a thin cotton nightgown. His father's bedchambers were a scant few yards away across the hallway.

Joanna only shook her head, giving him a slow and tantalizing smile. Barely seventeen, the girl looked and acted a good deal older, her body ripe and ready, her mind quick and shrewd.

Her family had been broken up early and she had lived by her wits ever since. She was eventually exiled from England as an indentured bond servant after being charged with public lewdness by the jealous wife of a nobleman who had befriended her. Alastair DeWitt had been taken with her from his first sight of her, his marriage to

Trientje DeWitt having long since foundered. He
had brought Joanna into DeWitt Manor as a maid
two years earlier and waited only a month before
taking her to his bed. What Joanna felt for old
Alastair was difficult to judge, for she was close-
mouthed about it. If she disliked his pawings, she
never let on. For his part, Alastair could not have
been more satisfied.

Now Joanna shrugged off the nightgown.

She stood before Schuyler, her eyes almost
closed, her full mouth parted slightly, her black
hair accenting the whiteness of her unblemished
flesh.

Schuyler swallowed hard, but said nothing more
as his eyes were drawn to the fullness of the girl's
up-turned breasts, the flatness of her ivory belly,
the juncture of her thighs above long, pretty legs.
He reached for her arms and pulled her down
beneath the canopy of his four-poster bed.

She made no effort to avoid his mouth, which
clamped hungrily down on hers. Soon he was
touching her flesh where he wanted to, where he
had to. He was not gentle. He did not need to be.
And she did not want him to be, although she
gave him no sign at all as to her desires before,
during or after their assignation.

When it was over, she left him abruptly. He had
barely stopped the furious thrusts with which his
passion climaxed when she was no longer beneath
him.

"Where are you going?" he demanded as the
girl put on the nightgown she had dropped by
the bed.

"Why, to sleep, Master Schuyler. It's after midnight."

Schuyler stared at her in consternation as she went quickly out the door and closed it behind her. He could not find sleep for many hours afterward; his mind was a jumble of thoughts and emotions.

What had prompted Joanna to come to him? Her response to his lovemaking had spoken of great passion. Yet she had said nothing, and had been so cold and aloof afterward.

Why?

When finally he slept he was still struggling to find an answer.

To further mystify Schuyler, for the next two weeks Joanna barely acknowledged his existence. She was polite enough when called upon to be—in the presence of his father or Magnus—but she managed to avoid ever being alone with him.

Then Schuyler returned from an evening at the tavern to find his bed occupied by her once again. Schuyler was dumbfounded and for a moment all he could do was stare at the girl, whose eyes were closed as if in sleep, the quilt pulled up to her chin.

Knowing the fair flesh beneath the quilt, Schuyler's pulse quickened. "Joanna?" he said softly. When she did not respond, he approached and stood next to the bed. He spoke her name again, this time noting that one of her eyelids seemed to give a slight flutter at the sound of his voice.

A faint smile appeared on his handsome face. It seems, he thought, that Father's mistress is a teasing wench. Well, if she liked to play, he would accommodate her. He grabbed the edge of the quilt and yanked it to the foot of the bed, revealing Joanna in all her glory.

Her eyes opened wide, but she made not a

sound. Nor did she attempt to cover up. Instead, she smiled and held out her arms to him. He resisted for a few moments, still wondering at her appearance in his room, then fell upon her and kissed her hungrily.

"I have been awaiting your return, Master Schuyler," she whispered, "with great longing."

Schuyler, holding himself above her with his long arms, shook his head in confusion. "Why?" he murmured, his eyes burning into her. "Why are you playing this infernal game with me? Why did you pay me a visit before? Why have you avoided me since? Why have you returned? You're an enigma, woman!"

"Make love to me," she said.

"Not until you answer my questions."

But as adamant as Schuyler tried to be with the girl, he soon learned he was weak and could not resist satiating himself with her flesh. Afterward, she curled up in his arms with a contented sigh.

It was easy to understand his father's lust for this slip of a girl, and why he would want to keep her for himself. But the thought made him scowl, for he did not like the idea of Joanna performing with his father as she performed with him.

"Now," he whispered to the girl, "you must tell me what kind of game you're playing. Why do you come to me when you are my father's . . . property?"

Joanna sighed deeply and buried her face in the coarse golden hair that covered Schuyler's chest. "Not now," she said. "I'm too tired."

He shook her, but she had gone limp. Finally he gave up, but to make certain she would still be there when he awakened, Schuyler eased himself out of bed and tiptoed over to the door to lock it. Then he hid the key under the mattress.

He stroked the girl's back until she turned over and again curled up against him. After a time, Schuyler fell into a deep sleep. He was still asleep when, early the next morning, Joshua awoke and slipped out of bed to dress and leave. She laughed softly upon finding the door locked, then reached into the pocket of her robe for a key, unlocked the door and left. She had keys to all the upstairs rooms of the DeWitt Manor house.

But afterward Joanna no longer avoided Schuyler, at least not when Alastair was absent. She went out of her way to please him, though never would she permit a discussion of the whys of their situation. Schuyler, thoroughly infatuated with her, finally resigned himself to enjoying her while he could, after weeks of swearing at himself for allowing her to sidestep the issue. Each time she left after paying him a visit, he vowed he would make her explain the next time. But he never did.

"What about my father?" he had demanded on a night when he knew she had come to him directly from his father's bed.

"Shhhh," she responded, placing her tiny white hand over his lips. "We must not speak of it, not now."

"But when? When he discovers us in bed? It might cause him a seizure of apoplexy!"

"The more reason we mustn't allow that to happen, darling Schuyler," she replied. "Now use me. My body cries out for you."

Hating himself for his weakness, Schuyler used the girl as she demanded and exhausted them both.

He looked for but did not find solace in his

music or his visits with his friends at the Golden Hawk. His growing guilt over the relationship with Joanna caused him to avoid his father completely. Fortunately, Alastair was kept busy by the press of business interests, making frequent trips to and from the city, and by his wife, Trientje, who had at last returned from her Connecticut visit to her sister.

Schuyler's unhappiness only increased with the approach of his scheduled June 1 departure to serve with Magnus in the British Army. He had become extremely possessive of Joanna and distressed over her continuing relationship with his father.

After supper in the family dining room one night, Alastair pointedly told Joanna he had just received some books about England which she might like to see. They were in his bedchamber and he would be glad to show them to her later.

Schuyler gritted his teeth over the thinly veiled invitation. He wondered at Alastair's aplomb, conducting his affair with Joanna under his wife's very nose. He stole a quick glance at his mother at the other end of the table. Still an attractive woman in spite of her fifty-plus years, Trientje DeWitt ignored the exchange between her husband and his bond servant. She sat contentedly sipping her tea—English tea, in spite of the Colonial non-importation policy—her expression and manner entirely unperturbed. Did his mother also have a lover?

The smile Joanna flashed Alastair as she thanked him for his "kind invitation" infuriated Schuyler so much that he excused himself and left. He stormed out of the house and went to the stable for a horse. As he rode toward the tavern, he called himself a fool for letting himself get involved with Joanna at the outset. He should have taken her when she offered herself, then quit her cold. How, he seethed, could she go from his father's bed to his, from accepting his father's withered, old body to . . . He let out a groan of anguish and spurred the horse to greater speed.

Halfway to the tavern, he was stopped by a redcoat patrol. Schuyler hardly believed it when the officer thrust a pistol under his nose and demanded to know who he was and where he was going.

"Schuyler DeWitt. I'm a loyal subject of King George, on my way to the Golden Hawk Tavern," Schuyler said.

"DeWitt?" the redcoat officer repeated. "Never heard of you. If you're such a loyal subject of the King, fellow, how is it you're not in the New York Dragoons?"

"I've just returned from college," Schuyler responded. "My father is Alastair DeWitt of DeWitt Shipping. Surely you've heard of—"

"Never heard of him or it," the officer said, still holding the weapon to Schuyler's face. "We'll just search you and make sure you're not a rebel spy."

"Ridiculous!" Schuyler declared, his voice rising in anger. "I shall be wearing an officer's uniform just like yours, sir, when I join General Clinton in June."

"A likely tale," the redcoat sneered. "Now get off your horse and empty your pockets or you shan't live to see June."

Given no choice, Schuyler dismounted and rummaged through his pockets for proof of his identity. When he produced a Yale identification letter, the officer scowled fiercely. "Isn't that the place where they preach insurrection? Where they encourage the shooting of British officers on sight?"

"That's Harvard," Schuyler said, "not Yale. It's in Boston, while Yale's just up the river in Connecticut." Schuyler spoke the truth; Harvard was a hotbed of anti-British sentiment. Yale, however, was little better. By the time Schuyler had completed his studies there, the anti-British feeling at Yale rivalled that at Harvard and Schuyler rarely spoke of his family's prominent status in Loyalist circles.

"That may be, but certainly the Golden Hawk is a center for rebel activity," the officer said in challenging tones.

"There's little rebel activity in all of New York at present," Schuyler retorted hotly. "And the tavern would have nothing to do with it in any case."

"It welcomes rebel sympathizers," the officer said. "We've just come from there and seen them."

"Ben Ballis welcomes Loyalists as well," Schuyler said. "Rebels have need of food and drink and the tavern owner has need of money."

"You're a smart one, aren't you? I should teach you some respect for your superiors."

"You are not my superior," Schuyler declared, glaring at the redcoat. "As for respect—"

Schuyler had barely uttered the last word before he was thrown to the turf beside the road, knocked unconscious by one swift blow to the temple from the officer's pistol.

When he awoke, he was alone except for his

horse, which had wandered a short distance away
to a pasture and was nibbling at the new spring
growth of grass. It was not until he was astride
the horse that the full memory of what had just
happened came to him. His aching head exploded
with angry thoughts, and he vowed to extract re-
venge from the British officer. The thought only
partially soothed his feelings as he completed his
interrupted journey to the tavern.

Ben Ballis summoned his young daughter to
put a cold compress on Schuyler's swelling temple
while he listened to the youth's recounting of the
attack.

"I recall the bastards," Ben said quietly. "Cocky
officer they had. Seemed itching for a fight, that
one. I almost had to throw him out myself. Thank
the Lord I didn't, for I have enough trouble trying to stay in business without having the British
Army on my back."

"He had cheek, but no courage," Schuyler said
ruefully. "If he's dismounted and given me a
chance, I'd have shown him a fight. I learned self-
defense at Yale and can stand up to anyone, as
long as they're not swinging a pistol or knife at
me."

"What you didn't learn, Schuyler," Ben said,
"is that there are those in this world who avoid
the rules like the plague. Surprise is the key to
their strategy."

After Ben left, Schuyler was approached by a
short, wiry black-haired man only a little older
than himself. It was Scott Laidlow, with whom
Schuyler had spoken on a few previous occasions
in the tavern. "I couldn't help hearing about the
trouble you had," Laidlow said. "Sorry about it."

"Thanks, but it could've been worse. Sit down and join me."

Scott had a willing ear as well as a friendly manner and Schuyler had liked him the first time they'd met. By the end of the evening, buoyed by a number of tankards of ale, the youngest DeWitt had confided his innermost thoughts to Laidlow. He had even spoken of his love for the beautiful Joanna. Finally, their conversation turned to the war.

"Have you heard about the French signing a treaty with the rebels?" Scott asked. "It's bound to complicate the war and give the patriots a real chance for the first time."

Schuyler frowned. "Really? When? My father will curse the French royally! He's . . . the family's in shipping and if the French come in, ships and all, we'll likely be put out of business."

"Your father's a Tory? Do you agree with his views?"

"Not entirely, Scott, but I suppose I'm a lot more Loyalist than rebel. And soon I'll be wearing a red coat myself. My father's opposed to anything that will change the way things were, actually. It's understandable when you consider his position, running an import-export business. The war has not been good for his business."

"Have you considered the other side of it?" Scott said carefully.

"My father scoffs at the rebels' view, Scott. He calls them ungrateful wretches, and feels they're entirely wrong. If he wore a redcoat uniform, no doubt he'd be a fierce officer indeed."

"What do *you* think?"

"My views are mixed. I've read Tom Paine's

pamphlets, *Common Sense* included, and heard the rhetoric. I can't deny the rebels make some good points, that King George and Lord North have committed some monumental errors in judgment. Still, the King has financed the colonies from the start and we shouldn't be nearly as well off as we are without his help. I don't believe he's wrong to expect a degree of loyalty from us."

"Then you agree that we should have put up with the ridiculous and unfair taxes to pay for the mother country's battles with the French and Spaniards? Or being given no voice in our own affairs? Or having people who know nothing of conditions here lay down the laws for Americans to follow?"

Schuyler had to smile at the emotion in Laidlow's tone and words. "I'd say you could serve on the rebels' Continental Congress, Scott," Schuyler said.

"I was in Boston and participated in a certain tea party," Scott said, "and was wounded by a British bayonet at Breed's Hill."

"My brother was at Breed's Hill," Schuyler said. "He's an aide for Clinton."

"Doesn't matter now, Schuyler. I'm no longer in the army. I got over my wound and now I make a living driving the stage between here and Rhode Island. I'm picking up a stage north to Providence tomorrow."

"How do you feel about the British now?" Schuyler asked, "and about Loyalists like me?"

The man grinned. "I'm talking to you, right? You don't see me getting angry when I talk about Breed's Hill, do you? I'm pretty well over it, I'd say. I still dislike the British and sure don't agree

with your father's or your views about the King's
right to loyalty. But I'm just a workingman now
and likely to remain so."

"If I were you, Scott, I'd watch out for that
British officer I encountered tonight. And hereabouts, anyway, I'd take pains to quiet my views
against the King. There are Loyalist radicals
around here who'd brew up some tar the minute
they found out how you feel."

"My friend," Scott said, "I thank you for the
advice. I shall remember it."

When Scott left and retired to his room at the
tavern, Schuyler wondered if any man who had
participated in the Boston Tea Party and been
wounded at Breed's Hill could honestly go back
to being a mere workingman again. Nonetheless,
Schuyler put such questions aside in evaluating
Scott. He was an uneducated man, yet an astute
one, Schuyler thought, and one with radical views
which had a sincere ring to them. Schuyler had
not been joking when he'd suggested Scott could
have been in the Continental Congress. But regardless of their differing political views, he hoped
their paths would cross again in the future, for
a good friend was difficult to find in these times.

Joanna was awaiting Schuyler when he arrived
home. She cried out when she saw the lump on
his temple and questioned him about it. He told
her what had happened, saying that it was "ironic
that I shall soon be joining Magnus and wearing
a red coat of my own."

Joanna grew silent, her eyes large and luminous.
"I had heard that," she said. "I . . . I had hoped
you would not go. Your father needs at least one
of his sons at home."

"My father," Schuyler replied, "wishes me to wear the uniform of the King. He will not hear of my not taking my place in the DeWitt military history, and those feelings are shared by my brother Magnus. As for you," he added quietly, "you care far more about my father's interests than about mine."

The girl was silent for a long moment. "That's not true, Schuyler," she said at last, and moved up against him. "It's you I care about." Her lips brushed his. "I would die if you were hurt while serving with His Majesty's army. And I will miss you. Terribly!"

Schuyler's anger evaporated and he kissed the warmth of her mouth, enjoyed the softness of her body once again. "But I must serve with the army, Joanna," he murmured "It is ordained and I must, regardless of my personal feelings."

"No!" The girl stood away, fire in her dark eyes. "You must not serve, Schuyler. You will not. Not if—" She stopped mid-sentence, her expression threatening.

"If what, Joanna? If I want you?" Schuyler's eyes locked with hers and told her she had made a mistake. "I don't have you now," he continued. "Only when you decide you can spare me an evening, often even then I can . . ." he hesitated, wondering if he should say the words which were in his mind decided to throw caution to the wind and continued "smell my father's hands on your flesh, taste his saliva in your mouth. I cannot abide what is happening, Joanna, how you play with both of us!" He turned away and started up the stairs.

"What would you have me do, Schuyler?" she

replied, lowering her voice, but blocking his path.

"How long will you continue to service him, Joanna? Why must you do it at all?"

"Service him? What an ugly way to say it!" The girl backed away, her face contorted in rage. "Very well, Master Schuyler," she declared. "Go to your brother! And may you both rot in hell!" She fled toward the servants' quarters before Schuyler could respond.

As he ascended the staircase to the second floor bedchambers, Schuyler wondered disconsolately whether he would ever again taste that willing mouth, ever again become a part of Joanna's wonderful body.

Arriving in his bedchambers, he cursed himself for a fool.

4

MAJOR MAGNUS DEWITT did not sleep well on the night before the British were to spring a trap on Lafayette's rebel detachment at Barren Hill.

Magnus was convinced the engagement could well be a turning point in the rebellion. Pulling it off could spark a rush of enthusiasm for Sir Henry Clinton and inspire him to ever greater victories during the campaign of '78. And, of course, it would dampen the spirits of the rebel soldiers to a degree that was difficult to assess.

And yet . . . Magnus had an uneasy feeling about the trap, the feeling that even though they had been as cautious as humanly possible, the rebel forces would somehow escape. He couldn't explain why he felt that way, nor would he admit his fears to anyone, but it was why he could not sleep.

Nonetheless, Magnus, in full battle dress, sat a horse beside Sir Henry Clinton as the army was readied for the charge up Barren Hill. To the north of their position was General Charles Grey and his cavalry, whose task would be to capture the rebels as they fled the scene when faced with the numbers and precision of the King's regulars.

With the first rays of the sun announcing the coming of dawn, Clinton personally gave the order to move up. Soon the air was echoing with the orders of Clinton's junior officers, and the long red line of soldiers, their Brown Bess muskets fitted with bayonets, began moving briskly through the trees and up the slope toward Lafayette's sleeping colonial soldiers.

As always, Magnus felt his heart pounding in cadence with the drums which now announced the British attack. Soon the first shots rang out and his heartbeat redoubled.

There was an excitement in battle unrivalled by anything in Magnus's experience. If he was not addicted to it, he relished each chance he was given to experience it. He almost wished he was once again a young ensign leading the first wave against the enemy. Almost—for even in a surprise attack, the number of casualties in that first wave was always formidable and, though loyal, Magnus had no special wish for death.

Now Magnus came back to reality with a start as the shots stopped and all that could be heard off in the distance were the shouts of redcoat officers and men.

He glanced over at Sir Henry, whose face was stormy, then at Sir William, whose presence was by special invitation from Clinton. Was there amusement in Howe's eyes? Magnus thought so.

"What in hell is happening up there?" Clinton roared.

"I'll ride up for a look, General," Magnus responded.

Clinton waved him on with his sword and Magnus prodded his mount into a gallop. The spring sun was blinding as Magnus cleared the trees and ascended the hill. In a matter of moments he came upon the advance units charging around an empty campsite and checking the trenches for the enemy.

"For God's sake, on to the river!" Magnus shouted. If the rebels weren't here, then they were at that very moment boarding boats to cross the Schuylkill for a race back to Valley Forge. Heedless of his own safety, Magnus spurred his horse westward down the hill toward the river.

His lack of ordinary caution nearly caused his death. A rebel musket barked and a musketball grazed his right thigh as he reached the river. The last of Lafayette's troops were in boats only twenty yards from shore as Magnus arrived. Behind him came the first wave of Clinton's army. The rebels fired from their boats and wreaked havoc on the redcoats' line with their accurate musket-shooting.

Magnus, furious at having been so careless as to take a wound, now hastily dismounted and took cover behind a rock. Moments later he was joined by redcoated infantrymen. He quickly commandeered a musket from one of the cavalrymen, then brought it to bear on the helmsman of a longboat fifty yards away. He grunted with satisfaction as his shot struck home and the man doubled over, then fell over the side and into the Schuylkill.

But the battle was over. The redcoat musketeers managed to wound a few of the fleeing rebels, but at a deadly cost to themselves. Lafayette's detachment was halfway back to Valley Forge before a fuming Sir Henry ordered a return to Philadelphia. What was to have been a glorious beginning for the Clinton regime had turned out to be ignominious defeat. Or at the very best, a non-victory.

Clinton seemed hardly to notice that his intelligence chief had been wounded. "How did he manage it?" Sir Henry demanded.

Magnus winced as the open wound on his thigh was cleaned by the British army doctor. "Must have been one of their spies tipped them off sir," Magnus said through gritted teeth. "He probably watched us form up early this morning, figured out where we were going and slipped out of the city just in front of us. Security's terrible at ingress and egress points, and half of Philadelphia seems to have passes signed by Sir William." Magnus had looked carefully around before completing his statement, but Sir William was nowhere in evidence. He had already left to go back to the city.

"We'll fix that, Magnus," Clinton said. "Starting tomorrow only passes with my seal are to be honored. And I want twice as many guards at every single in or out point in the city!"

Magnus did not point out that Sir Henry was closing the barn door after the cows had departed. Besides, he knew that the new security measures would make it easier to keep the direction of troop withdrawals secret when the entire army moved next month.

"How's your leg, Major?" Clinton inquired, suddenly aware that Magnus was hurt and might be lost to him for a few days.

"Could be worse, sir," Magnus responded. The doctor had just finished bandaging the wound.

"Your aide was fortunate, General," the doctor said, looking up with a smile. "The musketball struck in the fleshy part of the thigh and did very little damage. If it doesn't become infected in the next day or so, he should be fine. As it is, it will make walking a little difficult for only a day or two."

"I'm certainly glad to hear that," said Sir Henry. "For I have a strong desire to meet the spy who intervened to keep us from capturing the Marquis de Lafayette. Do I make myself clear?"

Rarely had Magnus seen such determination in Sir Henry's expression. He nodded. "I'll do my very best, General Clinton," he declared, wishing he could add, "but don't expect miracles from me. That spy's likely gone into hiding right now."

That Magnus's best would fall far short of turning up the culprit in the hectic days which followed soon became clear to the DeWitt heir. He called in his and Sir William's spies one after the other and questioned them carefully, but to no avail. It occurred to him that General Lee himself might have played a double game and alerted Lafayette, but he quickly discounted the idea, reasoning that Lee would have absolutely nothing to gain and could wind up a big loser by taking such an action.

Still, he found it vexing not to be able to turn up a single clue in the matter.

* * *

Back at Valley Forge, Lafayette was exultant over the Barren Hill fray as he reported to Washington. "I believe," he told the rebel commander, "that we did not please Sir Henry this day."

Washington, sober-faced throughout the report, now asked, "And how did you confirm the timing of the British attack?"

"Ah, we were fortunate, General," Lafayette declared. "It was one of our Philadelphia spies who brought the word. Bell was his name. He awoke me an hour before daybreak to inform me that Clinton was already on the move."

"Bell? Matthew Bell?" Washington said.

"That's correct," Lafayette said. "He said he decided to leave Philadelphia rather than chance a meeting with Clinton's intelligence chief, Major DeWitt. It was when Bell made his way out of the city that he found the enemy forming up for its attack. Bell did not know of our location, but he managed to find us with little difficulty."

"As did the enemy, General Lafayette." Washington's comment brought a look of unhappiness to the young Frenchman, but Washington pretended not to notice. "Major DeWitt? Yes, Matthew would want no part of him, for the major was there when Matthew was captured in New York. Too bad DeWitt's come to Philadelphia. Matthew's assignment here has paid off handsomely for us. He's given us much valuable information."

"Ah, General Washington, Bell outdid himself this time. His warning, though it came barely in time, saved the day. We were already crossing the river when the British arrived. Fortunately, the last of our boats were in the water away from shore—and the redcoats remain the worst of marksmen. I lost only a handful of men."

"And learned nothing of value." Washington's words were a comment, not a question, and again brought Lafayette up short.

"Only, I am afraid, that General Clinton lusts after a victory."

"You did well to return your detachment to us, General," Washington said, "so do not despair. Now, would you have Matthew Bell sent to me? He may have some information as to the British intentions in the new campaign."

But Bell's information was meagre. "With De-Witt in town, I've had to tread a narrow path," Bell said. "I can repeat a bunch of rumors, but not many facts."

"Speak the rumors, then, Matthew. Rumors often tell a story unto themselves."

"Well, sir, it's said that Clinton will pull his forces out of Philadelphia within a month and that he'll go by water. But then it's also said he'll stay in Philadelphia—and that he'll go by land, across Jersey, should he decide to leave."

"What do you think about Clinton's leaving, Matthew?"

Matthew Bell grinned at his superior. "It's probable, General—even though the work on the fortifications says they're staying." Bell doffed his hat and ran his hand through his dark, curly hair, his blue eyes remaining on his commander's face. "If I were a betting man, General," he said slowly, "I'd certainly bet on Clinton leaving."

"Why?"

"A couple of things, General. One is the way the

engineers are working on the fortifications. They aren't in any hurry and they aren't wasting any materials. In a lot of places, they're using the cheapest material they can come by. But the real reason I know they'll soon be on their way is their women."

Washington's eyes narrowed. "What about them, Matthew?"

Bell's expression became almost a smirk. "No way a man can keep bad news from his woman, General, and the Tory ladies of Philadelphia are suddenly a very unhappy lot. At least two of them have already left by boat for New York."

"Good work, Matthew. I'm inclined to agree with your assessment. The British must fear an attack on Philadelphia—or New York—by the French fleet. Such an attack could be devastating, were it mounted while the British forces are split and unreinforced. Therefore, it's perfectly logical for Clinton to consolidate his forces at one port or the other."

"And New York would be more valuable to them, General?"

"Of course. And Clinton is wise enough to try to make us believe they'll stay in Philadelphia. If we take their bait, we're frozen where we are and can't mount an attack while they're withdrawing."

Washington was silent for a few moments. Then he asked Bell, "How will they go, Matthew? By ship or by land?"

Bell shook his head. "I wish I knew, sir. They've been putting supplies aboard their ships and sending them somewhere, but that might mean anything. They've got enough ships to carry their army, but . . . well, you know how the wind is. If it stops, the whole army's becalmed for God knows how long."

"Shipping the troops by sea protects them from attack, except from the French," Washington said, as much to himself as to Bell. "And Clinton can have no idea where the French fleet is at present."

Before the interview ended, Washington shook Bell's hand warmly and wished him well. "You've done us two great services, Matthew," he said. "First in saving General Lafayette's army and now in giving me solid information regarding Clinton's intentions. I only wish you could go back to Philadelphia until the British leave. Information on what route they'll take when they leave would be invaluable to us, perhaps allow us to mount an attack successful enough to shake up the House of Commons, King George and Lord North."

"I've been thinking about that very thing, General," Bell said after a slight hesitation. "Only DeWitt knows me by sight in Philadelphia. I suppose I have a pretty good chance of avoiding him and still picking up information. So I'll go back if you want me to."

"God bless you, Matthew."

Bell laughed. "And keep me, too, General—safe from DeWitt and his Tory cronies. I'm still a young man with lots of years ahead of me."

"Agreed, Matthew. Exercise extreme caution. Can you make your way back through the British guards without difficulty?"

"I have a pass signed by Sir William himself," Bell said with a chuckle. "Anyway, I can get into the city without one. I know a way in that isn't guarded at all. I save it for emergencies."

"By the way, Matthew, our good friend John

Langley Hunter was asking about you. He's doing something for me in Rhode Island at present, but will be returning in a week or so."

Bell beamed. "If you see him before I do, General, tell him I'm locking horns with his old friend Magnus again." He chuckled. "And ask him if he's seen my sister, Deborah, in his travels."

It had been John Langley Hunter who, with the help of Deborah Bell, had saved Matthew from torture and probable death at the hands of the British little more than a year before in New York. Hunter, a tall, redheaded man who did well with the ladies, had long been sweet on Deborah, who taught school in Wethersfield, Connecticut. Matthew figured if John Langley had gone to Rhode Island, he was sure to have stopped off to see Deborah. He wondered if John Langley would wind up his brother-in-law. If the daring Hunter survived the war.

If any of them survived the war, he reminded himself. Matthew had managed to make it through his imprisonment and torture and the long winter at Valley Forge with the help of his love for a Tory woman, Coleen Page, only to learn that she had succumbed to pneumonia and died. He was just now beginning to recover from the blow. The demands of his assignment in Philadelphia had helped—that, and his now unshakable belief in the rebel cause.

5

O N THE DAY of the redcoats' unsuccessful try at trapping Lafayette at Barren Hill, Schuyler DeWitt was preparing to journey to Philadelphia to join Magnus and take up his commission. Magnus had sent him a message only a few days earlier, telling him he could defer joining the army until Clinton's forces returned to New York, though Magnus said nothing of when that would be. Schuyler considered his options and in the end decided to go to Philadelphia on the first of June. He wasn't anxious to join the army, but had found being at home had become increasingly intolerable. Joanna had been enraged when he insisted that he must take up the commission his family had secured for him and after that she had avoided him so efficiently that he had not seen her face in more than three days. The army, he had decided, would be a pleasure compared with spending any more time wishing for a bedchamber companion who would not put in an appearance. Perhaps, he thought, in Philadelphia he might meet a pretty belle who could make him forget Joanna.

On his last day home, he rode to the tavern to bid adieu to Ben Ballis and any of his friends who happened to be there. While there, he once more encountered Scott Laidlow, the wagon driver. He also met the redcoat officer who had struck him down with his army pistol—a meeting no more pleasant than the first, but with a different ending.

Ben was out when Schuyler got to the Golden Hawk, so the youth contented himself with a mug of ale while he waited. Schuyler had just finished his second mug when a British platoon trooped into the tavern, each man with a musket.

"Where is he?" demanded the burly redcoat lieutenant who had assailed Schuyler only a few weeks before.

Clyde Masson, a big, lantern-jawed mule of a man who tended bar for Ballis, raised his hands in a peaceful gesture to the redcoat officer. "Where is who, sir?" he replied.

"The rebel spy," the officer said, "the one who calls himself Laidlow. Scott Laidlow."

Schuyler listened quietly as Masson attempted to deal with the officer, who had swiveled on his heel and was looking around the room.

"I don't know a soul by that name, Lieutenant," Masson said, "but if I run across him, I'll certainly be glad to let you know."

Just then one of the redcoats who had been left outside came flying through the door. "We've

picked up Laidlow's tracks, Lieutenant Chambers,"
he declared. "He's heading for the river."

The redcoats were gone in a matter of seconds.
Schuyler drained his glass and wondered if Scott
was a spy. The man believed as the rebels did and
had even served and been wounded as a rebel soldier. But a spy?

Twenty minutes later, Scott Laidlow sauntered
into the room, calmly ordered a bottle of ale and
returned to a table with it. He did not at first notice
Schuyler, but Schuyler saw him immediately. It
took but a moment for Schuyler to decide he
should warn him, rebel or not.

"Well," Scott said, frowning as Schuyler finished
telling him about Chambers. "I have no idea what
they want with me. I'm not a spy. For that matter,
I'm not even a soldier anymore. You say the officer
was the same arrogant bastard who assaulted you?"

Schuyler nodded. "He has it in mind that you're
a spy, Scott, and I believe he plans to either take
you prisoner or—"

"Kill me?" Scott finished with a chuckle. "I suppose he might, though it's a fool thing to do to a
suspected spy. A dead spy can't name his superiors
or provide any idea of the information he's delivered to the enemy."

"Chambers isn't likely to be reasonable," Schuyler declared, "so I'd leave if I were you."

Laidlow grinned. "I'm delighted to know you
care enough to warn me, Schuyler, but I think I'll
chance it. Now tell me, how goes your romance?"

"I really wish you'd go, Scott," he said. But when
Laidlow shook his head, Schuyler sighed and gave
in. "There is no romance. Joanna asked me not to
go away to become a British officer. When I ex-

plained that my father and brother had given me no choice, she became angry and swore she'd have nothing further to do with me."

"And she hasn't?"

"Exactly," Schuyler said. "And tomorrow I'm leaving to join Magnus in Philadelphia. He's on Clinton's staff, the new British commander."

"I thought Clinton was in New York," Laidlow said.

Schuyler shook his head. "He and his staff sailed to Philadelphia earlier this month and Clinton took over from Howe. They'll be coming back to New York before long, I expect, and I shall be with them."

"How do you know that, Schuyler?"

Schuyler shrugged, suddenly realizing that what he had just revealed was not common knowledge. "Magnus sent me a letter in which he said I could either take up my commission in Philadelphia or wait for the troops to return to New York. I decided to go—because of Joanna and because I'm told Philadelphia is a beautiful place and this will give me a chance to see it."

"It is, indeed," Scott said. "I've been there. Last time I found the ladies bountiful and beautiful. As for the city—who really cares?" He laughed and Schuyler, feeling better for having run into Laidlow, joined in.

Then came the sound of horses outside. The two friends exchanged looks and Scott went to the window to confirm the fact that the redcoats had come back. He reseated himself at a different table and awaited the soldiers.

"You're staying?" Schuyler said.

"I've nothing to fear, lad, for I am no spy."

That Scott's assessment of his danger was wrong became apparent when the redcoats stormed in and Chambers spotted him. The lieutenant leveled his pistol and went straight to Laidlow. "You're now my prisoner, soldier," Chambers said, brandishing the pistol in Scott's face.

"I'm not a soldier, Lieutenant," Laidlow said cheerfully. "And as for being anyone's prisoner, I think not. My papers are quite in order—if you'll take the trouble to look at them." He pointed to a packet of papers in a leather pouch lying on the table.

For the first time, Chambers appeared unsure of himself. Lowering the pistol, he picked up the pouch and began leafing through the papers. The last paper in the pouch surprised him. "What is a spy doing with a pass signed by Sir Henry Clinton?" he demanded. "Who gave this to you?"

"Sir Henry himself, Lieutenant," Laidlow said. "And I am not a spy. Would Sir Henry give me a pass if I were?"

Chambers was considering that when his eyes settled on Schuyler and narrowed suspiciously. He dropped Laidlow's papers on the table. "How is your head, rebel clod?" he said. "Do you still insist you're a Loyalist?"

"You'd do better to confine your activities to battle, sir," Schuyler observed, "where you do not need intelligence to determine your enemy. You've made me your enemy, and if you wish to push me I shall be glad to cut you down before the eyes of your own men."

The words had the intended effect. The British officer raised his pistol and Schuyler sprang, knocking the weapon aside and slamming his right hand into the man's thick neck. As the officer doubled over, gasping for breath, Schuyler knocked him unconscious with an elbow to the jaw.

Chambers's men, who had been paralyzed by what was happening, now began to move in, their muskets at the ready. The leader, wearing sergeant's insignia, stopped at the sight of Scott Laidlow leveling a pistol at him.

"I am not a spy, and Mr. DeWitt will soon be Lieutenant DeWitt of the British Army, Sergeant," Scott said. "Your officer deserved the lesson he just received and I would suggest that you leave it at that. Otherwise, you may forfeit your life, Sergeant."

The redcoat's eyes went from Scott's pistol to his fallen commander. Ascertaining that Chambers was unconscious, a thin smile came to the sergeant's beefy face. "I have no quarrel with you, sir," he said, "and I can't say I'm sorry about what has taken place. The lieutenant has been needing a lesson such as this for a long time. I pray that he'll learn from it." Now he told his men to pick up Chambers and carry him out.

When the redcoats were gone, Schuyler thanked Scott for the help, but Laidlow grinned and said, "You didn't look like you needed any, Schuyler. Did you learn to fight like that in college?"

Schuyler shook his head. "Not entirely," he said. "I used to fight with Magnus and he showed me a few tricks."

"Like hitting someone squarely where it hurts?" Scott asked, running his fingers over his own Adams' apple. "Well, he earned what he got, I'd say."

"As his sergeant said, I hope Chambers learns

from it. It's soldiers like him who give the British Army a bad reputation."

Laidlow laughed. "Would that it was only men like Chambers who gave the King's soldiers a bad reputation in the colonies, Schuyler. I believe they'd be immensely popular—if only they'd stop trying to tame the so-called rebels."

Schuyler laughed. "There's no doubt which side you're on, is there?"

"After what just happened, there'll be some question as to which side you're on. Or I should say there would have been, were you not soon to wear a redcoat uniform."

"I'm just glad you're out of the war. Hate to have to worry that you were in my gun sights."

Laidlow looked at him for a long moment. "Perhaps one day you'll realize you've taken the wrong side. Perhaps not. Whatever is to come, I wish you good luck. I trust you'll survive to become a part of whatever this country will become when this war is over."

"Will you look me up then? I'll buy you an ale and we can reminisce."

Laidlow's face twisted into a frown. "I'll try, but I've a bad feeling about the days ahead."

"Let's hope you're wrong, Scott. Now let's have another round. We've two things to celebrate— what happened to our friend Chambers and my going away tomorrow."

Schuyler was barely sober when he returned home to find Joanna once more in his bedchamber.

"So," he said sarcastically, "you've decided to honor me with a fond adieu?"

"Then you are truly leaving?"

Schuyler met her eyes and decided they were sullen. He dropped his own eyes to her bosom and immediately looked up again, disturbed by the arousing knowledge of what lay beneath her gown. "Had you any doubt I would go?"

"I do not wish you to go," Joanna said.

"You've made your feelings known, lovely lady," Schuyler said. "The question is, why does it even matter?"

With that, the girl flew into his arms and tears overflowed her eyes. She sobbed against his neck as she told him, "Because I love you, darling Schuyler. Can you not see that? Have I not shown it? Made it plain? I love you! *Love you!*"

Schuyler wanted to hurt her as she had hurt him, yet found he could not. As Joanna huddled against him, he kissed away her tears, then tasted their salt again on her mouth. He tried to speak, but she shook her head and said, "Later, not now."

Once again he experienced the delight of her body and lost himself in it. When it was over, he again wondered if she could respond to his father as she did to him.

"Now," she whispered, "now you can speak."

Still breathing hard, Schuyler only smiled and kissed her nose. "You have stolen my breath," he said, "though I forgive you for it."

"Mmmm," she murmured, molding herself against him from shoulders to toes. "How can you bear to leave, darling?"

"I almost can't, Joanna. Yet think of how unbelievably sweet the return will be. I will live for it."

"You won't change your mind?"

"I cannot. I will not."

"Then," she said, "I will live for your homecoming, too."

"You're no longer angry?" Schuyler said. He had been prepared for another display of the girl's temper.

"Would I be in your bed if I were?"

"And you'll wait for me?"

"Yes. You are what I desire, what I need, what I want."

"What about Father? Can you—would you—?"

He did not have to complete his questions. "I do not want your father, not like this," she said. "You must know that. Yet I'm grateful to him for being kind to me and . . . I will try, darling. I can promise no more."

Joanna slept with Schuyler the remainder of the night. On the ride south the next morning, the youth heard Joanna's words a hundred times in his mind. He prayed she meant them. He prayed she would indeed wait for his return and relish it as he would.

The day was warm but comfortable, the countryside quiet and peaceful, and it set Schuyler to thinking about the war he was about to become a part of—a gruesome war, he had no doubts; a war in which no one was spared, if his brother Magnus were to be believed. Magnus said the rebels sighted in on British officers as often as on ordinary soldiers, knowing that the redcoats' attack would break and the troops fall back when a commanding officer fell.

He wondered if he would ever have to sight his Kentucky rifle on a rebel. He had hunted, of course, but certainly never for human beings. It was one thing to spill the blood of an animal, another entirely to open the bloodstream of a fellow man.

It was mid-afternoon as he neared Princeton and he thought about finding a stream to water his horse before proceeding to the Delaware. He was just about to unfold the map he carried of the Jersey territory when he heard the sound of musketfire off in the distance.

Deciding to have a look, he headed toward the sound until he was certain of its location, then began to skirt it until he found some high ground. Tying his horse to a tree, he climbed up the slope and looked down to see a group of redcoats trading shots with a comparative handful of straggly-looking, un-uniformed men. As Schuyler watched, the British officer in charge of the group ventured into the gunsight of one of the enemy riflemen and went down clutching his heart.

Schuyler judged the un-uniformed men to be New Jersey militiamen and decided that he might be able to help his new British Army comrades by using his shooting skill from his vantage point on the higher ground.

He quickly loaded his rifle and assumed the prone position Magnus had taught him. At his brother's direction, he had learned how to get off four shots a minute with accuracy—and his accuracy, like that of many of Washington's Continentals, was not common to the bulk of the British soldiers, who relied on massed musketry to wreak havoc upon their enemies.

Bringing his rifle to bear on the militiaman who had just picked off the British officer, Schuyler steadied the weapon with his left hand, sucked in a deep breath and fired. The man went down. But

Schuyler was already looking away as he quickly reloaded, then resighted, this time on a militiaman some distance away from the first one he had killed. His aim was good, but the man ducked just as he fired. He reloaded and sighted again. This time he picked off a second militiaman. Had he been watching the British soldiers, Schuyler would have seen them look up in puzzlement at the sudden gunfire from overhead.

Schuyler managed to pick off two more of the militiamen before they withdrew to mount horses for a fast gallop away from the scene.

Schuyler stood and called down to the redcoat soldiers: "They're on the run! Form up and give chase."

But the redcoat soldiers, leaderless except for a sergeant, had no taste for a chase. They were grateful to have escaped with their lives.

After the militiamen had raced away, Schuyler descended the hill and led his horse toward the redcoat group. When he reached them, he was astonished to see that the sergeant who greeted him was the same one who had been with Lieutenant Chambers.

Sergeant Jack Wilkins's eyes widened as he recognized Schuyler. Remembering that Schuyler was supposedly a redcoat lieutenant, Wilkins ordered his men to attention and snapped off a sharp salute. "Sergeant Wilkins, sir," he said, "and glad you're here to take command."

"Then Chambers is dead?"

Wilkins nodded. "Just before you arrived, sir. And if I may say so, sir, we might also have died were it not for your shooting. Thank you, sir. There's no question of where your loyalty lies. A pity the lieutenant didn't live to realize it. You're on your way to take up your commission, sir?"

"Yes, in Philadelphia." As it happened, the redcoats were also on their way to Philadelphia, where they were to become a part of Clinton's headquarters company, and so Schuyler agreed to lead them.

It was not until Schuyler accompanied Wilkins on a tour of the enemy dead that it was brought home to him that he had killed four men. Seeing their lifeless bodies lying there, bloody and motionless, brought a cold sweat to Schuyler's brow in spite of the warmth of the weather. He stared at them, in his mind reliving the moment when he'd sighted in on living men and taken the very breath from their bodies.

Wilkins noticed the expression on Schuyler's face, but withheld comment until he finished searching the dead militiamen. "First time you've killed, sir? You'll get used to it."

"Can you get used to it?" Schuyler said. "I was so intent on helping you that it never occurred to me that I was snuffing out lives. I doubt I'll ever become used to it."

Wilkins shrugged. "In war you have to, sir. In war, it's you or the other fellow—and you don't want it to be you. It's easier, though, when you're killing Indians or black men. At least they're different from us."

Schuyler wondered about that, especially about the blacks. That they were held as slaves made them no less than human. Schuyler had always been glad that his father did not hold slaves, though the old man did keep bond servants because they were cheap labor, if at times unreliable.

The sergeant's grunt caught Schuyler's attention and he accepted the packet of papers Wilkins handed to him. "Most are letters, Lieutenant De-Witt. One of your tasks is to screen such things for important intelligence."

Schuyler looked through the letters carefully. Only one seemed to have any significance, a letter from an officer in the rebel forces at Valley Forge to the dead man. The part Schuyler thought Magnus would be interested in was:

"The Prussian Von Steuben is working us on the drill field day and night, but to give the devil his due, we regulars are beginning to look and act like real honest-to-God soldiers. Maybe not as sharp as the redcoats, but plenty good enough, for my money. If nothing else, the drilling will get the men used to taking orders, so that we officers will be able to get them back in line after a break."

Schuyler had learned a lot from his brother about the weakness of Washington's army. Many of the rebels were excellent with a musket, especially those wielding the accurate Kentucky rifles. But they had little training or discipline and were nearly impossible to reform after they were broken by a charge from the British infantrymen. If Von Steuben could instill discipline in the rebels, they would become a much more formidable foe. Schuyler resolved to bring what he had learned to Magnus's attention the moment he reached the city.

The burials of the dead completed, the redcoats headed south once more, this time with a new commanding officer. Night had fallen by the time they reached the banks of the Delaware northeast of Philadelphia, and so they they stopped and made camp.

Tomorrow they would cross the river and enter the city. But Schuyler's mind was again on the dead bodies he had just left behind. His dreams were as bloody as the bodies had been.

6

JUNE SECOND DAWNED warm, cloudless and sunny, an auspicious beginning for the day that faced Magnus DeWitt. The first excitement came in mid-morning, when Schuyler reported in, accompanied by a redcoat sergeant who related the tale of Schuyler's bravery. According to Sergeant Wilkins, Schuyler had saved the brigade from extinction at the hands of a sharp-shooting band of New Jersey militia.

Magnus, stirred by the sergeant's tale, grinned broadly at Schuyler. "I'm proud of you," he told his brother, "and I'm certain Sir Henry will be as well. Come, let me introduce you."

Schuyler was welcomed warmly by the commander in chief after Magnus described in the most laudatory terms his brother's heroism on the British patrol's behalf.

Sir Henry's eyes glittered when his aide had completed the tale. "If even half of that is true, Lieutenant DeWitt, we're fortunate to have acquired the services of the second of Alastair DeWitt's fine sons."

"Magnus exaggerated the militiamen's numbers," Schuyler said. "They were outnumbered by our men, but they were winning because they were skirmishing from a considerable distance—perhaps a hundred yards—and were fine marksmen."

"Obviously you, too, are a fine marksman, Lieutenant. I'll be glad to have you at my side when we are in the field. You'll make a fine addition to my personal guard."

Magnus instructed one of his assistants to take Schuyler to the mansion in which Clinton's staff was billeted, then sat down at his desk to review the documents Schuyler had turned over to him.

As Schuyler had anticipated, Magnus found the letter about the rebels' training to be both interesting and disturbing. He wrote himself a memorandum about it, resolving to find out what effect the training was likely to have on the army's effectiveness.

In mid-afternoon, as British Army supplies were being loaded onto ships in the harbor, Magnus had another visitor—the tall, spindley messenger from rebel General Lee.

The message was short and none-too-sweet:

If I had been on your side, Major, I should not have missed taking Lafayette at Barren

*Hill. I will tell you that a spy named Matthew
Bell was responsible for forewarning Lafayette. I await your offer."*

Bell! Magnus muttered an oath. Bell was the
rebel spy that he and Whitehead had captured last
year. Only a miraculous rescue brought off by
Magnus's old friend—and enemy—John Langley
Hunter had saved Bell's neck. Recalling now how
he had served with Hunter against the French and
Indians only a few years before, and how he had
saved the redhead's life, Magnus cursed himself
for a fool. Hunter had repaid him by bedding his
fiancée, the beautiful Elvira. In the end, there had
been an aborted duel and Magnus had been left
brideless when Elvira went to England. There had
been a succession of women in his life since, but
none had thus far truly replaced the fair Elvira.

The memories were bitter and Magnus was hard-
pressed to bring his mind to bear on what he had
to do. When at last he did, he decided that the
first matter he had to deal with, after the courier,
was Matthew Bell.

"Go get yourself a meal," he told the messenger.
"I shall have a reply for the one you serve when
you return."

Sir Henry was conferring with the Earl of Car-
lisle, sent by King George to negotiate a peace
with Congress on something less than rebel terms
or, failing that, to bribe American leaders to wind
up the war. The earl was authorized to offer a
dominionship without independence, but that fact
had already become old news around Philadelphia
by the time he had arrived.

When Clinton was free, Magnus brought him

the latest message. The general grew red in the face as he read the missive, then rose from his desk and began to pace the floor. "So," he roared, "we *were* betrayed! I knew it. Damn it, I knew someone had tipped them off. Magnus, I want that man, that Bell. Find him and bring him to me. That's an order!"

"I'll try, sir, but I fear it's hopeless. The scoundrel has no doubt taken refuge with Washington at Valley Forge by now. You see, Matthew Bell is well known to me and I to him."

"I don't care where he is, Major," Clinton said hotly. "I want him! Have your spies kidnap him. I don't give a damn how you do it, but I want it done and before we leave Philadelphia."

"What about General Lee?"

"Write him that we'll have an offer to lay on the table by the first of July. I have no time to waste on him at the moment. By the way, you may begin passing along those phony letters. Let's hope that they convince Washington we're leaving by ship. There can be little doubt in the rebels' headquarters by now that we are leaving. The wagon train is growing steadily and our ships are riding low in the water with supplies. It seems that each of our men owns ten times his weight in baggage. How in the world was Howe ever able to muster a charge from men who were so heavily weighted down? When we consolidate our forces in New York, perhaps we can do something about it."

Magnus framed a response for Lee, then began laying plans to capture Matthew Bell.

Schuyler spent the remainder of his first day in Philadelphia exploring the streets and came to the conclusion that it was a beautiful city. That it was also filled with pretty women became apparent when Magnus took him to a party that night in the home of a prominent Tory family.

Schuyler, wearing his new British uniform for the first time, felt oddly out of place, though the ballroom was filled with red coats. The belles of Philadelphia found the handsome youth interesting, however, and gave him little time to miss Joanna.

Magnus pointed out various members of Clinton's staff to his brother, including Captain Andre, who had paid Clinton's headquarters a number of visits in his efforts to seek an assignment on the commander in chief's staff.

"He's a dandy," Magnus said. "Belongs on the stage, not in the King's army."

"I believe you envy him, brother," Schuyler chided, "and you shouldn't. Father is forever boasting of your exploits these past five years and I think well of you, too."

"You needn't butter me up, Schuyler," Magnus growled, "for your place on Clinton's staff is already assured. You will first be a member of his personal guard—a great honor—and the reason is your exploits at Princeton, which impressed Sir Henry a great deal." The pride in Magnus's voice was unmistakable. He had never thought his younger brother could or would command respect in the army except by owning a commission. He was delighted to learn he had been wrong.

In the days which followed, Schuyler was put under the wing of a veteran member of Clinton's guard, Major Edwin Tompkins, for indoctrination. Tompkins, who had distinguished himself at Breed's Hill and Long Island, was a quiet, reliable soldier who gave Schuyler all the information he needed to function in the efficient British Army, and especially in Clinton's elite personal guard.

Schuyler still thought of Joanna, each passing day failing to diminish the longing he felt for her. Only the deluge of new information and assignments from Major Tompkins made the days bearable. But nothing, it seemed, could do the same for the nights.

In the midst of British preparations to withdraw, Magnus too was busy, seeking the whereabouts of Matthew Bell. He learned that Bell had been seen with Washington in the aftermath of Barren Hill, but had vanished thereafter and had not been seen since. Deciding that Matthew's disappearance could only mean that he had returned to Philadelphia, Magnus disguised himself as a Tory businessman and spent two days visiting a number of taverns, places known to be meeting places for rebel spies. Magnus dawdled over his meals, his eyes alert for a glimpse of Matthew, his ears seeking words that might disclose Bell's refuge, but he met with no success. He could not know that he had been recognized by the owner of one of the inns and that the news had been passed along to Matthew.

Matthew wished he had the time to capture the infamous Tory and deliver him to Washington, but he had more important things to do. It was vital to Washington to learn whether the British would withdraw from Philadelphia by land or by sea. Even if Matthew could not learn Clinton's exact route, finding out which way he would go could place the rebels in a position to attack successfully. And Washington sorely needed a victory right now, with the campaign of '78 about to begin and the general trying his best to recruit more soldiers for the Continental Army. A victory now could add five thousand men to the military roster, Matthew knew.

Unknown to the British, or even to his fellow Patriot spies, Matthew had a number of local ladies reporting to him who were accepted by their fellow Philadelphians as either Loyalist or neutral and who were therefore privy to all the gossip which was bandied about at the social events. Because of the British officers' penchant for attending such affairs, and the looseness of their tongues following a few toasts to King George, it was not unusual for the ladies to pick up significant tidbits to pass to Bell through his sometime mistress, Molly Minton. It was a remarkably effective way of gathering intelligence. Matthew's trickiest task was translating the gossip into verifiable information and contacting Washington soon enough to make it useful.

Bell's success using his ladies was solid, though it had produced no spectacular coups. He had learned of Clinton's appointment as Howe's successor and personally carried the news to Washington on the same day Clinton received word in New York: One of Howe's staff officers had spent an evening lamenting the cruelty of fate which was soon to cost him his place on the commander in chief's staff, and the one to whom he had lamented was one of Bell's ladies.

In December, when a British attack on Washington's encampment at Valley Forge had seemed imminent, it was Matthew who had informed Washington that Howe would not attempt further offensive action before spring because he still had hopes of working out a peaceable end to the war. That piece of information allowed Washington to concentrate on rebuilding and retraining his army at Valley Forge in order to get ready for a spring offensive.

A bright morning sun streamed through the window to awaken Matthew, who had gone to sleep in Molly Minton's bed before that lady had returned from the ball to which she had gone. Patting the other side of the bed, he found his hostess was nowhere in evidence, and so he arose and dressed.

Molly was a red-haired beauty in her middle twenties whose husband had been killed while serving in the British Army during the Battle of Long Island. It was Molly, as much as anyone, who had helped Matthew recover his spirits after the death of Coleen Page, for Molly understood all too well the loss he had suffered.

"And what have your ladies found out, Molly?" Matthew said, finding her seated at breakfast in the kitchen of her Philadelphia home.

"What is it worth to you, Matthew?" the lady responded teasingly.

"I can get quite a few Continentals for you from General Washington if you've something good to tell," Matthew said.

Molly laughed derisively. "Continentals?" she exclaimed. "They grow less and less appealing with each passing day. The merchants would laugh at me if I tried to pay for something with them. I'm in need of something far more substantial than that."

"And you shall have it, Molly dear. But I must pay the general a visit today and I still have no hard facts to offer him. The British have put together a wagon train, which should mean that they'll travel to New York by land. But Clinton's clever and it could be a ruse."

Molly's eyes sparkled and her smile grew in intensity. "Give your poor widow-lady a hug, Matthew, and perhaps I'll give you something you'd like to hear."

Matthew embraced the redhead, then kissed the saucy mouth.

"The redcoats will go by water," Molly said, a twinkle in her eyes.

"*By water?*" Matthew could hardly believe his ears.

Molly gave a soft laugh. "By water across the Delaware, thence by land to Amboy and New York."

Matthew was ecstatic. "You're certain?" he said.

"Two different British officers let it be known and one of them is on Clinton's staff. Lucy, the one who was with him, says he was mortified that he'd let it slip and begged that she not repeat it to anyone."

Matthew gave her a grateful hug. "Now I must get going and pass this along to Washington."

"Tell him I shall personally assassinate him if he does not speak to the Congress about me."

Molly was a warm-blooded lady, but her Loyalist father, who had arranged her marriage to a prominent Tory, had instilled in her a healthy respect for property. Because of her husband's Loyalist status, the Continental Congress had annexed the bulk of her estates, and she was in no way patient over the return of her property.

"Don't worry, Mol. I'll speak to the general and I'm certain he'll take care of you. Was there any other information? Any indication of the route Clinton's men will take across Jersey?"

Molly shook her head. "Only what I've told you, Matthew. And they were pretty close-mouthed about letting even that out, so it's likely to be true."

Back in Washington's headquarters at Valley Forge, Matthew passed along his news, then found the general had received conflicting reports and ideas of how the British withdrawal would be accomplished.

"We have what appears to be solid information that the troops will be traveling by *sea*," Washington told Matthew. "But there is a faction on my staff which doesn't believe there will be any British withdrawal at all, in spite of what we've learned. General Lee, for one."

"*My* source is solid, General," Matthew said. "I don't care what you may have that says the British are going by sea. The Delaware is the closest they'll get to water. Forget that a member of Clinton's personal staff told one of my people that they were going across Jersey. All you really have to do is look at the British train—it's huge."

"The train could be a trick, Matthew. Like the fortification work to make us think they're staying."

Matthew shook his head. "There's no doubt in my mind that Clinton will be dragging his train behind him. He's going to too much trouble just to avoid a battle with us. As for General Lee—well, he's wrong and both of us know it." Matthew could have said more about Lee. He had observed Lee's odd behavior while the general had been held captive by the British, and he hadn't been altogether certain of Lee's sanity or of his loyalty. But if Washington trusted Lee, that would have to be good enough for Matthew.

Washington was silent for a minute, then passed a packet of papers to Matthew. "Look them over, Matthew," he said. "They're letters we've intercepted, and they seem valid. Each letter contains a strong suggestion that the writer—a member of Clinton's staff—will soon be embarking upon a sea voyage. Each letter came to us by a different route, so it seems certain that they weren't simply planted."

Matthew thought it over, then frowned and shook his head. "Seems that would only confirm that I'm right, sir," he said. "One of Clinton's staff people might be dullard enough to write a dangerous letter like that. Maybe even two, if you want to stretch it a bit. But four people? Not likely. Not even remotely possible, I'd say. Magnus DeWitt! Sounds like something he'd try to pull off. Probably used a double agent, maybe several of them, to get these letters into your hands."

"Magnus DeWitt," Washington repeated. "Yes, he always was a clever one. But I trust the agents who brought these to me implicitly, and I doubt any of them could be doubling."

"Then you don't agree with me about the meaning of the letters?"

"I just can't be certain."

"Would you like me to go back and see if I can find out for sure?"

Washington gave Matthew an appreciative smile. "Yes, Matthew, return and make the attempt. As for Mrs. Minton, you may tell her that I'll send word to Congress about her excellent work as soon as it moves back to Philadelphia after the British withdrawal. She may be sure that not only will all her property be restored to her, but she will share in other properties as well."

After leaving Washington, Matthew had just saddled his horse and was about to head back to Philadelphia when he was confronted by a tall, redheaded mountain of a man, a man who wore a familiar eye-patch.

Matthew Bell broke into a wide grin as he seized the man's hand. It was his old friend John Langley Hunter.

7

THE DAY after Matthew's visit to Valley Forge, Clinton's staff pronounced his army ready to leave. Clinton, pleased to learn from Magnus that the rebels were confused about British intentions, said, "Let's keep them that way." After a quiet conversation with his superior, General Perfection, Clinton ordered the withdrawal to be accomplished in the early morning hours before sunrise on the seventeenth.

Magnus had also learned that General Lee was opposing any action by the rebels against Clinton's retreating army on the grounds that they were a "superior force." Clinton laughed with glee at the report.

"Ah, yes, our man Lee! What's his status with the rebels?"

"As nearly as I can determine, he'll command the rebel army if it leaves Valley Forge to pursue us."

"That," Clinton announced, "is excellent. If we must be chased, I cannot think of anyone I'd rather be chased by than the good General Lee. You've had no further word from him—private word, that is?"

Magnus said no. "We told him we would make him an offer the first of July, of course, but by that time we'll be back in New York."

"It would be nice if Washington were to give General Lee command of rebel forces in the south, Magnus. Then, a new southern campaign could be immensely profitable for us and further discourage the rebellious pups. I must remember to consult the General about that."

Magnus tried to keep from smirking at the reference to Clinton's silent superior.

What was to be the final British social event of the occupation was held that night in a mansion near the former headquarters of the Continental Congress. All British officers were allowed to spend the night away from their units in order to wind up their affairs of the heart. But all were in readiness for evacuation and all were cautioned to be tight-lipped about the timetable and route of the withdrawal. An attack while the troops were being ferried to New Jersey would be disastrous. It was because of this extra precaution, with the officers' lives in as much jeopardy as the soldiers', that Molly and her ladies were unable to ascertain the time and exact route of withdrawal.

Molly met Schuyler DeWitt at the ball, however, and mentioned it afterward to Matthew, teasing him about the handsome lieutenant. Matthew's sole reaction was to ask her if Magnus had attended. He had not. If Matthew was displeased with Molly's teasing, he was much more disturbed by her inability to learn the hour and day of the British withdrawal.

Matthew paid a personal visit to the areas where the troops were massed, awaiting the signal to march. There was no question in his mind from what he saw that the British were ready to leave at any moment. But when? Matthew sent a messenger to Valley Forge to report what he had learned, then fell into an exhausted stupor the next night after satisfying Mrs. Minton's hearty sexual appetite.

He awoke just before nine, when Molly delivered a report she had just received—the British were on the move. Quickly dressing, Matthew rode for the river and, with sinking heart, saw that the banks of the Delaware were filled with troops, but that most of them were already across and on the far side. Clinton had moved out during the night.

Furious at himself for having slept through Clinton's withdrawal, Matthew galloped to Valley Forge and reported to Washington. While dismayed, Washington wasted no time with recriminations, instead immediately ordering Lafayette's brigades to head for Coryell's Ford to cross the river and pursue. He and Lee and the rest of the army would follow after Lafayette had crossed the Delaware. Only a small skeleton force under Benedict Arnold would be left to march into Philadelphia to take it over.

Matthew offered to ride with Lafayette and

serve as a scout and Washington promptly accepted the offer, since his best spy could be of no use in Philadelphia anymore.

Matthew was the first of Lafayette's men to cross the Delaware, and he headed the patrol which found Clinton's forces near Hopewell five days later.

Magnus rode beside his commander in chief as the huge, sixteen thousand-man army moved in two parallel columns through Jersey.

"We fooled them this time, Major," Sir Henry exulted. "Now they can attack any time they wish and we'll be ready."

But scouting reports soon indicated that the rebels had moved their army out of Valley Forge and crossed the river in pursuit. Worse yet, they were making better time than the British, but Clinton seemed not particularly worried. Magnus figured it was because of his "friend" in the pursuing rebel army, General Lee.

A cold sweat enveloped Magnus as a thought occurred to him: Did Clinton really have a friend in General Lee? Could the messages he had received possibly have been from someone else? Worse, could the whole thing have been some kind of involved subterfuge, designed to fool Clinton, to lull him into overconfidence?

Magnus thought seriously about cautioning his commander, but refrained from doing so. What, after all, could be gained? he thought.

Because Schuyler was in the commander's personal guard, Magnus was able to see him nightly and it appeared the youth was bearing up well under the strain which went with his commission.

That, Magnus thought, was good. Yet it seemed as if something was bothering his brother, though Schuyler had refused to admit it.

During the march, Magnus interviewed a steady flow of deserters from Washington's forces. However effective the rebels' new training, it had not ended the stream of men who knew they could earn hard British cash by crossing over. Both sides encouraged desertions, but the British benefitted far more than did the rebels.

On the twenty-sixth of June, an officer from Lee's staff deserted and had an interesting story to tell. Lee, the man said, was under orders from Washington to attack at his first opportunity, but was not inclined to do so and, in the officer's opinion, would not.

"You believe he'll refuse his commander's direct order?" Magnus had inquired incredulously. He could not imagine even a strange man like Lee taking so precarious an action on a battlefield. The man could get himself shot by a firing squad!

Clinton heard the tale with interest, then questioned the man himself to confirm the information. When he had finished, he called a staff meeting and announced that he would change his plans slightly because of the hot and muggy New Jersey weather, which was inflicting heat-exhaustion casualties on his troops daily. He would camp at Monmouth Courthouse for a day, then turn the army eastward toward the water at Sandy Hook, where the fleet was waiting to ferry the men to Manhattan.

Several officers, including General Cornwallis, suggested that the change in plans would give the pursuing rebels two chances to attack—one while

they camped, the second when they turned east
and had to abandon their two parallel columns in
favor of one because of the existence of only a
single road to the Hook.

"Have no fear," Clinton reassured his officers.
"I doubt the rebels will attack. But if they do,
it will not be well organized and we'll turn their
offensive thrust into a victory which will inspire
us all. You're to give chase to the rebels once you
have broken their ranks. Do you all understand
that?"

Magnus had his doubts about Clinton's strategy,
but dared not voice them. He wondered if Clinton had taken up the matter with his silent superior. In spite of the information they had about
General Lee, Magnus thought the two armies were
too close in number for either to win a major victory. And Lee was not the only American general;
among others, there were the daring Lafayette and
the indomitable General Wayne.

The day of rest at Monmouth passed unevent-
fully except for skirmishes fought by patrols stationed around the perimeters. The next morning,
three hours before sunrise, the march east to Sandy
Hook began, but it was past eight o'clock before
the entire British force was under way, strung out
for miles in a single column.

Two hours later, word came from the rear that
the rebels had attacked Cornwallis, and his staff
raced back to see what was happening. The news
brought the entire line of march to a halt and
Clinton sent a messenger forward to order Knyphausen to send reinforcements back to help Cornwallis.

By noon the news trickling back to Clinton's

headquarters was that Lee and his army had been put to rout, and the rebels were running for their lives. Clinton was jubilant. But then things changed, as Washington personally rallied the Continentals and mounted a counterattack. Clinton and his staff moved closer to observe and a cannon shot launched by Knox from Combs Hill narrowly missed dispatching the entire staff.

Then, unknown to Magnus or Clinton, a sharp-shooting Virginia platoon led by John Langley Hunter and Matthew Bell spotted Clinton's position and began sending a deadly hail of Kentucky riflefire down upon it. Three of Clinton's staff officers fell, mortally wounded, before anyone realized what was happening. A musket ball ripped through Magnus's hat just before Clinton ordered a hasty evacuation of the position.

By late afternoon Clinton had reached the conclusion that the victory he sought could not be obtained and so he broke off the engagement and made camp for the night. He expected that Washington would do the same and he was right. But he did not expect what came next. A spy who served on Washington's staff brought the news that Washington had ordered an attack at dawn the next morning—and that Lee's scattered army had been regrouped and was available for the attack.

"The man is mad!" Clinton roared when Magnus brought the news. "He must know he can't win."

General Cornwallis, who had been conferring with his superior, now broke in. "Neither can we, Sir Henry," he said. "Not with the present disposition of the troops and our need to protect our train. And not," he added, "with the rebels taking their punishment in a more orderly manner. It seems that now only the militia breaks and runs."

"Why not beat Washington to it, General?" Magnus suggested. "We could break camp just after midnight, when they're resting up for their assault tomorrow. If we did it right, we could put three or four miles between us and them. By the time they came after us, all they could do would be attack us at the Hook, where it would be suicide. The navy would cut them to bits."

Both Clinton and Cornwallis agreed that even though their men were exhausted from the heat of the day and the furious battle they'd just fought, it was their smartest move. And so just before midnight, they broke camp and quietly moved out.

Incredibly, as in the British withdrawal from Philadelphia, this one was not advertised by spy or scout. Washington was furious when, the next morning, he found the enemy had fled.

8

THE DAYS that followed the two-week British march across Jersey were hectic ones for Schuyler as he tried to settle in to army life. In spite of the fierce fighting at Monmouth Courthouse, Schuyler had played no role in it and felt somewhat cheated.

Magnus paid him a visit soon after they arrived in New York and told him of the rebels' startling personal attack on Clinton and his staff. Schuyler, stationed some distance away, had heard some shots from the commander's position, but had not known what was happening. "The rebels were smart to try something like that," he commented. "If they could have put Clinton out of action, it would be bound to have a demoralizing effect on our army."

"The Continental sharpshooters have been taking aim on our officers ever since Breed's Hill," Magnus said. "We've lost more officers in this war than in any we've ever fought." He laughed ruefully. "The bloody bastards knocked my hat off with a musket ball, Schuyler. A good thing this one aimed a little high or you'd have become Father's heir."

"I'm not at all certain I'd like to be his heir, Magnus, so take care of yourself, will you?" Schuyler had never resented his status as second-in-line to Magnus, primarily because of Magnus's age and experience but also because he was not inclined toward running the family's shipping interests.

Schuyler had been in New York for a week when he received a letter from Joanna. He could barely conceal his jubilation at what the girl had written.

Dearest Schuyler,

When will I see you again? I ache for you. When I am awake, I think of you. When I try to sleep, I wish you were at my side. When I sleep, I dream of you.

Would that I could ride there to see you! But Mr. Alastair would never let me go and, of course, I could not explain why I wish to go, why I need to go.

I have managed to sleep alone this past month, which has not pleased your father at all.

Will you get leave soon? I trust that you will—before I explode with desire. I will write

> _again and try to find someone to carry the_
> _letter to New York._
>
> All my love,
> _Joanna_

Schuyler read Joanna's letter a dozen times in the first few hours after he received it. His whole being was afire with the desire to ride home to see her. But leave was out of the question at the moment; it was rumored that the Comte d'Estaing's fleet of French naval vessels was on its way to New York to besiege the city . . . .

Five days later d'Estaing did arrive and his ships could be seen off Sandy Hook. Also, it was said that Washington had moved his army to White Plains so as to threaten the city and its forts.

Sir Henry was more upset than Magnus had ever seen him over d'Estaing's arrival and Washington's threatening position. He raged over the audacity of the rebels, over the "inadequacy" of Admiral Howe's naval forces, presently anchored in New York's harbor and outgunned by more than a third by the French. Most of all, Sir Henry was furious over the orders he had from London to reinforce the British army in the West Indies, where the French were also threatening.

At Clinton's staff meeting the day the French fleet anchored off the Hook, when Magnus told him he had a report that the French ships were too deep-draughted to get over the sandbar Clinton turned on his aide as if he had never known him or Alastair DeWitt.

"That does precious little to ease the pain, Major," he snapped. "If London had sent the ships I requested, we should outnumber and outgun those bloody frogs and I could order an immediate attack which would send them reeling. Or they wouldn't have bothered coming at all. As it is . . ." Clinton trailed off, then turned on Magnus with new anger. "And what happened to the spy Matthew Bell, Major? You were supposed to apprehend him, bring him to me. Why hasn't it been done? Can't you accomplish a simple thing like that for your commander in chief? If not, perhaps I shall have to find an adjutant who can. I understand Captain Andre from Howe's staff is seeking a position with me. Shall I give him one?"

Magnus colored, visibly upset. "I have simply been unable to locate Bell, sir," he said. "My spies have sought him for weeks and I personally spent two days in Philadelphia seeking him out. He's no doubt being especially wary, knowing of my desire to capture him."

"Then when will you bring him to me, Major?"

Magnus shook his head dismally. "Would that I could tell you that, General. I can only say that I will find him and arrest him on your behalf soon."

"And what of the good General Lee who was so useful at Monmouth Courthouse? Were it not for his efforts—or lack of them—we might have suffered a most unseemly defeat."

"I've bad news about Lee, sir," Magnus said. "He's been arrested by Washington and is to be court-martialed. Lord Sterling heads the court which will hear the charges."

"What are they?"

"I haven't yet learned what they are, sir, though I'm sure I will before long. I'm certain it stems from his actions at the courthouse."

"See that you find out, Major," Clinton said, "and

send your people to learn what Washington is up to. I cannot comply with Lord Germain's demand that I reinforce the Indies while Washington continues to threaten us here."

Magnus was sweating actively when he left Clinton's office after the staff meeting. Andre on the staff? That would be abominable, Magnus thought. And Andre had been Howe's spymaster, just as Magnus was for Clinton. There could be only one spymaster on a general's staff; he, Magnus DeWitt, held that position and would continue to do so.

Magnus sent for the day's deserters and was further disheartened to learn that there was only one. Ever since the Monmouth Courthouse debacle—which Sir Henry called a British victory, but which most considered either a draw or a rebel win—the flow of rebel deserters had dwindled to a trickle. Did the rebels now believe they could beat the Crown? It was a ridiculous notion, and one Magnus had never even seriously considered.

Questioning the lone deserter proved fruitless. He was from Maryland, uneducated, and seemed to know little beyond his own name. Matthew Bell's name meant nothing to him and he had no idea when Washington would attack New York.

Magnus ordered an increase in patrol activities in the area between the city and the rebel forces at White Plains. He hoped to snare a messenger with some vital piece of intelligence, but a week went by with no hard information coming in. The French fleet remained off the Hook, Washington remained at White Plains and Clinton remained in a turbulent state of mind. No word came from Lee and Magnus's doubts about the rebel turn-coat general came back in full force.

Would Lee have sabotaged the rebels during the Monmouth Courthouse engagement even though he had received no definite offer from Clinton? There was as yet little hard intelligence on Lee's actions during the battle, but there was no question that he must have disgraced himself if Washington was to court-martial him.

As July moved into its final week, three things occurred which would have a strong effect on Magnus DeWitt and the British war effort.

First, Sir Henry appointed Captain Andre to his staff to do what he termed "special intelligence" work. Magnus could have choked Clinton when he called the staff in to make the announecment.

Then word came that d'Estaing's warships had departed Sandy Hook for an unknown destination. Captain Andre favored the West Indies, he said, and Clinton seemed inclined to listen to his newest adviser. For his own part, Magnus wasn't certain, but he had a feeling Washington might well try a surprise attack at Newport. He did not voice that opinion, however, preferring to try for some hard information before committing himself. He accordingly put out requests to his spies to check the activities of the rebel forces in Providence.

The third occurrence was the unexpected ap-pearance of Lee's messenger while Magnus was lunching at the officers' club. Magnus looked up in surprise, then washed down the food in his mouth with a pull at his ale. He motioned for the man to sit down. "I was wondering if we would hear from your principal again. You have a message?"

The man said nothing for a moment, watching Magnus attack the remains of his meal. When the man did not speak, Magnus looked up again and saw that the messenger wore a smirk. "My principal wishes to meet with you," he said, "to discuss remuneration for his services."

"Where?" Magnus replied automatically. Then, "How can he meet me anywhere? It's my understanding that your principal is under arrest and about to be tried by a court-martial."

The messenger chuckled. "My principal is free to go anywhere he likes—except here, of course. We knew you would think he was Lee. The truth is that he's not. Now where would you like to meet with him?"

Magnus felt a surge of excitement. Not Lee? Then who? "This side of the Hudson?"

"North of here," the messenger countered, "but south of Washington's position at White Plains."

Obviously the man was with Washington, Magnus thought. "East of there," he said. "There's a tavern not far from my family's home, the Golden Hawk. It's not far from the river. Is your man known to the citizenry in these parts?"

The messenger shook his head. "That would be fine," he replied. "Tomorrow evening at eight o'clock?"

Magnus nodded. "Can your man provide me information on Washington's plans?"

The man grinned evilly, exposing a mouthful of blackened teeth. "Will the sun rise tomorrow?"

he said. "Yes, but he'll disclose nothing unless he receives a definite offer. He'll be at the tavern at eight o'clock."

Magnus was elated, though mystified by the identity of the rebel turncoat. Gates? Wayne? Greene? Who?

He thought about reporting his contact to Clinton, but decided to put it off until he had more information to pass along. Though Clinton had authorized no offer to the man, Magnus was certain he could make a provisional offer on the commander in chief's behalf. Perhaps a brigadier-generalship and a tidy purse of five or ten thousand pounds sterling.

The meeting would also give Magnus a chance to see his father and mother again and check on the health of the family's business interests. He quickly decided to obtain leave for Schuyler and bring him along. The youth had already distinguished himself while serving the King and could no doubt use a holiday.

As soon as he returned to his office, Magnus sent an aide to fetch his brother.

Matthew Bell's expression was one of pure joy when Washington and the tall, spindly Julian Stout explained how they had taken in General Clinton and arranged the capture of Major Magnus DeWitt.

"And you'll take him near his very own home?" Matthew exclaimed.

Washington smiled. "No, Matthew," he said. "*You* will take him. You and another old friend of yours, John Langley Hunter." Washington's smile vanished. "I'd like to think that Magnus DeWitt will tell us all he knows, but I rather doubt it. I won't have him hanged, though, unless I'm forced to. If he wears his uniform while meeting you, he'll be treated as a prisoner of war."

"And exchanged?"

"Not until war's end, for Major DeWitt is far too astute an adversary to be given back once we have him. Not, at least, if we can help it. I know that in your eyes he's a devil because he was instrumental in your capture, but you must remember that he was merely doing his job. I may well be placed in a similar position in the time to come. Does that make me a devil?"

"At least you're acting in a good cause, sir," Matthew said.

"Right or wrong, Matthew, is not material. Major DeWitt believes he's in the right. Wars do not prove who's right and who's wrong, merely who is strongest—or luckiest."

"Or perhaps smartest, sir?"

"Exactly, and that's why we must rid ourselves of DeWitt. He's much too smart for such a strong enemy to have in its ranks. You'll abide by my instructions, then, Matthew? Do no harm to the major unless it's necessary to save yourself?"

"Yes, sir. But I shall say my prayers tonight and ask that the bastard sheds his protective military cocoon to meet us in civilian clothes."

"You have that right, Matthew. I must tell you that I'll pray for the opposite, for I should hate to see a good man hanged."

"Especially if his name's Matthew Bell," came a husky voice from the entrance to Washington's tent. It was John Langley Hunter.

Matthew laughed. "It's good to have you with me on this one, John Langley. DeWitt could be a tough one to bring home."

"You couldn't keep me away, Matthew. I haven't seen Magnus since the end of the French and Indian War."

Bell frowned. "You're not still feeling beholden to him, are you?"

"Because he once saved my life? He also tried to take it once, so I suppose the score is even. We've left it at something like an armed truce." John Langley turned to Washington. "Do you have any more orders for us, General? If not, we'll be moseyin' along to get us a cup of . . . tea." He winked.

Washington laughed. "Drink all the tea you want, gentlemen, but don't get so filled with spirits that you forget where you've got to be tomorrow night and who you're to bring back to me."

Joanna was tired when the old man summoned her. Tired and bored with her life. If only Schuyler had chosen not to go to Philadelphia. Things would be different then—oh, so different. She wouldn't have to wash the day's sweat from her body for Alastair DeWitt, but for his youngest son.

She smiled as she thought of the note she had sent Schuyler in New York. "I ache for you," she had written. Not exactly true, she thought, though she did enjoy Schuyler's lovemaking more than the old man's. Anyone would be better than Alastair, who smelled like garlic and frequently took forever to get it over with. She wished his wife would service him once in a while.

Service him? Yes, Schuyler had been right to call it that, for that was certainly what she did. She had little choice, of course, since Alastair had made it clear when he took on her indenture papers that she was to be his mistress as well as a maid. He could have no complaint about the result; she had come to his bed whenever he asked it of her except when she feared that answering his summons would cause her to become with child. The knowledge of how to tell when she was most fertile was her mother's only legacy. It had served Joanna well, however, since she had lost her virginity before she was twelve, little more than five years ago.

For a time she had hoped she could coax the old man into somehow getting rid of Trientje and taking herself as his wife, but two things had become clear to her this past year: Alastair was content with the way things were and he wanted only the wife he had, whether she was cold or not. Joanna knew that. Trientje had contributed handsomely to the DeWitt fortune, and she guessed that Alastair's regard for his wife also stemmed from her willingness to accept what, for any other woman, would have been an intolerable situation.

Trientje knew her husband bedded Joanna and seemed to care not a whit. In fact, she had appeared to encourage it so she would not have to service her husband—something she had found distasteful from the start, according to Alastair. She treated Joanna no different because of her knowledge that the girl was her husband's mistress. In fact, she had once inquired of Joanna—in halting terms—if she "really enjoyed the disgusting things men do to women."

Joanna had, in her most childlike manner, politely informed the missus that she "adored" it, that she couldn't live without it and that she couldn't understand how a woman could not love it. Of course none of that was true, but Trientje DeWitt would never know it.

Joanna was warm-blooded, but had yet to meet a man who was truly her match, in or out of bed. A bond-servant she might be, but she was wise beyond her years. She knew what she wanted and was not averse to conniving to get it.

She had enjoyed both of Alastair's sons a great deal more than their father, though she only pretended love for Schuyler. She had set her cap for Magnus soon after she realized that Alastair would not change her status from bond-servant to wife, then die and leave her well-fixed. But Magnus, to her unhappiness, felt no more for her than she did for his father. So Joanna had cast a spell over young Schuyler, who was far more handsome than his brother. She wished he was his father's heir, but she knew she would be comfortably fixed while married to him, even though Magnus would inherit control.

Joanna DeWitt? She had dreamed of owning such a name ever since she had come to America. She laughed delightedly as she splashed some cologne on her body and donned a nightgown to prepare herself for her master's bed. Soon, she told herself, she would no longer have to humble herself. Soon she would go to bed only with her husband—if she chose to have no lover.

If she chose to have a lover, she would seek out her man with care. She would want a man whose every thought would be to satisfy her. She was certain she could find one, for she was young and beautiful. And if she could not hope to stay young, she was determined she would remain beautiful.

9

WHEN MAGNUS SUMMONED Schuyler to tell him to go home, Schuyler could have kissed his older brother. "Home? How good it sounds!" he cried. "How very good! I feel as if I've been away for a year or more."

"Our father will be glad to see you again," Magnus said. "And I'm certain he'll be pleased with how your military career goes."

"I've done nothing that others couldn't do as well, Magnus, but I thank you for the compliment."

The next morning the two brothers left New York for the trip up the Hudson just after seven o'clock. As they rode, Magnus cautioned Schuyler to wear his uniform and not change into other clothes while at home "lest the rebels take you and hang you for a military spy."

"Why would they do that, Magnus?"

"Both sides have many spies," Magnus explained. "Those who own a uniform, however, are subject to the severest of penalties—death—if caught spying while in civilian clothes. Other spies are more fortunate, for they're merely held prisoner. It's always been this way during wartime."

"Well, I'll do as you say, though I don't fear the rebels. They hold West Point across the river and White Plains, but we're not close to either."

"True, Schuyler, but we are close to their patrols. Ours, too. Rebel patrols have been harassing ours frequently, ever since Washington reached White Plains."

"Then we'd best keep away from the main trails. I shouldn't wish our leave to be interrupted by a rebel patrol."

"Nor I," Magnus agreed.

They encountered no difficulty during their journey and arrived home by late morning. Alastair was ecstatic at being visited by his sons and Trientje hugged them both warmly.

Schuyler's first sight of Joanna came when she served lunch to the reunited family. She passed him a note along with his food, telling him she would meet him in his bedchambers after lunch.

He could hardly eat, his desire for her was so strong. His father delayed things, however, for he was full of questions about the war and especially about Schuyler's participation in it thus far. Magnus talked freely about the war and his brother's exploits, but would not tell his father anything he wanted to know about Clinton's plans. "Sir Henry is in the middle of a campaign which can end the war within the year, Father," he said, "but I dare not reveal any part of it, not even to you." Nor did Magnus mention that he had to meet someone at the Golden Hawk that night to arrange a rebel sellout to the British.

While Schuyler was renewing his affair with the lovely Joanna in his bedchambers that afternoon, Magnus rode to the Golden Hawk to make certain it was a safe place for the meeting.

Inside, his uniform made him conspicuous in a room that was deserted but for a few locals. Ben Ballis was there and he greeted Magnus politely, though without particular enthusiasm; he disliked seeing uniforms of any color in his tavern because they usually caused trouble, even when worn by the sons of friends.

"How goes it?" Magnus asked the tavern's proprietor.

"Could be worse, I guess. Once in a while we get a patrol lookin' for a fight, and usually they find it. I try to discourage it. No matter what uniform they're wearing," Ballis added, looking pointedly at Magnus's red coat.

"I'm to meet a friend here early tonight," Magnus said. "About eight."

"Be better if you and your friend don't wear those uniforms. The local rebels check in here every night and they're a lot more anxious for a fight nowadays, what with Washington only in White Plains."

"I have to wear the uniform, Ben. Otherwise . . ." He trailed off, then added, "What if I leave off the coat? That be all right?"

"Better than nothing. Just make yourself scarce if you see trouble coming—for my sake, if not your own. I don't want to get my place burned down because of a showdown between a redcoat and a rebel."

As Schuyler lay in his bedchamber beside the woman he loved, he was completely happy. Or he would have been, were it not for Joanna's insistence that they keep their romance a secret from his father.

"I'll buy you from him," Schuyler said, his mouth against the girl's soft neck.

"He won't agree to it, darling. Not yet. And if you ask him and he says no, it will make things very hard for me here."

"But I can't have you continue as you are, as a menial. I'll bring you back to New York with me, whether or not Father approves. We can be married there."

"You can't, Schuyler. Not without your father's approval. Should he cut off your inheritance, it would be very hard for you, hard for both of us."

"Well then, what do you propose to do?"

She joked with him, trying to soften the anger she sensed. "Just be patient, my love. I'll speak to your father before long and tell him what it is we want. But not before I'm sure he will grant his approval."

"Has he been leaving you alone?"

Joanna's eyes met Schuyler's. "I believe he is tiring of me," she lied. "He hasn't summoned me to his chambers for more than thirty days."

"I'm glad—though I can't imagine anyone tiring of you."

"Let us hope that you, at least, do not, darling Schuyler. I would surely die!" Then she was sobbing softly against him. Schuyler did not notice that her tears were few.

A thought now occurred to Schuyler. "We'll get out of here for tonight," he declared. "I'll take you to the tavern, where we can eat and drink openly, as other lovers do. Where I can have you all to myself, without having to worry about Father finding us together in my bedchamber."

"I don't know, Schuyler. If he found out—"

"Shhhh," he said, kissing her. "You will go. From now on you'll do as I say, and I will be your Master Schuyler."

"Yes, Master Schuyler," she said.

Then they made love and Schuyler forgot about the army, about his father, about everything but the woman in his arms. Joanna dreamed about the life to come, about the free and wealthy woman she would be as Schuyler's bride.

Matthew Bell mumbled a silent prayer as he and John Langley Hunter awaited the arrival of Magnus DeWitt at the Golden Hawk Tavern. "No uniform," Matthew murmured, "please, let him wear no uniform." Next to him among the pines beside the trail, John Langley grinned, but said nothing.

At a few minutes before eight, Magnus rode by, wearing his full British uniform. Matthew cursed and glared at the man as he passed.

Now the two men followed their quarry to the tavern and watched Magnus tie up his horse. Then he removed his red coat and replaced it with a green one. Matthew smiled triumphantly.

Inside, Magnus took a seat where he could

watch the door. Then he ordered an ale, unaware that he was being observed through the window to the right of the door.

There were a number of people in the tavern, but not a uniform in sight. Magnus's stalkers walked confidently in, their faces averted from Magnus's side of the room. Although Magnus looked over the newcomers with care, he did not recognize them. Nor did he sense the threat they represented as he brought his tankard of ale to his lips. But a moment later he almost dropped the tankard in surprise at the sight of Matthew Bell and John Langley Hunter. Both of them wore smiles as they stood before Magnus.

"It's been a long time, Major DeWitt," Matthew said, "although I've followed your career with interest. Do you still hear from our friend Whitehead? And does he still specialize in torture?"

Magnus could only stare as he recognized not only Bell and Hunter, but the danger he faced. He was unarmed, his pistol still in his coat, and out of uniform—which made him a prime candidate for a hangman's noose. A rebel hangman.

"Well," Magnus said, forcing a smile, "and what is it brings you here? And you, John Langley?"

"We came for you, Major," Matthew said. "A pity you aren't wearing that pretty red uniform of yours."

"I am in uniform, Bell. I switched coats because the weather's a bit warm, that's all."

Matthew's eyebrows arched high and he stroked his beard as he turned to Hunter. With the movement, Magnus saw that a finger was missing from the rebel's hand and he suddenly remembered how intent Major Winslow Whitehead had been on capturing Bell. He knew for a fact that Bell had suffered torture under Whitehead. The question now was the price Magnus might have to pay for having taken part in Bell's capture, and for not having put a stop to the torture that had awaited the rebel.

"I don't see any uniform," Matthew said. "Do you, John Langley?"

Hunter lit a cigar from the candle on the table before responding. "I say it doesn't really matter much. Not if we can come to an agreement, Magnus."

"Just what is it you want?" Magnus asked.

John Langley took a chair at Magnus's left and motioned for Matthew to take the chair on the right. "Now, Magnus, can you give us an idea what your commander is up to?"

"All I can tell you is that Clinton is worried about the French fleet." Magnus searched the room with his eyes, seeking help from any quarter, but finding none. He knew he hadn't a prayer against Bell and Hunter unless he received help. Even Ben Ballis was absent.

"You mean the fleet that isn't there anymore," Matthew said wryly.

"Its destination is very important to us," Magnus said, but it was obvious that his words revealed nothing Matthew and Hunter did not already know.

Magnus smiled thinly, then coughed as Hunter's cigar smoke filled his nostrils. "How did you know I'd be here?" he asked.

"It seems," Hunter said, "you mentioned to a friend of ours that you'd be here tonight."

"A friend of yours?" Magnus stared at Hunter,

then at Bell. Could they be serious? He shook his head, realizing that they were. "Lee's messenger," he said weakly. "He was in Washington's employ all the time? Tempting us, using us. We even paid him! But . . . why did he give us Barren Hill? Lafayette's surveillance of Philadelphia?"

"You'll have to ask General George about that," John Langley replied. "I suppose he figured you'd expect surveillance anyway, so he gave you some."

"Then you, Bell, you didn't warn Lafayette as I had heard? He knew we'd be coming anyway?"

"Of course I warned him—but only a short time before he'd have pulled out anyway. He didn't expect you to get there quite as quickly as you did."

"You're wasting time, Magnus," John Langley broke in. "There's no point in going into the past—not even between you and me. We may have been friends once, but if we haven't squared our differences by now, I doubt we ever will. Just tell us what we need to know. That way you can die of old age instead of in a hangman's noose." He fished in his pocket for a piece of paper and then handed it over. "Here's a list of what we have to know, Magnus. Look it over. It deals with Clinton's plans for New England, New York and the South."

Magnus pretended to study the questions on the sheet of paper while trying to estimate his chances of escaping his two formidable adversaries. Would they shoot him down if he managed to get away even for a moment? Shoot him even though they wanted information from him? Magnus knew Hunter had better sense than to kill a goose that could lay golden eggs. But Bell might be another matter. And did they have a rebel patrol outside? Magnus's eyes suddenly widened as he saw two newcomers enter the tavern. One of them was Schuyler—in civilian clothes in spite of Magnus's warning. The other was Joanna Baker, his father's servant and mistress!

After wearing his redcoat uniform for more than forty days, Schuyler felt strange without it. He knew he could not have brought Joanna with him to the tavern if he had worn his uniform, however, for to have done so would have attracted far too much attention.

Remembering Magnus's warning about being hung as a spy if caught out of uniform, Schuyler had slipped the pair of pistols he had inherited from Lieutenant Chambers into his coat. He hardly expected to use them, but he felt more comfortable with them primed and ready.

He did not at first notice Magnus and his two companions. Magnus had told him earlier that he planned to call on an old friend who lived several miles upriver, so he was the last person Schuyler expected to see. When Schuyler did see his brother, he could hardly believe his eyes. Magnus wore a civilian coat, and after warning Schuyler against doing just that . . . Had Magnus taken leave of his senses?

Magnus had probably seen them, for he was looking straight at Joanna, though with no sign of recognition. Well, no harm done, Schuyler thought. Magnus would not be likely to tell their father that Schuyler was squiring Joanna around. And even if he did, Schuyler would be glad. He did not wish to return to New York without Joanna and he could not have her without facing his father and asking him to release her.

The room was noisy as Schuyler and Joanna took a table some distance away from Magnus, the girl with her back to her brother. Almost as quickly as he sat down, Schuyler's eyes were caught and held by his brother's. Then, when one of Magnus's companions half-turned in Schuyler's direction, Magnus looked away. The moment his companion turned back, Magnus immediately stared at his brother again.

"What's wrong, Schuyler?" Joanna asked, noting his discomfort.

"I'm not certain anything is," Schuyler replied, "but my brother is there—over there."

"Goodness! Will he give us away?"

"I don't think so. But he's acting strange and I'm not sure why. Those two men with him—have you ever seen them around here before?"

Joanna flashed a look at the men, then shook her head. "I've never seen them before."

"I swear he's trying to tell me something, Joanna. He warned me not to wear civilian clothes, so that I couldn't be caught by the rebels and hung as a spy, yet there he is, without his red coat himself and seeming to be the center of attention of two strangers. And he surely seems nervous. Do you see how his fingers play with his right earlobe, Joanna? I've never known him to do that unless he was bedeviled about something."

Joanna looked, then shrugged impatiently. "They seem peaceable enough. Must we worry about Magnus? I thought we came here to enjoy ourselves, Schuyler."

"I can't Joanna. Not now. Not until I'm reassured about Magnus, until I'm certain he isn't in trouble. I'll pay him a visit. If all is well, I'll return in a moment."

He arose and walked casually toward his brother's table. For reasons he was not sure of himself, he kept his hands in his pockets, his fingers on the triggers of his two pistols.

Magnus stopped him with an almost imperceptible shake of his head and Schuyler veered away, reaching the bar just as both of his brother's companions turned toward him. Out of the corner of his eyes Schuyler saw them throw him a quick look, then turn back.

Schuyler secured a drink for Joanna while he watched his brother and the two men, both of whom seemed far less uneasy than did Magnus.

Certain now that the men were rebels who had somehow taken his brother prisoner, Schuyler moved quickly back to his table. "Stay right where you are, darling," he said. "Magnus is in trouble and I must help him. I'll return shortly."

She started to protest, but he was gone before she could make herself heard.

As he continued to evade the questions from Hunter and Bell, Magnus prayed Schuyler would not misread his message. When the youth began walking straight for his table, Magnus had stopped him with his eyes and probably saved them both. When Schuyler left the tavern, Magnus thought they might now have a chance if the youth came back with help.

"Magnus," Hunter said now, "you've told us nothing we don't already know. The questions are clear. Answer them or ride to White Plains as you are."

"My dear John Langley Hunter," Magnus declared, "has it not occurred to you that generals do not reveal all of their reasoning and strategy to their inferiors? Sir Henry consults me, asks my advice on occasion, but rarely discusses the strategy he's considering unless I'm to be involved in some manner in its implementation. I have nothing to say about how he disposes of his navy, nor am I involved in the movements of the army. I deal strictly in intelligence."

"You're much too modest, Magnus," Hunter countered. "If you were a brand new staff officer, you might be kept uninformed. But not as a senior member of the staff and one who has held his position since before Clinton became commander-in-chief. You're far too valuable an adviser to be kept in the dark, Magnus. Now talk."

Magnus sighed. "Gentlemen, we're wasting time. I cannot and will not reveal anything of importance. What little I know will die with me."

"Indeed it may," said Matthew, regarding him expressionlessly.

"Behave yourself, Matthew," said Hunter. "It will be up to Washington to determine whether the major will be treated as an officer or a spy. Now let's get Magnus out of here before we lose him to a roving redcoat patrol. Magnus, will you come peaceably, or would you rather be executed here and now?"

"I'm unarmed, so it would appear that I've little choice."

"You lead the way, Matthew," Hunter said as the three men rose. "Magnus, you follow him and I'll be right behind you with my pistol at the ready. Make no mistake, I'll kill you if I have to. Don't force me to do so."

"I shall try not to," Magnus murmured as they picked their way between the tavern's tables to the door.

Schuyler's pulse quickened as he watched the three men rise to leave the tavern. He had reconnoitered the area to make certain there were no rebel patrols to help the men inside and was satisfied it was only the two of them against his brother and himself. Now, he thought, as he took his place, he would either make a grand fool of himself or save Magnus's life.

There was a stand of tall scrub pine near the door and there Schuyler concealed himself, drawing out his two pistols. Darkness had fallen, so there was no way Magnus's two captors could detect him before he had them covered with the pistols.

He cautioned himself not to be nervous, but found he was. He told himself he must be wary, yet hold his fire until he was certain he had to shoot in order to save Magnus. He had no desire to kill at close quarters. Though he had killed in battle, it was not the same thing.

His skin prickled as he heard footsteps on the hardwood floor of the tavern, then the sound of voices. The heavy oak door creaked as it was swung open.

Schuyler held his breath as he brought the pistol in his left hand to bear on the lead figure's form, only a few yards away. The man was dead if Schuyler pulled the trigger. But there was the other man to consider and Schuyler held his fire for the seconds necessary to get a bead on him. In a moment he had them both.

"Drop your weapons," he barked out, "for I can kill you both before you can fire."

Bell's arm came up and he was about to turn toward the voice when Magnus said, "Don't do it. My brother is a crack shot and you'll be dead before you can even take aim."

"And you will be too, Magnus," said Hunter from behind him. "If your brother fires at either of us, you're dead as well."

There was silence as the four men assessed their positions. It was Schuyler who broke the stalemate. "It's a draw. Since none of us can win, I'll guarantee your safety if you'll only put your pistols away and leave."

"Fair enough," said Hunter. "Let's go, Matthew. We'll have another chance at the major."

"I shall count to three," said Schuyler. "I'm armed and Magnus isn't. I am also a gentleman and I won't fire unless you force me to. Just lower your weapons and leave. You have my word that my pistols will be lowered as well." He counted slowly to three and lowered his pistols as he saw the two men move quickly up the path to where their horses were tethered.

"I'd suggest you retreat to the tavern, Magnus," Schuyler said, "before one of them decides to turn around and leave you dead. I believe the smaller one, Bell, would gladly do that."

Magnus was inside before his brother completed his suggestion. Schuyler remained in the shadows of the trees until he heard the sound of two horses heading away. Then he followed his brother, who first hugged him in gratitude, then began explaining who Bell and Hunter were.

Before Magnus could finish his tale, a redcoat patrol from New York came into the Golden Hawk. Magnus identified himself to the young lieutenant in charge and ordered him to take his men along the road to White Plains for several miles to seek out Bell and Hunter. The young officer was none too pleased with the prospect of postponing food and drink, but recognized Magnus's authority and left, returning an hour later to report he'd seen no sign of the hunted men.

When Magnus had completed telling Schuyler about Bell and Hunter, he turned to Joanna, giving her a disapproving look and shaking his head. "Now, Schuyler, as grateful as I am for your aid, what are you doing here with Father's bond servant? We both know she beds with the old boy. I don't believe he'd be happy if he were to know of your interest."

Schuyler threw Joanna a reassuring look, then met Magnus's eyes. "We didn't anticipate running into you here, Magnus," he said, "but . . . well, we're in love. I brought Joanna here because I wished to be alone with her, away from the house. It's as simple as that. I really don't care what Father thinks of me for loving her."

"Oh, come now, Schuyler, you can't be serious. The girl belongs to Father. He holds her papers— and her body as well. Even our mother doesn't dare dispute his right to make a mistress of her. If you wish to use her as your mistress too, perhaps he would agree to share her or some such thing. But I don't believe he'd allow you to take her for a wife." Magnus swallowed hard at the last, so distasteful was it to him. "I'm certain we can help you make a better marriage than with a bond servant."

"But I'm serious, Magnus. Joanna is the woman I want. I shan't give her up for you, for Father, for anyone!"

Magnus ordered a flagon of ale as he wondered if he should reveal to Schuyler that he, too, had bedded Joanna. As the ale arrived he decided that Schuyler's muddled state of mind precluded such an admission; he could hardly expect the youth to be reasonable. Time, he thought, would change things. Further argument would serve no purpose.

"Well," Magnus said, "regardless of that, you must take your time about things, Schuyler. You've just taken up your commission and must prove yourself in the army, and the girl has . . . responsibilities at home. After a time, I'm sure things can be worked out to your satisfaction."

Schuyler nodded. "We'll take no action just yet," he said, "though I'm hopeful that our time will come in the not too distant future."

"To be sure," Magnus said agreeably. "Now, I must again tell you how grateful I am that you chose to come here tonight—and acted so capably to prevent me from becoming a prisoner of the rebels."

"Or worse," Schuyler pointed out with a quick grin, "perhaps the victim of a hangman's noose."

Magnus smiled a little wanly. "I must agree there was a distinct possibility of suffering what General Clinton would call the indignity of being hanged."

"Let's hope you never meet with such a humiliation, Magnus. I really have no desire to spend my life trying to keep DeWitt ships scurrying about the globe."

"Yet someone must do it. Father won't go on forever."

Schuyler chuckled. "Let it be you, brother. You're far better suited for it than I."

Joanna did not agree with Schuyler, but she volunteered no comment.

10

WITH THE CONSOLIDATION of British forces in New York, the city, Long Island and Staten Island quickly became a virtual beehive of spies for both sides. Rebel spies could be found wherever there was a Patriot sympathizer, while British spies were almost as numerous as Tories.

Within a month of the British withdrawal from Philadelphia, Molly Minton took up residence in New York in a plush mansion obtained for her by Matthew Bell. She immediately went to work establishing her own network of non-loyalist ladies. And cultivating Magnus DeWitt—a task assigned her by Matthew.

"What if I must bed him?" she asked her lover, a smile on her face.

Matthew scowled before replying. "If you must,

you must," he said, "but pray wash yourself when you're expecting me, for I couldn't stand the Tory stench of him."

Magnus had barely returned from his nearly disastrous date with the no longer mysterious rebel "turncoat" when word came from Rhode Island that the Comte d'Estaing had laid siege to Pigot at Newport.

Sir Henry was bitterly caustic as he listened to Magnus's report on the "Lee" affair. "Perhaps, Major," the commander said, "if you had paid a bit more attention to your real spies, your adversary Bell could not have misled you. Then we might have learned in advance of Washington's plan to attack Newport."

Magnus did not remind Sir Henry that he was not the only one who had been taken in by the bogus turncoat. Or that it would hardly have mattered if Washington had made a public announcement of his Newport siege, since the American general had a clear naval superiority for the moment. The British were only fortunate that the French could not bring their men-of-war over the sandbar at Sandy Hook, for defending New York was not the easiest proposition an unsupported army could take on, as the rebels had learned in '76. Clinton had long ago sent for naval reinforcements for the fleet, but it was not until the seventh of August, a full eleven days after d'Estaing's ships set sail, that four ships of the line reached New York to bring Howe up to strength.

While Howe set sail for Newport to attempt to draw off the French, Clinton considered a piece of advice by his newest staff member, Captain John Andre, that he personally lead a large force north to fight Sullivan. Such a move, Andre maintained, was likely to be successful and could lead to the capture of the rebel's entire army, if the navy defeated the French fleet.

Magnus spoke against the plan, calling it a waste. "By the time you can board the troops and provision them, the battle in Newport will be over. There's no telling how well the inept French sailors will do against ours," Magnus said, "but they're unlikely to defeat us, and Sullivan will be forced to break off his attack and retreat."

"The rebels will not retreat," Andre declared. "They're determined to seize Newport. I have that on excellent authority."

"What authority?" Magnus snapped. He was certain Andre had no spy network or contacts which could have produced that information.

"Ah, but I cannot disclose my source," the handsome young Andre replied with a smile, "lest I endanger his life."

This enraged Magnus. "You would suggest that we—General Clinton's staff—cannot protect the identity of one of our spies or contacts? Sir, that is patently ridiculous!"

Clinton, though obviously enjoying the exchange, cut it off to discuss other matters. But less than a week later, without consulting Magnus further, the commander was assembling an army to sail for Newport on or about the twenty-eighth. When Howe's ships returned from a standoff with the French at Newport—a battle which was broken off because of a howling gale which sent d'Estaing fleeing to Boston—Clinton embarked his troops and sailed with them. Andre was in his entourage and so was Schuyler DeWitt, but Magnus remained in New York.

On the night before Schuyler and the rest of Clinton's personal guard were loaded on their ships, Schuyler was enjoying a tankard of Jersey flip in a New York tavern when he heard a familiar voice behind him.

"Well," said Scott Laidlow, "I see you've at last donned your red coat."

Schuyler's pleasure was genuine as he stood and shook Scott's hand. "Sit down, Scott," he said. "The flip's as good here as anywhere. And I'll buy you one, if you'll tell me what brings you to New York."

Scott's smile was wide as he dropped his bag beside Schuyler's table and sank down into a wooden chair. He winked. "Only a woman could lure me here right now," he said. "And a good woman she is, though I'll not tell such a handsome lad as you who she is, lest you take her away from me. And how goes it with your lady?"

"My brother learned about us and doesn't approve. Fortunately, he's promised not to pass along the information to my father. We're going to do that ourselves when the time is right."

"Well, at least you're stationed close enough to see her. All you need is leave for a few hours in order to go home, I should think. And with a brother on Clinton's staff, obtaining leave shouldn't be difficult."

Schuyler's answering look was negative. "Would that it were so easy. As a lieutenant in Clinton's personal guard, I'm not very high up the totem

pole and I warrant few privileges. The guard is
filled with far higher-ranking officers. As for Magnus, he won't interfere on my behalf unless I ask,
and that I won't do." Now Schuyler's look became
morose. "And soon," he continued, "I'll be . . .
some distance from here and unable to see Joanna
at all."

"I'm sorry to hear it, Schuyler . . . Say, is it true
that Clinton's setting sail to meet Lord North in
the middle of the Atlantic for a parley? I found it
incredible, but if you're in his personal guard and
he's taking it with him on a trip, then maybe it's
true after all."

Schuyler smiled and shook his head. "I can't tell
you much, but it's nothing like that. All I can say
is that I've no idea how long we'll be gone and that
I'll be too far away from home to visit Joanna."

"I know how you feel," Scott replied. "I miss my
own lady here in New York and that's why I'm
here—in spite of all the redcoats and Tory spies
who might try to make trouble for me because of
my old army affiliation. If I had my choice, I'd
take her with me wherever I go, but travel is getting more dangerous with each passing day."

"Do you have much trouble with patrols?"

"Not usually, though there's always a chance
some young officer trying to make a reputation
will chop you up and then plant something on you
that makes it look like you're a spy. But up 'til
now, anyway, I've been lucky."

"You're still taking coaches to and from Rhode
Island?"

Scott nodded. "Things are gettin' a bit hot up
there right now. Sullivan's gone against Newport,
you know."

"Will he be able to take it, do you think? Does he have enough troops?"

"He does unless Clinton reinforces the place with about half of what he's got here. Don't forget, Sullivan's got the French navy up there with all their cannon, along with about ten thousand men."

Schuyler frowned. There were about five thousand troops embarked for Newport. If Pigot had only about two or three thousand, Clinton would be outnumbered. Could Scott be mistaken?

After talking to Scott, Schuyler said his goodbyes to Magnus. He hadn't wanted to worry his brother about his conversation with Scott, but decided at the last moment that it might be wise to tell him after all. After he'd told Magnus that Scott reported rebel strength at Newport at about ten thousand, he wondered out loud if the British were sailing into a trap.

Magnus fell deep in thought over his brother's words and did not immediately answer. He sat behind his desk and strummed his fingers together absently as he considered what he'd just heard. "It's possible Sullivan has that many, Schuyler, although my information puts his strength at two to four thousand less than that. In view of what happened with the French fleet and the demoralizing effect its withdrawal is likely to have on the New England rebel militia units, I rather doubt Sullivan's strength is even five thousand right now. The rebel militia tends to be faint-hearted unless they've got the odds in their favor."

"Then you believe we have a chance?"

"I doubt if there'll be a battle at all, Schuyler. It's a witch hunt inspired by Captain Andre, who wishes to usurp my position on Sir Henry's staff.

Sullivan will pull out once he realizes what he's up against. He's a bumbler, but not crazy."

Suddenly Magnus had another thought. "You say this friend of yours—what's his name—Scott Laidlow—drives the stage to and from Providence? He must be privy to a great deal of intelligence. I'd like to see him, Schuyler, so that I can enlist his services. He might be a valuable addition to my network of spies."

"Not him, brother," Schuyler said with a nervous laugh. "His sentiments are not . . . that is, he's a former Patriot infantryman. Wounded in Boston, he was. He's only recently recovered enough to find work."

"Yet you consort with him? And he with you? Astonishing!"

"We're friends, no more," Schuyler said. "He holds no grudges against me, nor I against him because of our sentiments."

"A dangerous friend to have, Schuyler. He could be a rebel spy."

"But he isn't!"

"How can you be so certain? New York is infested with the rebel vermin."

"If he were a spy, he would have questioned me closely on my destination when I sail tomorrow with Clinton. But he didn't. In fact, he hardly seemed interested."

Magnus concealed his reaction to Schuyler's revelation that he had mentioned his upcoming sea journey to Scott Laidlow. So, the Patriot-sympathizer did not seem interested in Schuyler's trip, he thought. The man didn't have to be! Any simpleton could deduce where Clinton was going from the information offered and the present colonial situation. The only question was whether Laidlow could get the information to Sullivan soon enough to be effective. Well, Magnus thought, the very worst that would happen because of Laidlow's tip was that Magnus would look to Clinton like a prophet when the commander arrived in Newport to find that the enemy had fled.

He thought about warning Schuyler to say nothing of his conversation with Laidlow, but decided against it. His brother thought it an innocent conversation and it would be best if he continued to believe that. Magnus planned to investigate Laidlow and wanted no warning given him by his well-intentioned brother.

Magnus wished Schuyler Godspeed on his journey, then said, "Watch out for the rebel sharpshooters. They find redcoat officers fair game."

"And you beware of rebel troops," Schuyler responded with a laugh. "They're easily sprung with all the spies hereabouts."

On that same evening, Magnus had accepted an invitation to attend a small party given by a local Tory merchant and his wife. There was a sumptuous banquet, which Magnus enjoyed rather too much, and equally enjoyable company. He met a beautiful lady named Molly Minton during the evening, a woman who was a good friend of the hostess. She seemed vaguely familiar, but Magnus could not place her and gave up the effort after a while.

Molly, whose decolletage attracted every man in the room, was strongly attracted to Magnus—or so it seemed. First she drew him out on the floor of the ballroom for a dance, then she spent more than an hour chatting with him in a private room. He was certain she would have responded to an invitation to accompany him home, but Magnus, ever cautious and never more so than since the incident at the Golden Hawk, put off such an invitation for the moment. He found Molly charming and was charmed by her, but was truly concerned that she might be a spy—if only because she paid him so much attention when he was not, after all, known to be a lady-killer. Yet she had talked with him for quite a time and had managed to avoid the subject of the war altogether, and that a spy would not have done. At least not completely.

Magnus decided that Molly would make a delightful wife or a comely and exciting mistress. He resolved to make a few discreet inquiries about the good Mrs. Minton—widow, from what she said —before committing himself to any relationship with her whatever. It would not do for him to take a mistress who might be a rebel spy pretending to be a Loyalist lady. He knew such ladies had existed in Philadelphia and guessed that they must also have penetrated New York society, though he had no proof.

The next day Magnus paid a visit to Sir Henry's rotund American mistress, a pretty woman despite her weight. He asked her about Molly and was pleased to learn that she was already highly respected, although she was fairly new in town. Magnus was not yet satisfied and made a number of other inquiries, learning that Molly was a strong-willed beauty who had resisted long-term liaisons since the death of her husband, and that she was strongly loyal in her political sympathies, as had been her family and her dead husband.

Magnus accordingly took the lady to the theater. And on the very night that Clinton's troops were scheduled to arrive in Newport, he had dinner served to Molly in his rooms and then took her to bed for an evening that was even more delightful than he had anticipated.

Two days later came word that the battle for Newport was over, that Pigot was the victor without benefit of Clinton's reinforcements. Sullivan, it seemed, had abruptly withdrawn on the day before Clinton's ships arrived, and had headed back to the safety of Providence. In a pique, Clinton allowed General Grey, commanding the reinforcements, to sack the Patriot towns along the Atlantic coast from New Bedford and Fairhaven to Newport.

When he learned that his fears about Laidlow seemed confirmed, Magnus ordered his spies and double agents to try to find out what the man was and where he could be located. Another name, he thought, to go with Bell and Hunter.

Just before Sir Henry's return, Magnus learned of General Lee's conviction by the rebel court-martial on three charges, two of them stemming from the battle of Monmouth Courthouse. He was found guilty of refusing Washington's order to attack on the twenty-eighth of June and of misbehavior by making an unnecessary retreat. He was also convicted for disrespect because of the language of a letter he apparently wrote to Washington.

"So," Magnus told Clinton when he spoke to the commander the next day, "Lee really did help us, even though he wasn't our turncoat general. Washington had ordered us attacked, as our information indicated, but Lee never gave the command."

"The man's a fool," Clinton observed. "I thought him only eccentric when I spoke with him while he was our prisoner last year, but now . . . now it becomes clear that he sits upon his brains. Can Washington be so inept that he gives command to such idiots?"

"If he was, sir, he no longer is," Magnus responded, "for Lee has been suspended from duty for a year. By that time he'll be robbed of further command by the mere fact that the rebellion should be over."

Clinton smiled for the first time since his return to New York. "I hope you're right," he said and drained his wine glass with a flourish.

Now Clinton announced plans to take the South, starting with Georgia and the Carolinas, followed by Virginia. With the colonies thus split, he reasoned, the rebels' spirits would be dampened and their supply lines weakened. He could then move, if appropriate, against New England.

After receiving the applause of his staff for his announcements, Clinton then listened to Magnus suggest that they accelerate the rebels' economic woes by flooding the free zones with counterfeit Continental dollars made by a printer who had once worked for the Continental Congress, but was now in British employ.

The moment he voiced the idea, Magnus knew he had just eased himself back into Sir Henry's good graces. Clinton's face was sunny as he absorbed the idea and its potential.

"Magnus," he declared, "that's the most exciting idea I've heard since Howe decided to move against New York two years ago. As you know, desertions within the ranks of the rebels have been slowing in the past few months and that will never do. If we further devalue the money the rebels need to pay their men, many will again consider coming over." Magnus was instructed to make the necessary arrangements for the printing of the currency and decide how to get the newly minted money into circulation.

Magnus now redoubled his efforts to uncover the network of spies who reported directly and only to Washington. He had a strong feeling that Schuyler's friend, Laidlow, might somehow lead him to Bell and Hunter. But try as he might, Magnus got no leads on any of Washington's private spies for more than a month.

Schuyler went home to see Joanna on every occasion he could, and for his trouble grew more and more frustrated. The girl continued to put off the confrontation with his father.

By November, when the war went south for the winter with the British siege of Savannah, Schuyler almost wished he could go south and fight. New York, in spite of the many parties and the droves of willing women, was simply not where he wanted to be. He thought seriously about resigning his commission and even talked to his brother about it. Magnus was appalled.

They stood on the dock watching a five-thousand-man contingent of Clinton's army embark on ships for a trip to St. Lucia Island in the Indies to fight the French when Schuyler spoke his thoughts.

"I doubt you'll like what I'm about to say, Mag-

nus, but I'm so desolate that I fear I'm destined
to leave the army."

Magnus whirled angrily on him. "You would
dishonor our family by resigning? No DeWitt in
the past century has failed to serve with distinc-
tion." Magnus's expression grew stormier at his
next thought. "It's the wench," he said. "She put
such thoughts in your head. Correct? Damn! She's
a worthless—"

"Do not insult her, Magnus!" Schuyler's rage
now matched his brother's. "I haven't spoken of
this to Joanna and I don't intend to. What I've
said is my idea and mine alone."

"If she hasn't suggested it, brother, she has nonetheless inspired it. Of that I am sure."

Schuyler seized Magnus by the collar of his
jacket. "I warn you, Magnus, I will not tolerate
your insults, your preaching. I love Joanna and
I'll have her in the end. You've no right to interfere."

"You fool!" said Magnus. "I've a perfect right.
Now take your hands off me. We're attracting attention."

And they were. A redcoat sergeant waiting to
be boarded had noticed the young lieutenant attacking his superior and was walking toward them.
"Begging your pardon, Major," he said, "is everything all right? Do you need any help?"

Schuyler released his brother, glanced at the
sergeant and turned away. "It's all right, Sergeant," Magnus said. "We're brothers. It's just a
mild disagreement."

"Yes, sir. Sirs. I understand. I've a brother of
my own who's always threatening to wring my

neck." He laughed. "Only I've a difficult neck to wring—it's rather thick, you see."

Neither Schuyler nor Magnus shared the sergeant's mirth, though both had cooled off a bit as they walked back toward Clinton's headquarters.

But Schuyler did not wish to drop the subject. "Magnus," he said, "you must see that I have little of the soldier within me."

"I see nothing of the sort, Schuyler. You look like a soldier, and have on several occasions proven you can act like one. And perhaps saved my life in the process," he added.

"But I don't think like one, Magnus. And frankly, even if I did, it would matter little. I have too great a need for the woman I love. Joanna is my life!"

"She is a mistake, brother. A monumental one. I will not discuss her again with you. In time you'll know she cannot be your wife, that marrying her would be a worse mistake than resigning your commission. Think of what that foolhardy act would mean, Schuyler! Not only the loss of your privileged status as a king's regular, but also the loss of shares in rebel estates which will be distributed at war's end. Perhaps even a governorship."

"I want no part of a governorship, Magnus. Nor any share in rebel estates. Our family already has more than enough property to support both of us handsomely. You believe me a fool for loving Joanna? Well, perhaps I am. Yet what have you to look forward to, brother? You have no woman of your own—not even a mistress, as far as I know.

All you have is your precious commission and your espionage games."

Schuyler paused at the door to Clinton's headquarters and allowed his brother to enter before he continued. "I've no time for your army, brother. I wish to be free to write, to play my music—to love my lady."

"She is no lady!"

Schuyler shot him a black look, turned on his heel and left.

"Schuyler," Magnus called out quickly, "I—" But it was too late. His brother had gone.

11

THE FIRST SNOW of the winter of 1778-79 was falling on the December afternoon when Schuyler DeWitt rode slowly along the stage trail toward home. He had leave until the week after the beginning of the new year and was looking forward to a Christmas with Joanna.

Magnus had been delayed, though Schuyler really didn't care. Clinton had called a full staff meeting for the day before Christmas, four days hence, because of the start of the southern campaign. Schuyler cared little about the southern campaign and would be just as pleased if Magnus did not get home at all. They had not seen each other since their bitter exchange over Schuyler's love for Joanna and his plan to leave the army, though he had yet to renounce his commission.

Whether or not he would leave the army depended a great deal on Joanna, for it had been she whose surprise opposition to his leaving the army had caused him to stay. He really didn't understand her and had told her so.

"First," he had said, "you do not wish me to go into the army. You even fought me over it—remember?" She said nothing as she lay in his arms following a furious mating. "Now you do not wish me to leave the army even though there's nothing to hold me in it. Tell me why."

But she had been able to give him no good reason. She had only said, "Trust me, Schuyler, please. It just isn't the time."

According to Joanna, it wasn't yet the right time to confront Alastair DeWitt either. Would the right time ever come? Schuyler was beginning to wonder. Each time he obtained leave and came home to see her it was with the determination that he would finally force the issue. But each time he found himself unable to resist Joanna's spell.

Now he shook his head at his despairing thoughts and spurred his horse to a gallop as the snow-covered trail opened out east of the river.

Around the next bend, he had to bring his horse to an abrupt halt, for a stage was blocking the trail, its main axle damaged by a boulder left in the trail by a rockslide off the mountain to their right.

The coach's four passengers stood watching while the driver removed the boulder and repaired the damage. The sight of Schuyler's red coat drew a mixed reaction from the passengers. Two of the men, obviously Tories, beamed, while the other man glowered to show his anti-British sentiments. The woman's look was one of guarded interest.

Schuyler threw the group a half-salute in greeting. "Bad day to be having trouble of this sort," he observed. "Can I be of service?"

The driver's back had been turned to Schuyler, but now the man turned around, his hands still on the undercarriage of the stage. "Schuyler!" he said. "For God's sake, you do turn up here and there! You haven't by any chance got a patrol of the King's soldiers with you? I could use them right now. It appears I'll have to change axles."

"Just my lonely old self, Scott," Schuyler responded with a grin. "But I'll be glad to give you a hand."

"Give me two, for I shall need them both."

And Scott did. But after twenty-five minutes of struggling, the two men had managed to replace the axle with the spare one Scott carried.

The snow was falling heavily now and most of the passengers got back in the coach as Scott and Schuyler spent a few minutes renewing their friendship. The woman, however, tarried outside to thank Schuyler for helping with the problem. "I do appreciate it," she said. "I should hate to be stuck in this God-forsaken place."

Scott laughed. "Mrs. Clarissa Beauford," he said by way of introduction, "meet Schuyler DeWitt—Lieutenant DeWitt of the King's army. Schuyler lives not far from here, Clarissa, so watch what you say about this part of New York."

Schuyler found the woman's look of appraisal a trifle disconcerting, but managed a smile in return. "I hope you have a pleasant trip, Mrs. Beauford. Is your husband in New York?"

The woman's smile turned into a faintly mocking grin. "My husband is dead, Lieutenant De-Witt. I've just spent time with a sister in Rhode Island and now am to visit another relative in New York. Eventually I shall find my way home to Virginia. I've a plantation west of Portsmouth."

"Well, we'll be going soon, Mrs. Beauford," Scott said, "so you'd best climb back into the stage."

Watching the woman's ascent into the stage, Schuyler was struck by her easy grace. She was nearly as tall as he, with attractive, distinctive features and hair of a rich brownish red.

"Thanks a lot for the help," Scott said, interrupting Schuyler's thoughts.

"Will you be heading back this way after Christmas, Scott? I'll be here until about the eighth of January and then back to New York."

"Maybe I'll see you in New York. I don't expect to take another stage for a few weeks. I'm tired out and just want to spend some time with my lady."

Schuyler waved as Scott mounted the top of the stage and urged the horses forward toward the city. Then Schuyler headed his own horse north toward DeWitt Manor.

Back in Clinton's headquarters, Sir Henry was having a serious discussion with Magnus about the lack of security in recent months. "Major," Clinton stormed, "we must crack down on the spies who infest New York. Washington seems to know our plans almost before we make them. We could have trapped Sullivan at Newport were it not that he was forewarned!"

Magnus said nothing as Clinton ranted on, blaming every failure of his seven-month-old military campaign on rebel spies. Spies were not to blame for every one of them, Magnus knew, but then Sir Henry knew that, too.

"Have you any idea how they're breaching our security?" Clinton asked Magnus.

"The rebels have hundreds of spies in New York," Magnus replied. "In the main, they're civilians who merely pass on what they see and hear. But as irritating as they can be—and informative to the rebels—the worst spies are Washington's personal ones. These, I'm told, are few in number, but quite effective because they report only to Washington and he keeps everything they say to himself so there can be no leaks. Matthew Bell and John Langley Hunter are among Washington's spies. Another who may be is a stage driver named Scott Laidlow. I'm actively seeking all of them. I also have reason to suspect that a few ostensibly Tory women are on Mr. Washington's payroll."

"What are you doing about them?" Clinton asked.

"I can do little until I can catch them with evidence of their infamy, General," Magnus said. "But with that in mind, I have men watching the homes of a number of suspected local spies. Soon we'll be able to identify their visitors and check them against our list of known spies." Magnus's smile was thin. He was even having the home of Molly Minton watched, and that of Sir Henry's mistress.

Now Clinton began to pace the thickly carpeted floor of his office, stopping periodically at the window which overlooked the Hudson. At last he stopped and faced his adjutant.

"As you know, Magnus," he said, "I abhor violence outside of war. Hangings, for example. But I believe we need an act of violence if we're to discourage the local spies who haunt us. Do I make myself clear?" The general's look was dark as he affirmed his adjutant's conclusion. "Preferably one of Washington's people," he continued. "But the thing is, we have to teach them a lesson they won't soon forget, so get someone to the gallows, whether it's one of Washington's men or not."

"I can't hang a civilian spy, General. I must snare a military spy if I'm to comply with your orders."

"Exactly, Magnus, and quickly, for the southern campaign is proceeding at a good pace and will accelerate as the months pass. I don't wish it to be jeopardized."

Magnus was downhearted as he left to call on Molly, who was to travel home with him the next day to spend the holidays. How, he wondered, could he hang someone when he couldn't even find, let alone catch, one of Washington's spies? The closest he had come to one of the rebel general's men was when *they* had caught *him*—and he had gotten away.

Molly seemed to be the only cheering factor in Magnus's life, although she continued to resist his suggestion that she should share his quarters as well as provide him with bedroom sport. He felt nothing special for her beyond appreciating her unquestioned physical gifts, and he did not entirely trust her. Yet he was grateful for her.

* * *

It was getting late and Molly Minton was nervous as she sat in her drawing room and listened to Scott Laidlow outline the plan he had just delivered for Magnus DeWitt's capture.

In spite of what Magnus represented, she rather liked the powerful Tory. If times were different, she thought, Magnus and Matthew might well be the sole rivals for her affections. But this was war and she had allowed Matthew and Scott to convince her that the capture of Magnus by the rebels would aid Washington greatly in bringing the rebellion to a successful conclusion. And she wanted that, if only because of what it meant to her from a purely financial point of view. She had been promised a substantial amount of property by Washington for her help and she meant to get it. She would receive nothing, chances were, if the British won the war.

Molly was to ride with Magnus by coach to the DeWitt home, and now she knew that a rebel patrol commanded by John Langley Hunter and including Matthew Bell would stop the coach outside the city and take Magnus prisoner. Molly's task was to keep Magnus from pulling out a pistol and fighting for his life. "We want him alive and we want to stay alive, too," Scott told her.

Molly accepted the tiny derringer pistol Scott gave her and listened as he instructed her in its use.

"But I'm not sure I could shoot," Molly warned him. "To do that at close range might kill him," she said.

"You must be prepared to do it if necessary, Moll," Scott said. "Little in war is pleasant, of that you can be certain. Don't believe for even a minute that DeWitt wouldn't have you tortured on behalf of his King. He may not have tortured Matthew, but then he didn't stop it, either."

Molly nodded. She still found it difficult to believe that anyone could inflict torture on another human being, but she had seen evidence of it on Matthew's body.

Just then, the clock over her mantel struck seven and Molly started. "You'd best be leaving, Scott," she told him. "Magnus is quite punctual and ought to be here any time now."

"Don't worry, Molly," Scott responded, "DeWitt has never seen me. I could shake his hand without fear of his knowing who I am. And he has no knowledge that I'm a spy."

"I do not fear for you, Scott," she said, "I fear for me. If you were found here, perhaps they would put *me* to torture. What a dreadful thought!"

Laidlow could not help but chuckle. "Very well, Moll, I'll go now. I shouldn't wish to be the one to cause you such a horrible fate. If I'm not in New York when you return after Magnus's capture," he added, "don't worry about me. I have people to see and information to gather. Clinton is up to no good in the South and I must learn as much as I can about his plans. Clarissa Beauford, John Langley's sister, will carry a message to General Lincoln in Georgia if I can learn something of value. And I intend to!"

Scott Laidlow's exit from Molly's house, like his entrance an hour earlier, was observed by a Tory informer named Horatio Howe, whose activities had turned up a number of Patriot spies during the past two years. His service to the King, all of it undercover, had begun during General Gage's tenure as British commander in Boston, when he had often carried messages from Dr. Church of the Continental Congress, who now resided in a Connecticut prison.

Howe, a poor relation to the famous military Howe brothers of England, was immediately suspicious of Laidlow because he was young and out of uniform. If he was a Loyalist, Howe reasoned, he was no doubt a deserter; if a rebel, he could be a spy.

Knowing he had the special assignment of watching the home of Major DeWitt's mistress, Howe also knew the major would be along shortly and would want an immediate report. Accordingly, Howe stopped the major's buggy when it drew near the house and told Magnus of Molly's visitor.

Magnus was not pleased by the revelation, but neither was he dismayed. The man could merely have been one of Molly's other lovers, of whom, Magnus was certain, there had been many. Then again, he could be a spy. And that interested Magnus greatly, so he read Howe's description of the man several times to mentally compare it with other descriptions he had memorized. It sounded, he thought, like Schuyler's sketch of Scott Laidlow, though he couldn't be sure because he had not asked Schuyler to give a detailed description.

Magnus instructed Howe to continue to watch Molly's house and to report immediately to Magnus's headquarters for a small force of uniformed soldiers to take the man into custody should he show up again. If Magnus was away, he was to be contacted immediately.

As he made love to Molly Minton later that eve-

ning, Magnus made a decision which might well
have saved his life. He decided to take Molly home
not by coach, as he had planned, but by water.

And so the next morning he and Molly traveled
only to the river by coach, thence traveling upriver
in a small schooner Magnus arranged for. He
watched Molly's face carefully when he sprung this
surprise on her in the coach, but couldn't detect
any disappointment. In fact, he thought later, it
seemed as if she was greatly pleased by the change,
and enjoyed the trip upriver more than he did.

It was two days into the new year when Magnus
received a messenger at DeWitt Manor and learned
that his men had taken Scott Laidlow into custody.
They even had definite proof that he was a rebel
spy.

Magnus, elated, cut short his holiday and returned to the city the following day.

12

BACK IN NEW YORK, Magnus studied the reports of Laidlow's questioners with more than a little interest. A team of Magnus's best intelligence people had spent four days trying to wear Laidlow down following his capture.

The man, however, denied almost everything. He admitted to having known the favors of Molly Minton, but denied that he had any knowledge of the papers he carried, which, though bearing no signatures or names, left little doubt that their bearer had to be a spy. Laidlow's papers listed probable British strength in the South and was less than ten percent off. And worse, the papers told of Clinton's probable course of action in his southern campaign for the first six months of the year—and were entirely accurate. It was as if Laidlow had attended Clinton's staff meeting little more than two weeks before.

Astonishing? It was hugely disappointing to Magnus that anyone could have secured such accurate espionage information, so quickly and with so little apparent effort, so soon after the information's dissemination.

Now Magnus had Molly brought to his office on the pretense that he had a surprise for her. After seating her with a show of consideration and affection, he excused himself for a moment and left her alone. In a few moments, a manacled Scott Laidlow was brought into his office. Magnus watched the proceedings through a peephole from an adjoining office.

Molly frowned at the sight of the prisoner, but she showed no other sign of recognition. Laidlow looked at her lasciviously, his eyes on the ample bodice of her dress.

"Haven't we met, Moll?" the man said. Then he chuckled at the look he got from her. "I'd know that front anywhere!" He nodded imperceptibly.

Molly, however, did not immediately get the message. "Hardly, sir," she said, turning away. Then she turned back. "What did you call me?"

Laidlow laughed. "Why, what I always call you, lady—Moll. You honestly don't remember me? Your own . . . Scott, your cousin?"

Now there was recognition on Molly's face. "Cousin Scott? From Boston? But what are you doing here? In irons and in New York."

Scott made a face. "Actually, I was driving a stage until about a week ago. Had a run here and decided to stop in to . . . uh . . . see my favorite cousin. But I missed you. There was nobody home.

I went back a couple of days later and, well, the damned British arrested me as a spy. They wanted to know how I knew you and I told them." He lowered his voice as he added, "But I didn't let on that we're related. Doesn't sound right, y'know, so don't tell them. Okay?"

Now Magnus terminated the meeting. It looked and sounded as if Molly had no connection with Scott Laidlow except as a kissing cousin. But it was impossible to know for certain, of course, and if Molly had been exercising her voracious sexual appetite with a rebel traitor, it would not do for Magnus to have anything to do with her.

Once Scott had been removed, Magnus apologized to Molly for the surprise. "I needed to know whether or not you and this fellow were acquainted and in what way you might be involved. He's a spy for Washington, you see."

. Molly's surprise seemed genuine enough. She told him that she and Scott were barely related and had become close friends several years ago after her husband's death. She did not say how close and Magnus did not ask.

Later, Magnus personally interrogated the spy. Laidlow smiled throughout the session, though Magnus used every device he knew to break the man's icy calm and frighten him into telling the truth. In the end, Magnus found himself admiring the man. Even liking him.

"You are a spy," Magnus accused.

Scott shrugged. "I'm a stage driver."

"You carry information to the enemy."

"I carry passengers, sir. Also mail, on occasion, and yes, often personal messages."

"To the enemy?"

Scott's smile became radiant. "Who, sir, is the enemy?"

"The rebels."

"They are not my enemy. They've done nothing to me. I sympathize with them, you know. If you check my record, you'll find I served with the army at Boston—the Continental Army."

"And you still serve the Continental Army?"

"No, sir, I do not. I was wounded at Breed's Hill and mustered out. Since then, I've worked as a stage driver and nothing more."

"Then why do you carry intelligence which gives aid, comfort and information to the King's enemies?"

"I carry papers which were given me to deliver. I was told they were personal papers and that I should allow no one to read them."

"Who were you to deliver them to?"

"Which papers?"

"The ones which tell of British strength in the South—and Clinton's plans for a southern campaign throughout the winter months."

"You're not serious! That was what was in the papers I was carrying? No wonder you've brought me in for carrying them!"

Magnus studied the man, infuriated at him, yet admiring his audacity.

"Perhaps you'd be more cooperative if we were to put you to torture," Magnus suggested.

"I would immediately tell you anything you wish to know, Major," said the prisoner, "for I'm extremely faint-hearted and cannot stand pain."

"Such as your status as one of Washington's spies?"

"If you wish, sir."

"And the names of your fellow spies? Bell and Hunter, for instance?"

"As you desire, sir."

"And your military rank?"

"Now there, you've got me. If you insisted and made things really painful for me, Major, I guess I'd invent something, though you see, I have none."

"You have bedded your cousin?"

"Under torture I'd admit that, but no other way," Scott said. "Who would not like to make love to the charming Moll? She is indeed a lovely lady. Or hadn't you noticed?"

Magnus colored and turned away. Before he left the prisoner, however, he made one last try. "We will no doubt hang you, you know," he told Laidlow.

At which the prisoner frowned and dropped his defenses, but not by much. "Really? For what? You can prove no connection between me and the army. Therefore I'm not subject to being hung as a military spy."

"Nevertheless, Scott Laidlow, you're almost certain to be hanged unless you give us the information we seek. Sir Henry needs someone to serve as an example to other spies. I'm afraid you are to be it."

Laidlow said nothing for a short time, then again met Magnus's eyes. "You mean it, don't you?"

"I'm afraid so. My brother said you were a nice sort, and I must confess I agree with him. I can easily see why he considered you his friend." Magnus turned to leave.

"Give Schuyler my regards, Major," Scott said. "Tell him . . . tell him I would like to see him before . . ."

"I'll make sure he's allowed to see you, Mr. Laidlow, but I won't be able to deliver your message. I'm afraid I shall have to dodge him for a time because I have no answers to the questions he's sure to have for me."

Again Magnus started to leave and was stopped by Laidlow's voice.

"Did you know that Matthew Bell would be tortured when you captured him, DeWitt? I find it hard to believe."

Magnus was pale when he turned to face Laidlow. "I was younger then—and considerably more impetuous. I was never a butcher, Mr. Laidlow, but . . . I was there and could have stopped it. I should have shared the guilt. I do share it."

Clinton was pleased when Magnus reported that Laidlow had been apprehended. "We shall hang the blighter," the general declared. "Right over there," he added, looking out into the square to the right of the river.

"There's no doubt that he's a spy, Sir Henry," Magnus replied, "but I cannot prove he holds rank in the rebel army. He won't admit it and I'm not sure that he would own up to it even under torture."

"We'll hang him anyway, Magnus! It's only protocol that causes us to refrain from hanging civilians."

"And fear of retaliation from the enemy, sir," Magnus pointed out. "If we hang Laidlow, we may endanger the lives of many of our own civilian spies. And we may lose them entirely, for no amount of cash can compensate a man for running that high a risk of death."

"Still, we must deter the rebel spies, Major," Clinton declared, "no matter the risk. I will win this war, whatever the odds. To safeguard my men in the South, I need a hanging. Therefore I'll sign an order for Laidlow's public execution. See that the populace has ample notice of it. I want the square filled."

With a heavy heart and many trepidations, Magnus went about seeing to the preparations for Scott Laidlow's most inglorious moment.

Schuyler returned to New York nearly a week later than his brother. Angry over Joanna's continued refusal to face his father, Schuyler's heart was already heavy when he saw the posters hung around the city proclaiming the hanging of Scott Laidlow a week hence.

The youth shook his head in disbelief as he digested the news. Scott? To be executed? No, it could not be. It must not be!

He tried to see Magnus in Clinton's headquarters, but was told he wasn't in. When he went to Magnus's quarters, Magnus's man claimed he wasn't there, either. Nor was he at the home of Molly Minton, who seemed to have left on a trip in rather a hurry.

After two days of trying unsuccessfully to see Magnus, Schuyler visited the jail where Scott was being held. Surprisingly, after he had given his name, he was allowed to visit the prisoner.

Scott seemed in surprisingly good spirits and glad to see Schuyler. After exchanging greetings, Schuyler told Scott he had been trying for days to see his brother, without success. "He either can't or won't talk to me, Scott."

"He has no answers for you, Schuyler," Scott said, "and that's why he won't see you. He told me Clinton planned to hang me, even though they can't prove I was a military spy. It seems they need an example to frighten the rebel spies of New York."

"*Are* you a spy, Scott?"

Laidlow studied Schuyler for a moment before replying. "I haven't admitted that to anyone, Schuyler, and won't to you, either. I can tell you, though, that I have no military rank."

"Won't the rebels try to rescue you, Scott?"

Scott nodded and began to pace his cell. "Yes," he said, "they might at that, though I hope they won't. I'm sure you know how well guarded this place is. It would be futile and would not only leave me still a prisoner, but result in the deaths of my would-be rescuers. If I could get a message to Washington's headquarters right now, it would be to tell him that I die for freedom—that there's no reason for any others to lay down their lives for me."

"Don't give up yet, Scott," Schuyler said. "I'll speak to Magnus. Perhaps we can still do something. If he can't or won't help, I'll disown him as a brother. I'll free you myself, if necessary!"

"No!" Scott roared. "I won't have it, Schuyler. I see nothing wrong with your talking with your brother about me—though I know you'll be unsuccessful because it's out of his hands. But I will not have you risking your life to save me. It isn't necessary. And should you try, I'll refuse to go with you. Do I make myself clear?"

"I won't defy you, Scott, though I don't understand you. You want to die?"

"Of course not. But it's in the cards. It's my time. I can see that now, that there's no alternative. You can't save me, the rebels can't save me—only Clinton can. And he won't, because at this stage of the war my death is too important a symbol. And so . . . as the French say, *c'est la vie.*"

The visit with Scott was disturbing, but Schuyler became even more disheartened when his efforts to see his brother over the next two days proved futile. At last Schuyler tracked Magnus down to a tavern where Clinton and his staff were supping. Laidlow's execution was barely forty-eight hours away.

Magnus looked up with alarm at Schuyler's approach, but the youth stood next to his chair before he could even contemplate an escape. "I wish to talk with you, brother," Schuyler said, aware that Clinton and his associates were all staring at him.

"And you shall, Schuyler," Magnus said, "but not here and now. Meet me in my rooms later this evening, if you will."

"No, sir. I've been to your rooms often enough already, and you always seem to be unavailable or so I've been told by your man. I'll talk with you now, if you please."

Clinton focused inquiring eyes on his adjutant, but said nothing.

"Later," Magnus repeated, flashing his brother a steely-eyed look of warning.

"If you won't talk with me, perhaps General Clinton will," Schuyler said, meeting Magnus's stare with cold eyes of his own. Now he raised his voice slightly and added, "It's about Scott Laid-low."

"What of the spy?" Sir Henry inquired from across the table.

Magnus quickly rose from his place, almost knocking over a flagon of red wine in the process. "My brother," he said, "provided the information which led to my apprehending Laidlow. Please excuse us. I'll return shortly."

Before Magnus could get Schuyler away from the table, Sir Henry said, "The lad does well. Perhaps he ought to be on our intelligence staff. His talents are being wasted where he is." But Schuyler hardly heard Clinton's praise, for he was now seething at Magnus's insinuation that he'd had anything to do with Scott's capture. He had no chance to speak, however, until he and Magnus reached a small private room in the back of the tavern. The moment Magnus closed the door behind them, Schuyler exploded in a torrent of words:

"How dare you!" he declared. "I had nothing to do with your capture of Scott! To tell Clinton or anyone else that I did is an out-and-out lie! And now that we're down to it—by what right do you execute a civilian, spy or not? I spoke to Scott and he assured me he holds no rank with the rebel army. He shouldn't be a candidate for the hang-man's noose. What say you to that?"

"What care you for a rebel spy, whether he's connected with the military or not?" Magnus replied. "You are a soldier of the King, and should therefore be loyal to the Crown, not to a rebel of any stripe."

"King's soldier or not, I have a right to pick and

choose my friends. Scott has admitted to no one that he's a spy—*if* he is. I ask you again, by what right is he to be hanged?"

Magnus regarded his brother coolly and tried to compose himself. He was dismayed at having to defend such a dishonorable act as the proposed hanging of Scott Laidlow, yet knew he had to.

"I skirted the truth with Clinton just now for your good as well as mine," Magnus said. "You would have made me the laughingstock of his staff had I let you. And the ringing declaration you were about to make of your friendship with the spy might well have resulted in your mustering out of the King's army in disgrace."

"Disgrace? You are in disgrace, brother, not I! In less than forty-eight hours, it is you who will allow Scott to be hanged when he doesn't deserve to. For the last time, I ask you why."

Magnus met his brother's eyes for a moment, then looked away. "Yes, your friend will be hanged, Schuyler, and I regret it. But neither you nor I can do anything about it for it is Sir Henry's will. Did Laidlow *deny* to you that he was a spy??"

"No," Schuyler admitted, "but you yourself said the gallows are reserved for military spies."

"As normal protocol, Schuyler, that's true. But these are trying times and Sir Henry is under great pressure to bring the rebellion to an end. Rebel spies are everywhere. They somehow learn our plans almost before they're devised. Laidlow's death is to provide an example. Clinton wants the citizenry to think twice before it engages in any spying for the rebels."

"An example? A mere bloody example?" Schuyler could barely believe his ears. "Clinton would kill him only to set an example for others? My God!"

"I sincerely wish I could prevent it, Schuyler," Magnus said, "but I can't. Laidlow must die, and he will."

"It's murder! Cold-blooded, deliberate murder."

Magnus wished he could disagree. "Clinton is commander and has the power to do precisely as he wishes. I can disagree with him—and have done so in this case. Yet in the end, his orders will be carried out."

"He's a monster!"

"Normally, he isn't. I've known him as a kind man, one who despises cruelty of any sort, on any level. He's never allowed troops serving under him to hurt or maim indiscriminately. Once, in the course of my intelligence work I participated in the torture of a rebel. I neither instigated nor performed the torture, but I was guilty because I did not prevent it. Sir Henry went into a rage when he learned of it. It was not my most shining hour."

"If Clinton's so bloody kind, brother, then how can he justify such a heinous act as hanging Scott Laidlow?"

"I've outlined his reasons, Schuyler. If I had a choice, I'd reverse his decision, for practical as well as moral reasons. I don't believe that hanging Scott Laidlow or anyone else will provide the deterrent Clinton expects. Aside from that, I could easily like your friend Laidlow. He's capable and personable, a man I could respect greatly but for the war."

If Magnus thought his brother would be placated by his last remark, he was stunned by the savage attack Schuyler now launched.

"So," the younger DeWitt roared, "you would be Scott's friend? You could respect him? Like him? You hypocrite! You're no less monstrous than Clinton, no less guilty than he of the murder to be committed by your hangman and yourselves."

"I've argued with Sir Henry, done all but pleaded with him—but to no avail. His mind is closed on the subject. He won't even discuss it. Nothing I can do will save Laidlow."

"And what if his friends attempt to rescue him? You said yourself they have spies throughout the city."

"Laidlow is too well guarded. Should any of his compatriots make such an attempt, they'll be caught and no doubt hanged with him."

Schuyler now cursed his brother, Clinton and finally the King. "I tell you now, Magnus," he declared, "that if this hanging takes place I'll abandon my commission immediately. I'll never forgive you for playing a part in Scott's death."

"Please, Schuyler, don't talk foolishly. Consider your actions with care, for they will not only affect you now, but for all time. Your entire future is at stake here."

"Go back to your murdering friends," Schuyler muttered. "They're *your* future, not mine." He was gone before his brother could respond.

Promptly at dawn two days later, Scott Laidlow was removed from his cell and marched to the newly erected scaffolding in the square near Clinton's headquarters.

Security at the jail was as tight as Magnus had said it would be, and neither Schuyler nor rebel rescuers could get anywhere near Scott prior to his date with death. It was Magnus who issued orders that Schuyler was not to be allowed a second visit with Laidlow; he did so out of fear that Schuyler might try to rescue the man. Schuyler did try to see Scott again, after concealing a pistol and a bayonet under the cloak of his uniform. When the guards would not permit his entry into the jail, Schuyler spent the remainder of the night drinking in a New York tavern.

The scene of Scott's hanging became indelibly etched in Schuyler's mind, though his head was still dizzy with the after-effects of his drinking of the night before.

New York's large Tory community turned out in numbers to view the hanging of the Patriot spy—and so did an even larger number of rebel sympathizers. The Tories were raucous and derisive as Laidlow was marched up the steps of the platform to the gallows. A hush settled over the watchers only when he was allowed to speak his final thoughts. He had worn a smile as he marched toward his doom, but now the smile was gone.

Laidlow's voice started out low and raspy, but quickly gained strength and rang through the square. "One day," Scott said, "perhaps we will again be friends with England, our mother country, and its king—in spite of the atrocities being committed in his name."

The redcoat officer who was in charge of Scott's squad of escorts stepped forward to silence him, but he was stopped by the cries of protest from the watchers. At last he shrugged and retreated.

"I don't want to die," Scott continued, his voice ringing out in passion, "but if I must, then I will die for liberty. Not for what the King would have us believe is liberty—which is merely acquiescence to the might of the King's cannon—but for liberty from the whims of a tyrannical king."

The square came alive with sound at Laidlow's speech, and again the British officer moved threateningly toward the prisoner. "More words like those," he told Laidlow, "and I'll have to run you through with my bayonet."

Laidlow simply shrugged. "I faced the British at Breed's Hill as a soldier," he said. "Today I'm no longer a soldier, but I'll try to die as bravely as one. Where I'm going, I'm certain I shall find both Tories and Whigs—in quantity."

There was laughter at that.

"I urge all of you out there to cast off old ideas and attitudes and see the new light in America— the freedom light which will soon burn brightly for all of us!"

Laidlow's speech was brought to an abrupt end when the redcoat officer produced a handkerchief and gagged him. There were angry shouts from the onlookers, but the die was cast and Laidlow's last words over.

Schuyler swallowed hard at the sight of Scott being led to the gallows and the noose being fitted around his neck. Tears stung his eyes as a black hood was pulled down over Scott's face. Schuyler turned away, but found he could not keep from turning back immediately. He didn't see Clinton flutter a red handkerchief in the window of his office across the square, but he did see the result. And hear it.

Schuyler's senses screamed as he heard the sound of the trap door beneath Scott Laidlow's feet being sprung and falling away, and as he saw

his friend's body go limp, his neck broken by the
rope and the force of his fall.

There were a few yells from the Tories among
the crowd. But for the most part, the watchers
were as stunned as Schuyler.

Schuyler was drunk when he rode out of New
York later that day. He wore his uniform, but only
because it made it easier to get past the British
guards at the entrances and exits to the city. He
had resigned and no longer had any official status
with the military.

When Schuyler reached the Golden Hawk Tavern near his home, he changed into civilian clothes
and stuffed his uniform into his saddlebag. After
replenishing his supply of whiskey and watering
his horse, Schuyler rode slowly along the trail to
DeWitt Manor. It was nearly midnight when he
got there—after stopping twice to disgorge the
contents of his stomach and sober up a little.

The house was dark, except for his father's
second-floor bed chambers. Schuyler tethered his
horse inside the stable and was walking back
toward the house when he heard a familiar sound
coming through his father's slightly open window.
A laugh. Joanna's laugh.

He frowned and stared up at the shaded window
just in time to hear the laugh come again. But he
could make out no movements. Nor could he hear
his father's voice.

He let himself into the house as quietly as he
could, took off his boots and proceeded up the
staircase to the family's living quarters. At his
father's door, he paused to listen. The bed creaked,

was silent, then began to make regular creaking noises.

Schuyler sucked in a deep breath and nudged open the door.

Alastair DeWitt's rotund body lay in the middle of his four-poster bed. Astride him was Joanna. She was naked and beautiful, her eyes closed as she rode the old man, the old man who was the father of the man she said she loved. The old man who owned her indenture. Who owned her body.

Schuyler again tasted vomit in his throat as, for the second time in only a few hours, his senses recoiled from the outrage and pain of the sight he witnessed.

"Aye, girl," the old man croaked, "do not stop. I am nearly there!"

If Joanna heard him, she gave no indication of it. She continued to ride the old man at her own pace, for her own pleasure, Schuyler thought, rather than his. Her long hair half-covered her firm young breasts and her flesh glistened with sweat.

It was an arresting sight, but one that paralyzed Schuyler. He tried to cry out in protest, but no one heard, for it was only in his mind. Not until the girl changed her pace and began going at the old man furiously did Schuyler's voice come alive.

"No! No! No!" He screamed out the words that brought both the man and woman to turn to him, their faces ashen.

"Schuyler!"

Both Joanna and his father pronounced his name at the same moment. The girl hastily disengaged herself from Alastair DeWitt and jumped to the floor to clutch a gown to her body, as if to hide herself from Schuyler.

To hide herself? Schuyler could hardly believe it. He glared at her, stalked over to her. "Bitch!" he said, striking a series of stinging, open-handed blows to her cheeks.

Alastair DeWitt, uncomprehending at first, suddenly came to life. "What are you doing, boy? Who gave you leave to burst in here like this? This is my house, not yours. My mistress, not—" Suddenly he fell silent as the truth began to dawn on him.

Schuyler gave Joanna one last hard slap, which she accepted without a whimper. He cursed her for a whore. "Why?" he demanded. "How could you? And you were actually enjoying him!"

By now Alastair was as angry as his son. He was till naked as he got to his feet and tried to wrest Schuyler away from the girl. For his trouble, he was thrown to the floor by Schuyler with an ease that belied the old man's great weight. He struck his head as he fell and appeared to lose consciousness.

Joanna glanced at Alastair, then shrieked at Schuyler with such fury that she was able to squirm out of his grasp. She raced to the wall of the bedchambers and seized a pistol Alastair kept there.

"Get out of here, Master Schuyler," she declared, leveling the pistol at him, "before I blow off your bloody head! I should do it anyway, for daring to strike me that way."

Schuyler stared at her. Could this be the woman he had loved? "You could do that?" he said. "You could kill me? After I've loved you? After I've offered you your freedom and the comforts a good marriage could bring, in spite of your wretched indentured status?"

"I gave you far better than you could've given me," she said. "It was all I could do to put up with your impatience, your jealousy." She glanced again at the old man, who was still unconscious. Then she continued, the pistol still pointed at Schuyler, her breasts heaving.

"I do not need you, Schuyler. I never loved you any more than I do your fat old fool of a father. The reason I kept putting you off was because I sensed the old man might yet take me for his bride, once he'd rid himself of your mother."

Her voice had dropped to a near whisper with the last and she took a step closer to him as she added, "And tonight, Alastair told me he would rid himself of Trientje and marry me." She laughed. "So you see, Master Schuyler, I wasn't merely enjoying bedding the old prune—I was reveling in it! Now, would you like a go at your step-mother-to-be while the old boy's out of it?"

Schuyler brought up his arm with such speed and fury that she never saw it coming. He knocked the pistol out of her hand and sent it spinning across the room. The girl fell backward on the bed, too surprised to react.

With an agonized cry, the youth fled the room. In moments he had descended the staircase, gone out the door and retrieved his horse from the stable.

He was trembling as he rode toward the tavern trying to decide where to go from there. At the very moment that he decided to bypass the tavern and turned his horse south, his father suffered an apoplectic seizure. The old man had heard every word of Joanna's confession.

By morning Alastair DeWitt was dead, but Schuyler DeWitt did not know it. He was already halfway across Jersey, headed south.

PART TWO

PART TWO

1

SCHUYLER WANDERED toward the sunny American southlands at an increasingly leisurely rate as the winter of 1779 turned into spring. He went from tavern to tavern, drinking heavily and giving in completely, if quietly, to self-pity.

While he heard occasional reports of the taking of Georgia by the British, he paid little attention to them, concentrating instead on the whiskey he consumed in substantial quantities. He had no idea where he was headed, he only knew that he wished to be as far away from Joanna and his father as he could get.

From time to time he had run-ins with trouble-seeking rebel or redcoat patrols, but he managed to forestall any serious trouble merely by showing himself to be what he was—a drunk capable of harming no one but himself. They laughed at Schuyler DeWitt, but they left him alone.

In early May, Schuyler was awakened in his quarters at an inn in Portsmouth, Virginia, by the sounds of several thousand marching soldiers. He got out of bed at the sounds of cannon and musket fire, staggered to the small window of his room and stared out in disbelief at what he saw: There were columns and columns of redcoats passing on the road outside. In the three years of the war, there had as yet been no British campaign in Virginia and that was one of the reasons Schuyler had decided to head for the former Jamestown colony.

Across the way Schuyler could see the harbor. It was filled with British ships, where yesterday there had been only cargo boats and a few privateers, all of which had vanished during the night.

Schuyler stumbled to the chest of drawers for the bottle of whiskey he had secured from the innkeeper. He brought it to his mouth and a shudder raced through his body as the amber fluid slid down his parched throat. He was about to go back to bed when the sounds of battle outside intensified. He was to learn later that the British had run into a troop of the Virginia militia while they were looting Portsmouth and the Virginians made a staunch stand before being routed by the invaders. The redcoats sacked the entire area in the next few days, sinking scores of ships and seizing tobacco cargoes with little or no local opposition from the citizenry or militia.

Fearful that the British might put his establishment to the torch, Hannibal Shomes, the innkeeper, went out of his way to placate the officer corps of the marauders, serving meals after hours and putting out his best stock of liquors. For his part, Schuyler wanted to stay out of the way of the British, all of whom had no doubt been stationed in New York. They probably wouldn't recognize him now that he had grown a beard and mustache, but he dared not take the chance.

For the first two days, Schuyler managed to stay out of sight by pretending illness. But on the final day the British stayed in the area, Schuyler roused himself and made an appearance in the public room of the inn. He was scraggly and unkempt as he picked his way through a room crowded with redcoat officers.

As he sat down at the ebony black pianoforte near the window of the tavern, Schuyler was cold sober, but he felt an incredible urge to somehow thumb his nose at the King's officers. He wondered if he could get their attention by playing "Yankee Doodle," a rebel song of some note.

As he was debating that piece of infamy, however, his thoughts were interrupted by the entry into the room of a tall woman with deep red hair. She was on the arm of a British general—General Mathew, it turned out, who commanded the British force which had pillaged the area.

She was stunning and looked somehow familiar to Schuyler, though he could not immediately place her. When he began to play, she looked up, stared at him for several seconds, then smiled, but he looked away and tried to concentrate instead on his playing.

The woman applauded enthusiastically when Schuyler concluded, and so did a number of the others in the room, but he was still puzzling over her because she did not seem to be a typical loyalist lady. He got up from the piano and walked straight to her table, bowed and kissed her hand.

He was about to introduce himself by a fictional name when she told him she had enjoyed his playing and called him "Schuyler." "You must again visit my plantation," she added, turning to the general, who wore a frown as he looked Schuyler over. "Don't you agree, General Mathew?" the woman asked him.

Schuyler was aghast, wondering how she could know his name. She *had* seemed familiar, but he still could not place her.

Then, as the general smiled and said an insincere "Yes, of course," to her question, Schuyler remembered her. She had been a passenger in Scott Laidlow's stage the day he'd run across Scott broken down north of the city. His recollection was that her name was Clarissa. A widow from Virginia, she had said.

"Well, Clarissa," Schuyler said, "I must be going. Send a messenger when you'd like me to call."

He was pleased at the look of surprise his remark brought to her face. She had obviously not expected him to recall her as she had him. He was glad he had remembered her name, though there was pain in the flood of memories which she now triggered in his mind. Memories of Scott Laidlow. And of a gallows.

An hour later Schuyler was half-drunk in his room when there was a knock at his door.

"Lieutenant DeWitt?" The voice was unmistakably that of a woman, Clarissa.

He wove unsteadily toward the door and opened it.

She was smiling. "You have a good memory,

Lieutenant DeWitt," she said, "I congratulate you. And at the same time, I am flattered." She was past him before he could invite her in.

He liked the musky fragrance of her as she swept past. She sniffed the air and allowed a quick look of disdain to show on her face as she recognized the smell of alcohol. Then she turned to face him as he closed the door.

"The last time I saw you, Lieutenant DeWitt, you were a dashing, young redcoat officer who wasn't afraid to get his hands dirty and who didn't smell at all of alcohol, though it was late in the day."

"You're obviously partial to English officers," Schuyler said. "As for the whiskey—I've only recently discovered its delight. I'd offer you a drink, but I'm afraid I have no glass to pour it into."

Clarissa Beauford shot him an odd look, then smiled. "Where is the bottle?" she asked, her eyes sweeping the room. "Get it for me, please."

He looked at her questioningly but then shrugged and obtained the bottle from his chest. She took it from his hands, unscrewed the cap, smelled it, then wiped the neck of the bottle on the skirt of her gown before bringing it to her lips. Schuyler's eyes grew large as he watched her take a deep swallow of whiskey with no apparent effect. Then she recapped the bottle and handed it back.

He started to take a drink himself, but thought better of it and put the bottle away. "So what is it you wish with me?" he asked her. "And why the subterfuge this afternoon about visiting you again?"

"Where is your uniform?" she asked. "Are you a deserter?"

"Would it matter?"

"In a way, though probably not as you may think."

"I resigned my commission. I am now a free man. I belong to no army, to no one but myself."

"Why did you resign your commission, Lieutenant? Did the woman have something to do with it? The one called Joanna?"

Schuyler's surprise showed. How could this woman know about Joanna? "You sound like my brother," he murmured.

"I trust I don't look like him," she said with a laugh. "But tell me, Schuyler, *did* the woman break your spirit? If she did, I shall not be pleased, for I wish to know you better. And I really do have a plantation—actually a tobacco farm—not far from here. If you will, I'd like you to come visit me."

"How do you know so much, Clarissa? First you speak of Joanna, then of my brother—as if you know of them."

"Scott Laidlow was a very good friend of mine," Clarissa said. "He told me many things, among them the story of your love for the bond servant your father kept as mistress."

"Did he also speak of my troubles with Magnus?"

"He said you were very different from your brother, except that both of you are quite intelligent. I already knew you were handsome."

"You say you were a good friend of Scott's, yet you consort with the British—as you did with the general this afternoon." He reached for the whiskey bottle, but she stayed his hand.

"You've had enough, haven't you?" She said the words so gently that he could not have taken offense. "Scott also consorted with the British," she reminded him, "even with you. Like Scott, I am my own person. I do as I wish. I was with Mathew this afternoon because I hoped he would prevent his army from coming to our plantations and destroying our tobacco crops."

"And did he?"

Clarissa Beauford smiled brilliantly. "You shall see for yourself, Schuyler, that he did. And I did not have to bed the good general in order to stay his hand. I merely told him our plantations were supplying British-held New York with tobacco. That satisfied him—though he did wish to visit my bedchambers as well."

"And was that the truth about supplying New York with tobacco?"

Clarissa laughed. "Do I look like a loyalist girl to you, Schuyler?"

He slowly shook his head and gave her an admiring look. "No, and I'm not surprised the general slept alone in spite of his desires," Schuyler said.

"You are sweet, Lieutenant DeWitt. Now, you'd best start packing your things. I've just issued you an invitation that I withheld from the general and I expect you to take it up." She laughed lightly, as she added, "Though I must say that you, like the general, will sleep alone."

It was impossible to refuse the irrepressible Clarissa Beauford. An hour later, Schuyler found himself in an upstairs bedroom of the woman's white plantation house some fifteen miles west of Portsmouth. He still had his whiskey bottle, but he didn't drink from it. Instead, he fell into a heavy sleep without even bothering to remove his rumpled clothing. The next morning he woke and found that he was no longer dressed, though he couldn't remember anyone undressing him. Upon arising, he found a new suit of clothes set out for him. It fit him perfectly.

Downstairs, he was startled to find Clarissa eating breakfast with two men, both of them familiar to Schuyler. Both were dressed in civilian clothes. One wore an eyepatch and had hair the same red as Clarissa's. The other man was slightly shorter, with jet black hair and blue eyes. Clarissa introduced the men as her brother John and his friend Matthew.

Schuyler swallowed hard as he reached out to shake hands with John Langley Hunter and Matthew Bell. They were the same two men who had tried to capture Magnus. And Clarissa said one of them was her brother?

John Langley smiled at the look on Schuyler's face and turned to Clarissa. "Told you he'd recognize us."

"It doesn't matter," she said.

Schuyler glanced from one man to the other and wondered if he was to pay with his life for misjudging Clarissa Beauford's intentions. Even though she admitted carrying messages for the rebels, he had never expected her to be tied in with the notorious Bell and Hunter.

"Clarissa," Schuyler said, "did you get me here to arrange my funeral?"

She turned to Schuyler, her expression serious. "No one's here to arrange any funerals, Schuyler. They want something else entirely, but I hope you'll forgive them—and me—if we get to it in sort of a round-about way."

Schuyler shrugged. "Do I have any choice?"

"None at all. Now tell me, what did you think of what happened to Scott?"

He grimaced at the memory and took a deep breath before answering. "I was ashamed of my uniform, Clarissa, and still am. Or would be, if I were still wearing one."

"How do you feel about Magnus?" Matthew asked.

"He's my brother, though I lashed out at him for not saving Scott's life. I disowned him for it and resigned my commission. Both he and Scott told me that the hanging was Clinton's doing."

"And so it was," John Langley Hunter said. "Whatever Magnus is, he's no fool and hanging Scott Laidlow was a blunder—for ever so many reasons. Magnus had to know that hanging was only going to fire us up."

"Which doesn't bring Scott back," Schuyler bitterly observed.

"He was our brother in his beliefs," John Langley said, "and we would have saved him if we could. But we couldn't. He was a victim of the times and of Clinton's mistaken belief that men can be frightened into giving up their liberty."

"What do you think of the rebels' view of liberty, Schuyler?" Clarissa asked gently.

"It's a bit academic now," Schuyler said. "As I see it, the King has probably granted too little real liberty and you rebels probably want too much. I'd say the King has himself to blame for bringing on the revolt, though I believe there are some patriots as much to blame as King George."

"Agreed there are some bad ones among us," Matthew said, "but you must admit none of them has the power of German George! None of the colonists can take the very bread out of our mouths merely by issuing a proclamation."

Clarissa held up her hand to quiet Matthew's indignation. ""Schuyler, why did you take the King's side in the war? Out of conviction? Or was it something else?"

Schuyler was surprised at their conciliatory attitude. It seemed terribly important to them that they learn his motivations. Well, he thought, perhaps it was time he learned them too. None of it had been clear to him when he was attending college and it had only seemed to grow less apparent since. The affair with Joanna and the unconscionable hanging of Scott Laidlow had severed his ties with the DeWitt clan and set him adrift.

"I had no iron-clad convictions about the politics of the revolution, Clarissa," Schuyler said. "Of course, my brother and father were Tories through and through. And I sympathized with the view that we owed our good life in the colonies to England and King George, and that the rebels were perhaps guilty of ingratitude. I hardly felt strongly about the issue, though. Certainly not enough to lay down my life for King or country.

"Magnus bought my commission and urged me to take it up, although I hadn't asked him to and wished he hadn't. I wasn't ready for any kind of responsibility and had no wish to become a soldier anyway. I resisted Magnus and my father as long as I could, but then I finally gave up and became a King's soldier."

"And how do you feel now?" Clarissa asked.

Schuyler grinned. "You wish to hear me say I

now hate the King and everything he stands for? That now I'm a dyed-in-the-wool patriot, willing —nay, eager—to serve my country against the oppression of the cruel German George?" He shook his head. "I can make no such statements, for I do not feel them. Anger and frustration are what drove me out of the King's army, not political conviction. Scott's death caused a fury in me I had never known I could feel. I still feel it, against the King, his commander—even against Magnus, though I'm convinced now that he was powerless to stop the hanging. As I watched Scott die, I knew I would never again serve his killers." He paused to look at Bell, Hunter and the beautiful Clarissa Hunter Beauford.

"I thought Scott's death was the crowning blow —until I reached home to find that the woman I loved was not only unfaithful but was a bloody whore. Learning that, I left home and came south. My thoughts since then have been a trifle dulled and by my new-found taste for whiskey."

Clarissa, her dark eyes soft with compassion, reached across the table to take Schuyler's hand. Bell and Hunter did not betray their thoughts. That, Schuyler thought, was probably what made them such good spies.

"Now that I've bared my very soul to you," Schuyler said, "would you be good enough to tell me why it seems to matter to you? Are you so desperately in need of soldiers that you'd recruit a man who has no wish to be a soldier at all?"

Bell and Hunter exchanged glances and looked uncomfortable, but Clarissa merely smiled, her eyes focused on Schuyler's.

As Schuyler took in the warmth in her eyes, he

suddenly understood his situation. His mouth fell open and his expression became one of pure incredulity. "Good God!" he said at last, "I believe I know what it is you wish of me. You think to recruit me, not as a Patriot, nor as a soldier, but— as a bloody spy! You wish to have me spy on Clinton by returning to seek a position on his staff!"

Clarissa looked smug, but the two rebel spies showed their newfound respect for Schuyler De-Witt by the amazement on their faces. He had put his finger on precisely what they had in mind.

2

WHEN MAGNUS returned from his home in Hastings after spending three months arranging his father's burial and business affairs, he was not at all happy to find Captain John Andre in his office with his feet up on the desk.

Andre hastily removed his feet when he saw Magnus, then explained that Clinton had ordered him to take charge of Magnus's espionage work during his absence. Two days earlier, Andre told Magnus, triumph in his voice, he had received a message from a "prominent American officer who wishes to come over to our side."

Magnus received this piece of news with utter disdain. Let Andre make a fool of himself, he thought. Did the rebels believe they could pull the same trick twice? He told Andre he could handle the matter on his own, but was to report on his negotiations to Magnus as they occurred. After Andre had reported the rest of the business of the past three months, Magnus dismissed him and sat back in his chair to think.

Things could not easily be worse, he decided, what with his father dead, his brother góne heaven-only-knew-where and Clinton placing his trust in an incompetent like Andre. Thank God for Mother, Magnus reflected. Although she had never meddled with Alastair's management of the family business, a thorough knowledge of it had been ingrained in her by her Dutch parents before she married. With Alastair's somewhat perplexing death, she had stepped in to take over, thus freeing Magnus of any need to resign his commission to handle the DeWitt business interests.

Magnus absently scratched his head and lit the pipe he had taken to smoking in recent months. Once again he considered the two things which had been bothering him the most: where Schuyler had gone following his disappearance and what had brought on Alastair DeWitt's fatal seizure. Magnus had wondered if Schuyler had played any role in their father's death. He had also wondered whether Joanna might be lying when she said she had no idea what had happened. After all, she was his father's mistress and could have been in his bed the night he succumbed. Yet she said she had not and Magnus more than half believed her; she could have nothing to gain by hiding the truth.

Schuyler. The youth could have played a part in his father's death, though Magnus had no idea what. It was known that Schuyler had come home the night Alastair died, because the tavern-keeper had seen him. But no one had seen him at home. Trientje had been away and Joanna and the other servants had been sleeping—or so they claimed.

Schuyler. He had been livid over Scott Laidlow's execution and had left his resignation with Magnus's man. He had left no message, only the resignation. Magnus had hoped that his brother would come to his senses before too long, and had quietly arranged for an indefinite leave to be granted him so that the resignation would not have to be submitted to Sir Henry. Magnus still hoped Schuyler would walk in one afternoon, apologize and re-join the army, though his hopes were growing fainter with each passing day. He prayed no harm had come to his brother, wherever he was.

Schuyler had not seen Joanna the night his father died—or at least that was the girl's contention. Magnus was inclined not to believe Joanna on that one, though he was puzzled as to why she would lie about it. Schuyler would certainly have tried to see Joanna. It was possible, of course, that she had not wished to see him, that they had quarrelled. She was strong-willed and hot-tempered enough to keep him away if she didn't want to see him.

And to see a man she wished to see, Magnus thought ruefully, recalling the scene in his bedchambers on the night Alastair was laid to rest in the family graveyard not far from the house. Magnus had been shocked to find Joanna in his rooms. He had not wished her there and had ordered her to leave. But the bold wench had immediately used her wiles to make him desire her, and soon he had claimed her as she so obviously wished to be claimed.

The girl had been better than Magnus remembered. Far, far better. Magnus used her ruthlessly and she had reveled in the use. He had ordered her to do things which would have repulsed many a woman, yet Joanna had performed to his taste and with an ardor he had never before experienced. The first few times he had taken the girl, he had felt a trifle odd, knowing she had been his father's and his brother's mistress. But thereafter he found himself more and more bewitched by Joanna, until he had been tempted to bring her back to New York with him. He had decided against it, primarily because he felt she would be far too great a distraction and would cause him to shirk his duties with Clinton's staff. Now, as he tried to gather his thoughts and get down to business, Magnus wished he had not left the girl in Hastings, that he had her to look forward to when his day of work was done.

Moments later, an aide came in to inform Magnus that Sir Henry wished to see the latest intelligence on the rebel fortification at Stony Point, not far from West Point on the Hudson. Fortunately, Magnus had an up-to-date report on conditions there, furnished by a rebel deserter Andre had interviewed only a few days ago. Was Sir Henry considering attacking Stony Point? Chances are he was, Magnus thought, so he looked over the information he had with special care, trying to anticipate the general's questions. Within five minutes Magnus knew he and General Perfection would agree that Clinton could take Stony Point if he so desired, with perhaps five thousand men.

As he hastened out of his own small office toward the much larger one of Sir Henry Clinton, Magnus hoped his general would not ask who had obtained the information which now resided in his mind.

Clarissa Beauford was quiet as she sat in her drawing room listening to Schuyler play the pianoforte. Two weeks had passed since she had found him in the tavern near Portsmouth and convinced him to come home with her. She had sent for John Langley and Matthew, who were setting up spies for General Lincoln because of the impending attack on the Carolinas by Clinton's southern forces. John Langley and Matthew had responded with alacrity, but Schuyler had flatly turned down their suggestion that he return to New York to become a rebel spy.

"I can't entirely espouse your cause," Schuyler had told them. "And even if I did, I couldn't use my own brother as you propose. We have often disagreed, but we still share the same blood and heritage. To spy against him would have the effect of denouncing it. Neither he nor my father would ever forgive me. And I couldn't blame them."

It was at this point that John Langley told Schuyler about his father's death. He hoped it might somehow release the youth to join the rebel cause and spy against his own blood, but instead it upset Schuyler immensely.

Clarissa soon realized that Schuyler would not change his position on becoming a rebel spy without a compelling reason and she kept her brother and Matthew from forcing the issue. "I believe that Schuyler needs some time to adjust to his new circumstances," she told them, "and to get over his need for whiskey."

Schuyler had been grateful when they relented and stopped posing their incredible proposition. Clarissa suggested to John Langley and Matthew that they attempt to learn what had happened to Schuyler's would-be bride, and then set out to charm him herself. It soon became apparent to her that Schuyler had yet to get over his love for the DeWitt bond servant. That did not deter Clarissa in her quest, however.

Schuyler spent considerable time sketching the Beauford farm, playing the pianoforte and riding. But he seemed to spend no time at all noticing Clarissa's charms and she was rapidly losing patience with him as June moved into its second half.

Then, several days before the end of June, John Langley sent word by a rebel messenger that Schuyler's Joanna had taken up with his brother Magnus.

Clarissa sprang it on Schuyler right after supper that night, first telling him about Clinton's successful attack on Stony Point.

"By the way, Schuyler," she said, "my brother learned something about that girl that might interest you."

"Joanna?" Schuyler's attempt to sound casual failed miserably.

"You're not going to like what he found out, but here it is. She's taken up with your brother, Magnus; he's just brought her to New York and installed her in his rooms."

Schuyler was stunned, the color draining from his face as he repeated, "Joanna? In New York? With Magnus?"

It was some time before the youth regained enough composure to discuss the matter, and even then it was only with great difficulty. "Well," he told Clarissa, "I suppose I should have expected Joanna to take up with Magnus. Her prime interest, after all, is in making a good marriage. And what could be better than marrying Magnus, my father's primary heir?"

Schuyler was hurt by the revelation, though he tried to conceal it. That night he took to his room, brooding over his fate, and the next day he seemed lifeless and morose.

Clarissa tried to rouse him out of his lethargy but found she could not raise his spirits. For more than a week Schuyler did not sketch, did not play the piano, did not even leave his room except for an occasional meal. On those occasions, Clarissa tried to engage him in conversation, but he stubbornly maintained his silence.

Then, as quickly as his reclusiveness had begun, it came to an end. He walked into the dining room one morning and apologized to Clarissa for his "truly poor behavior this past week or so." But he still refused to talk about the war, and especially the possibility of working on the rebels' behalf. "Let's not speak of it, Clarissa," he told her. "You know how I feel."

In mid-July Governor Thomas Jefferson, an old and good friend of the Hunters, paid a visit to Clarissa, who introduced Schuyler as a friend of her brother's.

After Schuyler left them alone, Clarissa told Jef-

ferson who Schuyler really was and how important his brother and Matthew Bell felt he could
be to the rebel cause—if he could be persuaded to
lend his aid.

Jefferson thought a bit, then had an idea. "You
say the young man attended Yale, in New Haven?
Then perhaps he'd be interested to know that
Clinton has taken to ordering his redcoats to pillage and burn a number of northern villages,
among them Norwalk, Fairfield and New Haven
in Connecticut. I hear Clinton's been hung in effigy by the Yale undergraduates."

They told Schuyler and he was aghast. "You're
serious, sir?" he said. "Clinton actually ordered
such raids against civilians?"

Jefferson nodded. "General Grey led the troops
and it's said that a number of his soldiers took
advantage of helpless women of the village."

"You can't be serious, Governor!" Schuyler said.
"New Haven?" Schuyler was rocked by this piece
of news. It had taken him weeks of agonizing to
decide that he must stay out of the war and away
from Magnus and Joanna. He was afraid of what
he might do if he were placed in contact with
them. He was not a killer, but . . . the feelings
he had for Magnus and the woman he had loved
were stronger than any he'd ever known. With
time he might learn to deal with his contempt—
his hatred—for both his brother and the woman.
With time.

In spite of Clarissa Beauford's eagerness to help
her brother and Matthew Bell get him involved
in the war, she had been most gracious and patient with Schuyler and he was grateful. That she
was alluring and charming, he had also noticed,

but he did not feel aroused. For though he liked and admired the Beauford woman, he felt only gratitude toward her and needed nothing more from her than her understanding. In Joanna's wake, he felt quite unable to be stirred to desire.

Until now Schuyler had remained a trimmer in thought, not actually favoring either side in the colonial revolution against royal control. When he took up his commission with the British it was not out of any fervent belief, but because it had been procured for him, imposed upon him. Even the outrage he had felt over Scott's hanging had not caused him to side with his friend's cause or to hate Clinton's. But Jefferson's words and the images they summoned set fire to his emotions. Redcoated soldiers, perhaps even men Schuyler had known and served with, attacking helpless women in New Haven, burning their homes, stealing their possessions, raping, killing . . .

"Clinton has gone berserk!" Schuyler declared emotionally. "Why does he act the part of the monster if he means to restore respect for his king?" Schuyler bit his lip in anger. "Surely his advisers could have made him see reason. They would have cautioned him. My brother wouldn't have gone along with atrocities such as you've described."

"I'm truly sorry, Schuyler," Jefferson said, "but we have reliable information suggesting that Clinton's advisers not only approved but instigated these actions because the people of Connecticut have long been against the King. They seek to beat down the people's spirit."

"You were here when the British devastated Portsmouth and pillaged the Virginia coast," Clarissa added. "I'm gratified that women and children were spared here."

Schuyler tried to recall what Magnus's attitude had been toward such war tactics as Clinton was now engaging in. He vaguely recalled a discussion of the topic, but could not bring back Magnus's viewpoint. "You're certain of your facts, Governor?" he asked. "You couldn't be mistaken?"

"Not in the slightest," Jefferson replied.

"Well, I thank you, sir," Schuyler said. "The information is horrifying, but it may help me reach a decision I must make in a very important matter."

Schuyler was later to confess to Clarissa that his decision had actually been ordained the moment he learned of the activities of the British army in Connecticut.

"I don't know which side is right in the politics of the Revolution," Schuyler told Clarissa the day after Jefferson visited the Beauford farm, "but it's now apparent to me which side is wrong in its conduct of the war. I'll help your cause, Clarissa, because I believe we must not—cannot—allow innocent people to be slaughtered, whatever the cause."

The woman threw herself against him, hugging him. "You're doing the right thing, Schuyler," she said. "And when this war is history, you'll be one of its heroes. I'm certain of it."

Schuyler looked into her dark eyes and enjoyed the fragrance of her hair. "You've been a jewel, Clarissa, and I shan't forget you. When I reached your home I was wallowing in self-pity. You've brought me out of that and I'm eternally in your debt." He stroked her red hair, then gave her a squeeze.

"As for being a hero," he said with a smile, "I leave that to others, such as your brother, Matthew Bell, or their General Washington."

"*Our* General Washington," Clarissa corrected.

"Perhaps," Schuyler said. "I'll do what I have to do without worrying about becoming a hero. I only wish to help bring the war to a close, so that we can all go about living our lives again."

"I believe our country has a bright future ahead, with or without the King, and I trust we'll soon be permitted to get on with it."

Two days later Schuyler was huddled with John Langley Hunter and Matthew Bell aboard the sloop *Glory* on the James River. In those two days Schuyler had learned as much about the business of spying as any spy of the time—or so John Langley claimed.

"Washington's got the best group of hand-picked spies anybody could have," Hunter said, "and what we find out is for his eyes only, so we never have to worry about picking up information that'll be wasted because of a leak at headquarters. General George's staff isn't perfect, but the general sure as hell is!"

"What about Scott Laidlow?" Schuyler asked.

"They got lucky," Matthew Bell said. "Picked him up because they were watching Molly Minton's house in New York. The only reason they were watching her was because she was cultivating your brother and he wasn't sure of her."

"They got lucky and Scott got unlucky, right?" The two spies had to agree.

Schuyler got something else from General Washington's two master spies—a broader perspective on the war and information on each side's military objectives. He could never have learned it as a common soldier, officer or not.

"It's amazing," Schuyler told his mentors, "how similar the objectives are for both sides in this war. The King's army seeks to win battles so as to convince the populace in America that they cannot win the war, while Washington's purpose is to present a formidable army against the British legions so as to convince England's people that they cannot win the war. In the end, it seems to be a war which will be won and lost not on the battlefields, but in the minds of the peoples of America and England."

Hunter looked at him with a slow smile. "I've never looked at the war that way, Schuyler, but I believe you've got it figured. Magnus was quick like you when we served together years ago."

"Thank you for the compliment, John Langley . . . Speaking of my brother, there's one thing I must make clear—I will neither participate in nor allow any further attempt on Magnus's life. Right or wrong, he's my brother and I value his life as I do my own. I'll spy on him and try to help defeat what he represents, but I'm determined that he'll survive."

"You just neutralize your brother, Schuyler," Hunter said. "Then we won't need to kill him."

Schuyler shook hands with both men as the sloop got ready to sail. He was startled to receive a last-minute visitor—Clarissa Beauford. She wished him good luck and said, "I'll pray for your success, Schuyler. And for your return here one day, that I may see you again."

Schuyler smiled. "I'm glad you want to see me

again, Clarissa, though I can't understand why. I was quite a trial to you for a time there. Had I been you, I believe I would have tossed me to the wind. Yet you didn't. I'm grateful. You're a warm, generous, wonderful woman."

"You were never a trial to me, Schuyler. I'm glad to have met you and pray I will meet you again. Do take care of yourself and come back so that I may see you under happier circumstances."

He kissed her hand, then touched her lips with his in a featherlike kiss. "I'll be back, Clarissa, for I have found something here. I look forward to my return."

Clarissa stood on the dock and watched the *Glory* sail out to sea, then walked slowly to her carriage, her heart heavy. She already missed Schuyler DeWitt.

3

JULY 16 was not a good day for General Clinton, his staff or Magnus DeWitt, for word came that General Anthony Wayne had stormed and taken Stony Point early that morning. Worse, he had stolen a page from the British tactics of war by doing it with bayonets alone! Considering that Clinton had only just taken the Hudson River fort himself on May 30 and had spent more than a month improving its defenses,Wayne's victory was more than a little demoralizing.

Only two days, later, however, Magnus was rescued from his doldrums by the visitor who arrived in his office. It was his brother.

For a moment, Magnus could only stare at Schuyler, who wore civilian clothes and needed a shave badly. Then he stood and came around his desk to take his brother's hand. Schuyler, who had even more reason to be apprehensive than Magnus, was grateful for his brother's conciliatory gesture.

"In spite of your stubble, you look as if your holiday did you no harm, Schuyler," Magnus said. "But where have you been? I've been greatly concerned and have had my spies keeping their eyes open for you ever since you disappeared."

"I've traveled far, Magnus, and been to a great many places. So many that I won't bore you with the details. Suffice to say that I'm back, without regrets about my travels."

Magnus hesitated, his eyes taking in the clothes his brother wore. "Have you lost your uniform?"

Schuyler had to smile. Only his brother would ask a question like that. Yet he had counted on it, after discussing it with Matthew Bell and John Langley Hunter. "Have I a use for my uniform?" he said.

"If you wish to wear it again, you can," Magnus responded. "I hoped that you would change your mind, and I took the liberty of withholding your resignation from Sir Henry. Instead, I obtained an indefinite leave of absence for you."

Schuyler pretended surprise, even though his brother had told him precisely what he had expected to be told. "Well," he said, "thank you for your foresight, Magnus, for I do wish to wear it again."

"Much has happened since you departed, Schuyler. And I'm afraid little of it will be welcome to your ears."

Schuyler's smile vanished. "I've heard about Father's death," he said. "It's the main reason I'm returning to complete my term in the King's service. I fear he may have died because of my decision to resign from the army."

"He was upset when you told him?"

"Extremely. I've never seen him more so. . . . I'm greatly saddened by his death and feel personally responsible."

"To be sure, Schuyler, we are all saddened. But don't burden yourself with the responsibility. He was not a well man, after all. Many different types of shocks might well have brought on his final seizure."

Schuyler merely shrugged. Now, he thought, Magnus must tell him about Joanna. If Schuyler did not accept Joanna's new status as Magnus's mistress, he would not—could not—be accepted by Magnus on his intelligence staff. "How's Mother?"

"Our mother has held up remarkably. She hasn't forgotten her early Dutch training in business affairs, and she's become the overseer of DeWitt Shipping. And performing quite capably, I'm happy to report."

"Perhaps Father's death wasn't the worst of blows to her."

"No one could blame her if she despised him at the end," Magnus admitted, "but . . . I must tell you something now that is not easy for me. The girl Joanna informed me that you and she have fallen out. Is that true?"

The tension in the room was almost unbearable and only Schuyler's strength of will let him get through it. "True enough," he said as easily as he could. He cleared his throat, which had suddenly gone dry. "While I haven't forgotten her, I no longer desire her, though I still think her a delightful girl. She's still with Mother?"

There was relief on Magnus's face, but also a telltale flush. "Not precisely," Magnus said. "She is . . . What I mean to say is . . ."

Schuyler chuckled, as much to ease his own tension as his brother's. "You need not go on, Magnus," he said. "I should guess you have taken Joanna as your own—am I right? Well, do not fear my wrath. I, of all people, can well understand your decision." Schuyler had rehearsed the lines on a number of occasions, trying hard to keep any possible bitterness out of his voice.

A faint smile appeared on Magnus's face, the color receding with the knowledge that the worst was over. "You're most discerning, Schuyler. Yes, Joanna is now with me. I wished to spare her any potential wrath from Father's widow and . . . I do work quite hard for Sir Henry and she's been able to provide me with some distraction. I don't plan on marrying her, of course, but I'll certainly provide for her when I tire of her."

Schuyler smiled at that, knowing full well that the scheming girl had the intelligence to bring about whatever she wished. Magnus, he thought, might have met his match at last in the lovely Joanna.

The two brothers dined together that evening, both of them in uniform now. Magnus, in an expansive mood, asked if Schuyler wished to remain in Clinton's personal guard or preferred other duty.

"To be truthful, brother, the guard is dull. If there's something else more exciting, I believe I would prefer it."

Magnus grinned. "You wouldn't like to command a platoon of dragoons, I take it." It was one of the most interesting assignments in the King's army, but one of the most dangerous as well.

Schuyler shrugged. "I leave it to you," he said. Magnus wouldn't dare allow him to accept such a dangerous assignment.

"Perhaps I have just the assignment for you, Schuyler. Sir Henry has seen fit to allow me to expand my staff of intelligence people, so I now have an opening. Would you like to fill it? It will be both interesting and invigorating, yet should not subject you to more danger than is appropriate at the present time."

Schuyler fell silent for more than a minute, from time to time searching his brother's face with steely eyes. "I'm not certain I can involve myself in intelligence work, Magnus," he said at last. "Not after what happened with my friend Scott Laidlow."

Magnus frowned. "That still bothers you? Well, I suppose I can't blame you, even though Laidlow was a rebel. The whole affair was a dreadful mistake and even Sir Henry realizes it now. I warned him against it then. I told him I was afraid we would lose some of our most capable spies, that they would fear the rebels would learn a lesson from us and begin to execute our spies—and that's exactly what seems to have taken place."

Schuyler looked away, his eyes on the few civilians among the redcoats populating the dining room in which they were seated. Were they spies of one sort or another? he wondered. He waited for his brother to exercise friendly persuasion. It was not long in coming.

"I insist, Schuyler. You must join my staff! Put the Laidlow affair out of your mind. It will not happen again. The work I have in mind for you will not be difficult, nor too time-consuming, for I don't believe in over-working anyone but myself. I'll make few demands upon you, only that you do what I ask capably and earnestly."

"Well . . ." Schuyler pretended to waver.

"Good, it's settled then," Magnus declared with a smile. He reached across and patted his brother on the back. "You'll be a fine addition to my staff, Lieutenant DeWitt. And a most appreciated one."

"I shall be glad to work with you, Magnus, but don't expect miracles from me. I've no experience in your game, you know."

"True enough, but you have intelligence. And if there's one thing I need around me, that's it. I'll teach you all that I've learned over the years. You can bank on that."

Magnus was true to his word and in the months to come spent many hours personally training his brother in the arts of espionage and counter-espionage. Schuyler discovered that there was little to choose between Magnus and rebel spies Hunter and Bell. All were remarkably astute and their methods were similar, though each side had some advantages over the other. The chief advantage the rebels had over Magnus was their commander, General Washington, who was an able spymaster indeed, especially as compared with the cautious Clinton. Magnus's advantage was mainly financial; he was able to pay his spies in hard cash rather than in worthless Continentals, and he never had to draw from his own funds as Washington did.

In the next few months Schuyler had few opportunities to pass along truly important information

to George Stationer, his New York contact with the
rebels. He learned that Clinton was to withdraw
his troops from Newport and abandon the Rhode
Island fort, but the news was of little consequence
to Washington because he had no sea power to
atack Howe's troop-ferrying armada.

But then, in late November, Schuyler learned
from Magnus that Clinton would extend his southern campaign to South Carolina by besieging
Charleston early in 1780. Clinton would sail with
General Cornwallis immediately after Christmas.
Magnus, however, was to remain in New York with
his staff because of his ongoing investigation of
rebel espionage activity in New York and Long
Island.

Schuyler immediately paid a visit to Stationer.
The Tory merchant's dry goods store was only a
short distance away from Clinton's headquarters
and was frequented by most of Clinton's staff because of its large selection of goods—many of them
imported from England on DeWitt ships. Schuyler thought the last piece of information was price-
lessly ironic when he learned it from John Langley
Hunter back in Virginia. No one, Hunter told
Schuyler, knew the hard-nosed Stationer as a spy
except Washington and two hand-picked couriers
who were "completely reliable." Stationer was actually despised by rebel sympathizers in the city,
and few of them would do business with the so-
called Tory.

Schuyler was browsing in Stationer's store,
awaiting the proprietor's personal attention when
he was taken quite by surprise by a voice behind
him.

"Well, I'd forgotten how truly handsome a man

can be in even a British uniform," came the sultry
voice of Clarissa Beauford. "I do believe, though,
that you'd look even better in a different color—say
blue and buff and red?"

A smile lit Schuyler's face even before he half-
turned to see the tall beauty. He could not have
been more pleased, especially now, when at long
last he seemed to have ejected Joanna from his
thoughts. His evenings had been lonely and not
helped by the knowledge that Magnus, at least, had
someone to go home to each night. Schuyler had
met a number of attractive women in the city, but
none had appealed to him.

"Clarissa!" he exclaimed, his eyes feasting on the
full-bosomed beauty of John Langley's sister. "You
look ravishing. I wish I'd known you were in New
York. I'd have come to see you."

"As a matter of fact, I was just going to ask Mr.
Stationer to tell you I'll be in New York for a time.
I've already moved in with another widow-lady not
far from here."

A British colonel Schuyler had seen around Clinton's headquarters moved past them, his eyes ap-
praising the woman with open admiration. He was
about to address Clarissa when she noted his attention and hurriedly took Schuyler's arm. "Come on,
darling, we have other places to visit."

She swept him outside before he could protest.
But Schuyler didn't mind. Stationer's place was
very busy at that hour and his news would keep.
Outside, he asked her what was happening in the
South and learned that the French had agreed to
send aid should the British move against the Carolinas. It was surprising news, considering that two
months earlier d'Estaing had joined the rebels in

besieging Savannah, only to sail away little more than three weeks later when warned of the approach of a nonexistent British armada.

"Well, let's hope that this time the French back up their talk with action, Clarissa," he said, "for I've learned that Clinton will sail with an attack force for Charleston in less than a month. If he's successful the loss of South Carolina is almost sure to follow."

"Well, that is important, Schuyler! A good thing you've joined our efforts, for General Lincoln will be anxious to learn of the British plan. He's been ill, John Langley says, but apparently is all right now."   ....

"Will you wait here for me while I get this news to George Stationer?" Schuyler asked. "I'd like to show you around the city."

"With pleasure," she said, and watched Schuyler re-enter the dry goods store.

After passing along the intelligence to Stationer, Schuyler warned him that it should be given to no one but Washington, "for there are spies everywhere."

Stationer's eyes were always cold and now they seemed icy. "I should guess you'd be knowing that better than anyone, sir," he said, "with your brother the British spymaster."

Schuyler's smile was thin. Regardless of what Hunter had told him, he found that he neither trusted nor liked Stationer. Fortunately, Schuyler's post on Magnus's staff placed him in a position where he was privy to the very reports that would give Stationer away, were he a double agent. Schuyler had checked out Stationer's file in Magnus's office and found he was considered "friendly, but neutral and not open to intelligence work." Magnus had explained that the decription meant that he could be relied upon not to work for either side.

"If I could only put more of our citizens in that class," Magnus had explained to his brother, "I could rely on our security a great deal more."

Now Schuyler left Stationer and returned to where Clarissa awaited him outside. "And how is life in the beauty of Virginia?" he asked as she took his arm. "Quiet and peaceful, I trust, with no more visits from General Mathew."

"Nor from a certain Mr. DeWitt, either," she returned. "Life has been dull and unexciting."

"Perhaps you would rather have Clinton send you some excitement?" he asked with a laugh.

"Only if Clinton sent you," she said.

"Yet it was you who was instrumental in convincing me I should leave Virginia and come back to New York. Now that I've acceded to your wishes, you would send me back to Virginia? Truly, you *are* a woman! A most vexing one, as well as a most attractive one."

Clarissa's smile flashed brilliantly. "Though I'm past the age of blushing, I would do so if I could at such a kind comment."

"You'll let me take you around New York?" he asked.

"Of course. I'll need to know it quite well, as it happens. You see, I'm to take the place of a friend of Matthew Bell—Molly Minton. She's in Savannah now, after almost being detected by your brother. But she still works for the cause."

"You're to be a spy, Clarissa? It's a risky business. My brother has been remarkably successful in detecting rebel spies, and I don't like the thought of your visiting a British prison ship. I doubt you'd enjoy it."

"Then I shall have to be remarkably successful too, shan't I? With your help, Schuyler, I'm certain I'll have no problem in remaining out of your brother's clutches. Shall we go?"

While Schuyler was meeting the newest spy in New York, Magnus was reviewing a growing file of correspondence between the ambitious Captain Andre and a would-be American turncoat. The man was calling himself "Gustavus," but his real identity was as yet unknown.

Magnus was far from convinced that this new suspected traitor was not just another of Washington's ploys to trap him or to make British intelligence look foolish. Therefore, he had not as yet allowed Andre to report on the traitor's approach to Sir Henry. After the previous deception orchestrated by John Langley Hunter and Matthew Bell, Clinton's skepticism might even surpass Magnus's.

Not until he could be more certain of the traitor's legitimacy would Magnus present Clinton with the facts. Then the commander's General Perfection would not have a chance to foul things up. He might not have to report the matter to Clinton at all for sometime, thanks to the impending voyage to Charleston after the holiday. By the time the commander returned from the South, Magnus hoped to have unmasked the traitorous American general, or at the very least to have found proof that he was real.

Magnus had other plans as well, however. He was determined to unearth the gaggle of rebel spies who infested Manhattan and Long Islands and who were keeping Washington so well informed on British army activities. Catching Scott Laidlow through Molly Minton had convinced Magnus that women were both the strength and weakness of the chain of rebel spies. He could not prove Molly had been working with Laidlow, though he was certain she had been. Her flight for an unknown destination had proved her guilt beyond any question; it had also convinced Magnus he had to uncover other ladies who played the spy game.

Consequently, he was keeping a number of "Loyalist" ladies under watch, just as he had Molly Minton. If he was lucky, perhaps Bell or Hunter would wander into his snare. If not, the ladies could at least provide leads to other rebel spies who were now well hidden. To be certain that the ladies he placed under surveillance and the spies to whom they reported were not alerted by loose talk, Magnus handled the surveillance quietly and told no one what he was doing. The Tories he used as watchers were told only that the ladies were suspected of having lovers who were rebel spies. Any suspicious visitors were to be followed so that their identities could be determined, but they were not to be apprehended.

Magnus began attending parties and balls regularly. There had been a noticeable increase in the number of such events in recent months and he was sure it was caused by spying ladies. He watched the goings-on at the parties carefully and made copious notes on which important Tories consorted with those he suspected as Patriot spies.

After a time, Joanna began to protest the many

evenings he left her alone. He explained to her
that he was trying to track down "leaks in important matters of state." When she said she had no
idea what he was talking about, he told her in plain
English that he was keeping his eyes on ladies
he suspected were spying. He cautioned her, of
course, to say nothing of his suspicions.

She had flung herself into his arms and kissed the
top of his head, which was balding badly, before
pulling his face into her bosom. "I will say nothing, Magnus darling," she declared, "but it would
be nice if you would allow me to go to at least a
few of these parties with you. Then neither of us
would have to be lonely."

Magnus had, of course, flatly refused. He refused
again when she put it to him a second time, one
day later. After three more requests which he managed to refuse, she became insistent and finally
threatening. Faced with losing her company in the
bedchamber, Magnus at last acquiesced.

So it was that she was present when Mrs. Clarissa Beauford was introduced by Lieutenant
Schuyler DeWitt of the King's army to New York's
Tory-dominated society, an event duly noted in
the *Royal Gazette* a few days later.

Magnus almost choked on his sherry when he
saw his brother enter the ballroom with the tall,
red-haired beauty, for Schuyler had shunned such
events since his return. And although Schuyler pro-
fessed to be over Joanna, Magnus had continued to
worry that he was not and that it would ultimately
cause trouble between them. As he downed the remainder of his sherry, he said a silent prayer, his
eyes on Joanna, who at the moment was looking
elsewhere, a look of pleasure on her face.

Schuyler was just as surprised to see Magnus at the affair. After all, Joanna was awaiting his brother in his rooms. And if one had Joanna, who needed others?

Now he caught Magnus's eyes and waved. He wondered what his brother might think of Clarissa. One thing was certain—by introducing her to his brother himself, he was keeping Magnus from any possible suspicion of Clarissa. He pointed Magnus out to Clarissa, but then paled as he recognized the striking beauty next to him.

"God!" he exclaimed, "he's brought Joanna!"

Clarissa's eyes opened wide. "Dance with me, Schuyler. I want to get a look at her."

Schuyler readily obeyed. He tried to keep his eyes away from Joanna as they waltzed past her, though he couldn't help but admire the flesh strikingly set off by the light blue chiffon gown she wore.

"I am envious of her, Master Schuyler," Clarissa announced as they continued their dance.

Schuyler winced. "Please don't address me that way," he said. "That's what *she* called me on occasion. I didn't like it then and don't like it now." He paused, selecting his next words with care. "As for your envy, it's quite unnecessary, for you are much fairer than she—in every possible way."

"Thank you for your compliment, Schuyler. But whatever that girl's status as a bond servant, no one can deny she is comely. I can well understand your fondness for her—which apparently persists."

Schuyler grimaced to show Clarissa her observation was incorrect, then wondered if he would have to introduce her to both Magnus and Joanna. Perhaps a hasty withdrawal was better strategy?

Clarissa made up his mind for him. The dance had come to an end while he was thinking and her voice brought him back to reality. "It is time I met your brother and former lover, Schuyler," she said, smiling.

"I'm not certain it's wise," he replied.

"Why, Schuyler? Because your infatuation continues? Or because of your brother's preoccupation with spies? I see no reason why the first should bother you if it doesn't bother me—and it doesn't. As for the second, you said yourself that Magnus would be far less likely to suspect me as a spy once he'd met me as your paramour."

"I can't disagree with your reasoning, Clarissa. It's just that I don't wish to see Joanna again. I'm afraid I might not be civil to her."

"Take heart, Schuyler, for I am a lady and I will see to it that you act like a gentleman with her."

Schuyler and Clarissa approached the corner where Magnus and Joanna were seated. Schuyler felt rather than saw Joanna's eyes upon him. He introduced Clarissa as "one who is very near and dear to me," and could not have felt more uncomfortable as he did so. He drew small comfort from the fact that Magnus seemed quite as uncomfortable over the situation as he.

As the orchestra began to play, Clarissa asked Magnus if he would dance with her. Startled, Magnus had little chance to refuse and Schuyler and Joanna were left alone.

For the first few moments, Joanna would not look at Schuyler and so he was able to look her over boldly. He came to the conclusion that she could not have looked better. Magnus's attentions had not harmed her beauty in any way; quite the contrary was true.

Now a thought occurred to him and it inspired a question he could not hold back. "I understand Father had a seizure after I left, and that you lied to Magnus about your presence when he had it. And also about seeing me. What brough on Father's attack—your lovemaking after I departed?"

The girl turned toward him, her icy exterior suddenly volcanic. "It was you who killed him, you bloody bastard! You and your damned jealousy, your barging in on us. He overheard what I told you, and the next thing I knew he was doubled over in pain. Then he died. Just like that. Your fault, not mine!"

"Did he say anything before he died?"

"Not a thing," she said. "Nothing at all. And he died without leaving me taken care of as he'd promised. Can you imagine? And with you gone, there I was, fending for myself again. I did the only thing that made sense. Magnus has been very kind to me ever since, thank the good Lord."

"Suppose I tell him what a liar you are?"

"And what good would that do you? Anyway, you'd also have to tell him it was you who brought on the old boy's attack by breaking up our little session. He hasn't asked me about it since you came back, so I know you haven't told him. It's a good thing too," she said warningly.

"You needn't fear, Joanna, for I won't tell him. But I will tell you this—Magnus will not marry you. He is not as young and foolish as I was."

Joanna laughed. "We shall see about that, Master Schuyler," she declared. "Mr. Magnus is a fine,

fine person. I've a feeling he will do just as I wish him to do. Though I confess I haven't yet made up my mind whether I wish to marry him at all. One cannot foresee what opportunities might come along, you know."

As she spoke, Joanna's eyes were sweeping the room, looking over every man in it. Schuyler had no chance to respond, for just then the dance ended and Magnus and Clarissa returned.

When he and Clarissa were again alone, she asked him if he was over Joanna.

"She's a harlot," he declared, "and I can't understand how I could have been deceived by her for so long. She only seeks what is good for her. She cares not a whit who she hurts in the process. I would almost enjoy strangling her pretty neck."

"A pretty one indeed," Clarissa said. "But you're not quite over her and I wonder if you ever shall be."

Clarissa's final words cut deeply and Schuyler tried vainly to put the lie to them later that night when he took her to the house in which she was staying. He kissed her, but it was with a passion he did not feel.

Clarissa dismissed him with a frown. "You're a dear, Schuyler, and I'm not sorry or ashamed to say I enjoyed that. But you aren't kissing me because you wish to. It's only because you're trying to deny Joanna. Don't kiss me again until you do it for desire alone."

Schuyler protested, but admitted later in the privacy of his own rooms that Clarissa was right. Joanna was still under his skin and he had no idea what to do about it.

The next day he forgot this problem, however, when he learned, quite by accident, that his brother and John Andre were negotiating with a turncoat rebel general.

4

New Year's Day in 1780 found Sir Henry Clinton on the high seas with an army bound for Charleston, South Carolina, while Magnus DeWitt was closing in on a rebel spy ring which kept track of the movements of British ships from Long Island for General Washington.

With Clinton gone, there were few secrets for Schuyler to glean at his headquarters except what might come from Magnus or Andre, and little came from either source. Certainly not from his brother, who seemed to keep much of what he knew to himself.

Schuyler had discovered that Magnus had a safe in his office where he kept certain files, among them one containing memos Magnus had written concerning an American general who was report-

edly bargaining with the British. Schuyler learned
of his brother's files by sheer luck, having arrived
early the morning after his meeting with Joanna
to find the door to Magnus's safe ajar. His brother
was in, but had apparently made a dash for the
privy right after opening the safe. Magnus had
instructed his orderly to admit no one to his office.
The orderly, however, did not believe Major De-
Witt's order would apply to his own brother, so
Schuyler was not barred from entering the room.

Seeing the safe open, Schuyler searched it and
soon was excitedly examining the file pertaining
to the unnamed rebel traitor. According to Magnus's rather cool reports, the affair being handled
by Andre for some reason which he did not account for. As soon as Schuyler had made sense out
of the memorandums, he put them back in the file
and the file back in the safe. Then he replaced the
door in approximately the same position it had
been in earlier and left, telling the orderly to mention to Magnus that he would be back later.

Wondering what Washington would say when
he learned one of his generals might be selling out
to the enemy, Schuyler returned to his rooms and
procured the invisible ink John Langley had given
him before he'd left Virginia. It took him nearly
an hour to write a coded message on the back of
a handbill circulated with the *Gazette* a week
earlier. When he was finished, Schuyler signed his
spy signature, the number 731, then added 727 to
indicate he was writing from New York. Only
Washington, he had been told, knew what his
number was.

After he had left the handbill with Stationer for
delivery to Washington, Schuyler had time to con-

sider the meaning of his discovery. An American general might well be in a position to lose the war for the Patriots! Of course, as Schuyler had pointed out to Washington in his report, since no name was mentioned it was likely Magnus did not yet know who the man was. And there was also the possibility that the traitor might turn out to be not a general at all, but a lesser officer hopeful of improving himself. In any case, Washington could do little with the information just yet. The general could only be watchful of his important staff members.

When Schuyler got back to Magnus's office, his brother was in high spirits. That very day, Magnus said, they would be taking into custody a rebel spy who had eluded them for years. The spy was known to most of Clinton's staff officers, yet no one had ever thought him less than a loyal subject of the King.

Schuyler felt a chill race down his spine. Who, he asked, was the man?

"Why, none other than Morrison, who runs the Broadway Coffee Shop," Magnus declared. "If I hadn't intercepted a message that mentioned the establishment, I would never have suspected him. His name wasn't printed on the message—only a number, 743. But the way the message is phrased, there's little doubt he's our man."

An hour later, Robert Morrison was in custody and being questioned. And not at all happy about it. He swore he was more loyal than the King himself, but could say nothing to prove it.

"What will happen to him now?" Schuyler asked Magnus as they left the man's cell.

"He'll be imprisoned on the *Jersey,* poor devil,"

his brother said. "I shouldn't wish to be in his shoes."

"The prison ship out in the bay? What's wrong with it?"

"I'm told conditions on it are bad, but . . . Morrison was a spy and knew the risks, so don't waste too much sympathy on him."

The next day Schuyler made some discreet inquiries about the *Jersey* and learned that a sentence aboard it was often a sentence of death. That the *Jersey*, like the other British prison ships, was filthy and rat-infested, and that each day began with a call to "cast out your dead." Not a happy way to meet your maker, Schuyler thought, imagining the scene below decks of the *Jersey*, half-naked, scrawny, sweating men in irons, fighting to survive. Men with little hope. Men who shared John Langley Hunter's dream of seeing America free of its English king. Schuyler vowed he would rather die than be taken to such a place as the *Jersey*.

In the weeks to follow, Schuyler saw Clarissa Beauford from time to time, usually at a party or ball, though he was rarely her escort. He felt an odd pang when he saw her in the arms of one British officer or another, but judged it fear for her safety rather than jealousy. She had slipped easily into New York Tory society and the spot vacated by Molly Minton in Washington's New York spy network. She had hosted several parties in her first three months in New York. According to Stationer, she had passed along a number of valuable pieces of intelligence, among them that the British had known that d'Estaing was coming to besiege Savannah long before the French admiral's arrival.

* * *

Two weeks after Schuyler had notified Washington about the ongoing secret negotiations with an American general, he received instructions through Stationer to meet John Langley Hunter in an old barn near Fish Kill, north of the city. Schuyler was both surprised and pleased that Clarissa's brother was in the north again. He had a healthy respect for the tall, eye-patched rebel spy, and liked him, too.

The next day Schuyler rode out of the city to keep his date with Hunter and found the man awaiting him in the agreed location. "Your sister sends her regards, John Langley," Schuyler told him after they'd shaken hands. "She's so capable a spy, I'm not sure you need me anymore."

Hunter chuckled and shook his head. "Agreed that Clarissa's a smart woman, Schuyler, but we could never replace you. Washington is pleased with your work, if not with what you've discovered. He's not happy that one of his officers is planning on going over to the enemy."

"I can understand that. I was a bit shocked myself."

"What General George wants to know, Schuyler, is who the bastard is."

"I'm not sure my brother knows who the man is. In his memos he refers to the man as Gustavus— a fictitious name, I think. There is no American general named Gustavus, is there?"

Hunter shook his head. "None at all, and I'm not sure there's even an officer around with that name. What about Andre? Do you think he might know?"

"If Magnus doesn't know, I doubt Andre does. Though maybe they both know and simply aren't writing the name down for fear of its being discovered."

"Can you get it out of your brother?"

"I don't know, but frankly, I doubt it. He tells me little these days."

"You no longer have his confidence?"

"I guess I do, but Magnus takes his work entirely seriously. He says, 'Talk too much, keep too little quiet and your grave will be dug in public so you can reveal no more secrets.'"

"Good thinking, but it doesn't help us much. Too bad he's such a dyed-in-the-wool Tory. I'd rather have such a formidable enemy on our side for the duration of this bloody war!"

"You could more easily persuade Lord Howe to scuttle his ships," Schuyler said with a laugh. "Even if the British lose the war, I doubt Magnus will ever capitulate. Not in his mind."

"What then, Schuyler? The general is livid over this. That's why he recalled me from South Carolina, even though Clinton's preparing an attack on Charleston. Fortunately, the good Sir Henry's pace in such matters seems to rival that of a snail and your warning came early enough to give Lincoln a head start in tightening the city's defenses."

"If one of them knows the traitor's identity, then they both do. It will be more difficult to obtain the information from my brother than from Andre, so I'd think our best course of action would be to set Clarissa upon him. Andre is a vain sort and fancies himself a ladies' man through and through. If Clarissa could charm him, perhaps she could loosen his tongue enough to learn our man's name."

John Langley's pleasure in the suggestion showed. "If anyone can charm the rascal she can,

Schuyler. Set her on Andre right away, for we have no time to waste. General George keeps much to himself, but there are times when he must confide in his staff generals. Until you and Clarissa learn the identity of the traitor, he can confide in none of them."

"The only thing that bothers me is using Clarissa. She has a pretty neck and I'd hate to see it stretched by a hangman's noose if she's discovered."

"Not likely they'd do that. She's a civilian."

"So was Scott Laidlow."

"But he was a man and you couldn't blame them for believing he was still Army. There's no way she would be Army. They might throw her on a prison ship, but they wouldn't hang her."

Schuyler shuddered. "That," he said, "would be worse. Much worse. They're an abomination. If I had any say, I'd have them all sunk."

"We've thought of attacking them to free the prisoners, Schuyler, but they're heavily armed and usually have naval pickets guarding them. We'd lose more men than we could save."

"Perhaps it would be worth it. There are thousands of your fellows lying in filth on those ships, more dead than alive. Even Scott's fate was better than that."

"Well, let's hope neither fate will be Clarissa's," Hunter said.

"Or ours?"

Hunter laughed. "Agreed. Tell my sister I said she should charm Andre out of his pants—but to make sure she doesn't do it for nothing. She must find out what he knows."

Schuyler frowned, but did not say what he was thinking, contenting himself with agreeing.

Clarissa did not hesitate to accept the assignment Schuyler gave her when he returned from meeting her brother. She told Schuyler she had rebuffed Andre several times in the past few months because of Schuyler's contention that Andre had little power on the staff.

"Can you now get in his good graces?" Schuyler asked. "It's important to learn what he knows."

"I believe I can. But I must warn you, he's a very attractive man. Perhaps I'll fall in love with him."

"Perhaps you will," Schuyler said, recognizing that she was teasing. He laughed. "But if you do, find out what he knows first and pass it along. Agreed?"

"Agreed," she said.

Clarissa was able to get close to Andre with little difficulty but was unable to learn anything from him. John Langley learned no more in White Plains than his sister did in New York. He was unable to gain a single clue as to the identity of the mysterious "Gustavus." With Charles Lee back in South Carolina, sitting out his exile by command of the Continental Congress, there were no likely candidates among Washington's generals. Or so it appeared.

Schuyler tried to get Magnus to talk, but with little success. He approached the subject by asking his brother if he thought Bell and Hunter had stopped trying to capture him. A momentary flicker on Magnus's face confirmed what Schuyler already suspected—that he was probably still worried that Andre's traitor might not be a traitor at all, but simply another try by the rebels to capture him.

"They caught me once, but I can tell you they won't capture me again. Certainly not by such a crude method as they used before."

"One which might well have been successful," Schuyler pointed out with a quick laugh.

"I cannot deny that," Magnus said ruefully. But he remained close-mouthed except when word came in April that Clinton had blockaded Charleston and cut off Lincoln's escape routes. Then Magnus became exuberant.

"Schuyler," he declared, "soon we'll own the entire South. When we do, perhaps the idiots of the Continental Congress will begin to see things more reasonably. Then the rebellion will be over and I can retire to look after the family's interests."

"Perhaps there will be no interests to look after, Magnus."

Magnus didn't find Schuyler amusing. He threw his brother a sharp look. "And what do you mean by that?" he asked. "Of course there will be interests to look after! DeWitt Shipping has carried on throughout two wars and will hardly be affected by this one's end, unless . . . Are you suggesting we might lose the war? Ridiculous!"

"It's been four years since the rebellion began, Magnus," he said. "The King was certain in 1775 that there would be no rebellion here that his army couldn't suppress, and yet it's still going on."

"We've won battle after battle," Magnus replied. "Breed's Hill, New York, Jersey, Brandywine, Philadelphia, Savannah—I could go on and on."

"We won the battles, but they're only contests of strength between armies. We have yet to beat our main opponent—the people's will to resist. A victory in Charleston will make little difference to the people in the North. Our occupation of New York and Long Island hasn't killed rebel resistance in Boston or the rest of New England."

"You sound like a rebel sympathizer, brother."

"But doesn't what I'm saying make some little sense, Magnus?"

Magnus contemplated his brother's remarks silently for some time, his pleasure at the reports from Charleston dissipating. He shook his head sadly. "I can't deny the validity in some of what you say, Schuyler," he said at last. "You're indeed wise for one so young. But even granting all those factors, wars are fought by armies and not people. Our army is far superior to that of the rebels, in numbers, in training and in ability. And we pay our men regularly, on time and in gold. Whereas the rebels, when paid at all, receive worthless script, some of which is of *our* minting."

"Yet our superior army can still be beaten by the rebels and is—often enough for the patriots to take heart and fight even more boldly."

Now Magus launched into a blistering indictment of the rebels which reminded Schuyler of the kind of tirade Alastair DeWitt had often loosed at his two sons. But Schuyler's mind was on something Magnus said moments before—about the currency of the rebels. He waited for his brother to end his monologue and watched for an opening to ask the question he framed in his mind. When it came, Schuyler jumped in.

". . . and so, dear brother," Magnus said, "we

will continue to win battles and keep the rebels from any sort of unified economy by splitting the South from the North and keeping import-export trade to a bare minimum."

"If what you've just intimated is true, Magnus," Schuyler now broke in, "about our printing rebel currency, we are to be congratulated! I'd never have thought of that! A great idea—was it Clinton's?"

Magnus beamed. "It was my very own, Schuyler." And he proudly revealed details of the British counterfeiting operation known only to himself—including the lone defect in the British bills, a tiny dot hidden by the bills' artwork.

Schuyler's ensuing message to Washington caused the general to make an immediate trip to Philadelphia to confront the Congress and its finance people with the truth about the Continental dollar.

But as March of 1980 turned into April and the weather became less blustery, the identity of the turncoat general remained unknown to Schuyler and Washington's spies.

5

CLARISSA BEAUFORD was pleased by the brilliance of a hot morning sun which awakened her on the first day of spring. New York was dreary in the winter and she was not happy with the way things had been going, either in her effort to get information from Captain John Andre, or to win the affection of Schuyler DeWitt.

Schuyler. He had paid her little attention except when she sought him out and had yet to respond to her not-very-veiled invitation the night he had kissed her to spite his former love. She had spent many nights savoring that kiss and wishing it had been real.

As for Andre, she thought him superficial and dull, though he was handsome enough. She knew he had little difficulty finding receptive Loyalist wenches in New York to sleep with, and many of them even bragged about bedding him. But Andre had not yet oiled his way into her boudoir. She had hoped it would not be necessary to allow Andre bedchamber privileges in order to get him to open up, but had now reached the point where she thought she would have to. She did not at all like the conclusion she had reached, but knew it was the right one, that she had been putting it off for some time now.

The thought of sleeping with Andre dampened her spirits by reminding her that she was to entertain him that very evening in the town house she had secured last month, the one she now occupied. She supposed she should not feel badly, since so very many Patriots had already made far greater sacrifices. But she did.

She reached a sudden decision to visit Schuyler at Clinton's headquarters and was immediately cheered up. She jumped out of bed and dressed quickly in her prettiest outfit.

Magnus DeWitt was in excellent spirits in spite of the presence of John Andre. He had just learned that General Benedict Arnold had been found guilty by a rebel court-martial on charges of misusing government transportation in Philadelphia and of granting an illegal pass through the lines to a Tory woman.

"If you're correct about the traitor's identity, John," Magnus said, "Washington's affirmation of the court-martial verdict ought to make Arnold's colonial tea taste bitter indeed. If he had reason to sell out his cause earlier, he has substantially more now!"

"Agreed, Major," said Andre. "There's little question in my mind that Arnold is our man and that he's wriggling on our line. All that remains is for us to reel him in. Of course, we must have Sir Henry's authorization to make him an offer."

"We shall have to wait until the general returns from South Carolina, for we dare not risk a message. Were Washington's spies to intercept it, we would lose our fish. I assume you've been discreet about our secret?"

"I couldn't have guarded this piece of intelligence more closely were it my sister's virginity, Magnus," Andre said with a laugh. "I wouldn't reveal it under torture."

As Andre left Magnus's office, he came upon Clarissa Beauford engaged in conversation with Magnus's orderly. Andre frowned when he heard Clarissa ask for Schuyler DeWitt. But then he smiled, pretending not to have heard, and interrupted.

"Well, Clarissa," Andre said, "I hadn't expected the pleasure of your company until this evening. Have I mixed up my dates?"

Clarissa's face reddened. "Oh!" she said, "your office is not . . . that is, I thought—I had stopped in to see Schuyler DeWitt, an old friend."

"Will I not do, madame? If I'm not as tall as Lieutenant DeWitt, I do outrank him. And I'm also in intelligence work, as are he and his brother."

"Really?" Clarissa said lamely. "I confess I do not understand such things. Is that where battle plans are drawn? That requires intelligence, I should think."

Andre laughed. "We draw no battle plans here, fair lady, but if you'll allow me to escort you to a nearby inn, I shall be delighted to explain. I didn't believe you'd be interested in such things as intelligence work."

"Like many modern women, I have a variety of interests, Captain, but . . ." Clarissa paused as if to think over Andre's invitation, wondering suddenly if she could manipulate the man's jealousy of Schuyler to make him confide in her. "Well, I had promised Schuyler that I'd lunch with him, but he isn't here and . . . You won't tell him I declined him in your favor, will you?"

Andre beamed. "It will be our secret," he said, taking her arm and steering her out of the office, thence outside the headquarters building. "I will hold our secret as inviolate as those which we intelligence officers hold most dear."

Clarissa laughed nervously as Andre guided her slowly toward the inn just east of the waterfront. "Your work must be exciting," she said. "Schuyler tells me he works at detecting enemy spies and it is very difficult work. Our informers are quite ineffective, according to him."

Andre's eyes lit up. "Ah, but on the contrary, madame," he said. "If I could tell you what I know, you would have to agree that we British are better at intrigue than the rebels could hope to be."

"How can that be? Schuyler told me the rebel spies have been difficult to detect. And because of them, we have had far fewer victories than we ought to."

By now they had reached the inn and were soon seated in a quiet spot at the rear. Clarissa was delighting in baiting Andre. Even though it would not work in Schuyler's favor with Andre, she knew she was doing the right thing for the cause. Each time she spoke Schuyler's name—attributing importance to him and, of course, great knowledge in the espionage game—the captain's flesh seemed to color noticeably. And he would try to top whatever credit she had accorded to Schuyler. If Andre told her little she did not already know, his tongue had become far looser than in all the time she had known him.

Just before she left him following lunch, she had an inspiration and said, "Schuyler DeWitt interests me more than any man I've ever known—except for you, of course," she added with a smile. "He is so handsome, so witty, so intelligent. And best of all, he respects me more than most men do a ladylove. Schuyler trusts me with great secrets and that has pleased me greatly, for if a man is to win my favor, he must respect me and show that respect by trusting me."

"Secrets?" Andre's expression was one of incredulity. "I don't understand. The lieutenant is privy to little of a truly secret nature. He's but a . . . a junior staff officer and quite unimportant, really." He paused and regarded Clarissa with a look that told her he was thinking of what he could say that would impress her—and ready her for his bed. Then he grinned. "Milady," he said, "this very evening I will prove how very much I think of you by sharing a secret of such great magnitude that Sir Henry himself knows nothing of it!"

Clarissa tried to look shocked. "I shouldn't wish to see you cause difficulties for yourself, John. Please don't tell me anything which might get you in trouble with your superiors."

"You needn't fear, Clarissa. What I plan to tell you will cause me no difficulties at all—though it is

vitally important to our winning the war. I'll have
to ask you to promise me you'll never speak of it
to anyone, of course."

"And you will have my promise, Captain. You
have it!"

That afternoon Clarissa managed to get word to
Schuyler that she had to see him and he paid her a
visit. Schuyler was surprised, pleased, then aghast
at what Clarissa told him.

"I hope you're not overestimating the value of
what Andre is willing to tell you, Clarissa. I have
the feeling that you are. But in any case, I trust
you'll reconsider your idea of bedding the rascal.
It's most clever of you to use me to pry open his
mouth, but . . ."

"It seems he wants me badly, Schuyler, and
while I don't want him, I do want the information
he can give me. I'm convinced he will only release
it if . . . I allow him in my bed."

Schuyler hated the images Clarissa's words were
provoking and his expression showed it. "I'm opposed to it," he said, "Your favors are worth considerably more than mere information, however
important it may be to the war." He was deadly
serious.

"Really, Schuyler?" she said, her voice more than
a bit sarcastic. "Truly, I've had no offers nearly as
good."

Her words shook him and he stared at her sharp-
ly. She was angry and her fury seemed directed
solely at him, though he couldn't understand why.
He moved to her side and tried to take her hands,
but she clasped them together and resolutely kept
her eyes from his face.

"Clarissa," he said softly, "I don't know why you're angry with me, but I beg you not to be. As to the dandy Andre, I pray you will reconsider and not bed him to get his information. There must be other ways to obtain it. I implore you to refuse him."

"What would you have me do? Let this chance to collect the information slip away? Desert our all-important cause? No, Schuyler, I must do what I can to aid my country. I am no longer a virgin, so I surrender little of value."

"What you surrender is of extraordinary value, my love! Your body! Your honor! I don't want you to do it and I . . . I order you not to!"

"Your love? Ha! You *are* presumptuous, Schuyler. You have shown nothing for me—no regard, no affection. Nothing, sir! As for your order, I reject it, for it is contrary to the cause for which we both work."

Before Schuyler could frame a response, Clarissa told him he must leave immediately because Andre was due. Disconsolate and unable to think of anything to say which might influence her, Schuyler left. But he found a place not far from Clarissa's house and remained there for the rest of the evening, noting with disgust Andre's seven o'clock arrival and one o'clock departure.

6

It was painful for Schuyler to watch Captain Andre take his leave of Clarissa early the next morning. He could not see Andre's face clearly, but was certain the man's expression was smug. The scoundrel . . . Schuyler would gladly have run him through.

As soon as Andre rode away, Schuyler walked slowly to Clarissa's door. He was about to knock when he heard something from the other side—the sounds of a woman crying.

It was Clarissa. She let him in and immediately fell into his arms, sobbing against his neck. She wore bedclothes, a fact that was not lost on Schuyler, who found it both chilling and exciting.

When Clarissa was at last calm enough to speak,

he listened gravely to the torrent of words she loosed.

"I've failed, Schuyler! Oh, how I failed! Damn, damn, damn! He knows who the traitor is—I'm certain of it. Yet I didn't get him to speak the name. Couldn't get it out of him. He promised. Told me he would speak of it after—oh, God! How could I know it would turn out like this? I took him at his word as a gentleman and officer and let him bed me in my very own bedchamber. Let him remove my . . ." She began to cry once more. "Then I made him talk, even as he was touching me. For a while I thought he was going to tell me what I wanted to hear. He said he was working at bringing an American general over to the British side. That he expected the man could aid the King's forces greatly. That he had to be careful not to alert the other side—for they could prevent the man from delivering anything of value to the British. Then, he . . ." She trailed off and cried furiously. Schuyler comforted her, or tried to. He held her face against him and stroked her long hair, which spread over her shoulders and back. The picture she had been painting was disturbing.

"What happened then, Clarissa?" He was still praying she hadn't actually allowed Andre to bed her.

"He told me he could no longer talk. That he had to lie with me before continuing. I didn't want to. Oh, Schuyler, I hated every moment of it. Yet I was certain that I had him, that all that stood between me and the information we need was his lust."

"So he had his way?" Schuyler's voice cracked as he forced out the question.

Her response was a new torrent of tears. At last she calmed somewhat and began drying her eyes. "What a fool am I!" she said, drawing away from Schuyler.

Schuyler watched her in silence, his eyes drinking in parts of her he had never seen. Though her substantial breasts were covered, they were unencumbered by corsetry and not only could he see their sweet fullness through her bedclothes, but he had felt them flatten against him as he held her. What she had told him made him forlorn, yet it was also arousing his desire for her, a desire he realized he had long denied.

Now she was more composed as she faced him, swaying a bit as she stood before the easy chair in which he sat. "I was wrong, Schuyler. He was too smart for me. He didn't name the traitor. He said that to do so would be unwise, and dangerous for me. That I might be in danger of being killed for the information. He said only that the man was important enough to affect the outcome of the war."

Schuyler swallowed hard. Not only had Clarissa failed, she had given herself to Andre for virtually nothing. He was sick over it. He could not meet her eyes after her confession, and turned away. "Well," he said, "what is done is done. The dandy got what he wanted for a pittance—as I was afraid he might. I warned you he would!" Suddenly a new thought struck him and he whirled angrily on her. "Did you enjoy it, Clarissa?" he roared. "How can I tell you how desolate you've made me!"

He was at the door before she realized he was going. "Don't leave me now, Schuyler," she said, "not this way."

"No, Clarissa," he returned, "I must go. When my anger subsides, I will see you again. But that will take time."

He slammed the door behind him, oblivious to Clarissa's cry for him to return. That night Schuyler became drunk for the first time since Clarissa had befriended him in Virginia.

In the months after Clarissa's conquest by Andre, Schuyler met twice with John Langley Hunter. The first meeting came in May, immediately after the fall of Charleston.

Hunter was not pleased, but neither was he surprised by Schuyler's and Clarissa's failure to learn the identity of the traitorous American general.

"Whoever the bastard is, he's a damnably clever one," John Langley told Schuyler. "General George has made a point of having long chats with each of his generals—except Lincoln, of course, since he's in the South. But he still has no idea who the traitor is."

"Well, if it's Lincoln, he's already joined the enemy—as a prisoner—for we just received word that he handed his sword to Clinton at Charleston last week. No doubt Clinton'll bring the general to New York when he returns from his victorious Southern campaign."

Hunter's surprise was plain to see. "Lincoln—captured? We . . . Washington thought we could hold Charleston against Clinton and had instructed Lincoln not to surrender, no matter what the cost." Now he stood and began to pace. After several minutes, he returned to face Schuyler. "There's one other thing," he said. "Matthew was in Charleston. I hope to God he got away."

"I'll look over the prisoner lists when they arrive from South Carolina. And try to keep them away from Magnus if I can."

"If you see Matthew's name or any name containing the first four letters—'Bell'—you get somebody to let me know as soon as possible. Matthew might lie about his name. Call himself Bellring, Bellnor or something like that, so Magnus won't pick up the fact that he's a prisoner. He'll keep the 'Bell' in his name, though, so I can figure out who he's pretending to be."

"Smart idea, John Langley. What about the spies whose names I gave you last time? Any luck in running them down?" Magnus had dropped three names when he told Schuyler about the British counterfeiting scheme and Schuyler had passed them along to Washington by way of Stationer.

"We've identified two and have a good idea who the third one is. We'll leave them alone for the time being though, so we can use them later."

"Use them? How?"

"As long as they don't know we're on to them, we can use them to either plant or confirm false information we want to feed to the British. Washington's a master at it. A couple of years ago he tricked both Clinton and Howe. Had them believing he was going to attack both New York and Philadelphia at the same time—at a time when we couldn't have attacked anybody, we were so weak. Because of what he did, we weren't attacked by either Clinton or Howe and had time to regroup our forces. General George is a damn wizard sometimes!"

"Judging from what's just happened down

South," Schuyler said, "it looks as if the Continental Army could use a few more Washingtons to replace some of his generals."

"You may be right, Schuyler. And don't forget the one who's figuring on becoming a redcoat general or whatever. We still haven't found him."

"No chance that Lincoln could be him?"

Hunter shook his head. "No chance. He's been in the South since before the British began negotiating with the traitor and that's just too far away from New York for him to be in touch with the enemy here." He grinned. "So keep on trying to figure out who the traitor is and have Clarissa do the same. She okay?"

Schuyler masked his confusion by trying to match John Langley's grin. "Still trying to prove she's the best spy of the war," he said.

"And likely to do it, too, Schuyler. In my family the men fight and the women spy." He looked at Schuyler thoughtfully for a moment. "Clarissa had to grow up pretty quickly as a child. I was off fighting the French and Indian War with your brother and General George, and since our mother had died there really wasn't anyone to look after her. She can take care of herself pretty well, Schuyler, so I wouldn't worry too much. That's not to say that we don't all need some help from time to time . . ."

Clinton returned to New York in early June, having left General Cornwallis to mop up in the Carolinas. But he brought with him no prisoner list, though he did bring rebel General Lincoln as a prisoner.

Buoyed by his great Southern success, Clinton

made a triumphant pronouncement at a banquet arranged in his honor several days after his return to New York. "Now that we've secured most of the southern half of the country, the rebels will find it difficult indeed to continue to fight this outlandish war. And I intend to hit them even harder up here—to remind them that they must capitulate!"

Less than a week later the British commander dispatched General Knyphausen to Elizabeth in Jersey with a large force, instructing him to "show the rabble we mean to make them exceedingly uncomfortable." Knyphausen was met by a force of Continentals, but the skirmish near Springfield proved little more than that Clinton meant his earlier words about hitting the rebels in the north as well as the south.

But now important news reached New York from English spies in France: part of the French fleet was on its way to America, carrying troops under the command of General Rochambeau which would land at Newport and hold it for the rebels. On the very same day, Andre brought Magnus a new message from the turncoat American general, offering to arrange for the delivery of an important command in exchange for a generalship and a large amount of English pounds. Equally important, the traitor confirmed news of the impending arrival of the large French fleet in Newport in "about July" and suggested that the British fleet had enough arms to surprise and rout the Frenchmen.

The news prompted Magnus to speed up delivery of the facts of his and Andre's correspondence with the traitor to Sir Henry, along with their conclusion that the traitor was, in fact, General Benedict Arnold.

"Arnold?" Clinton said disbelieving. "He's a bloody hero and most competent general—not like Lee! I cannot believe your assumption is correct."

"Everything points to Arnold, General," Magnus said, "including his handwriting, which I've had analyzed by experts. And he has had some trouble with his superiors—the members of the Continental Congress, mostly. The man simply isn't liked and as a consequence, he's been passed over for promotions and not given his due."

"Do not misunderstand me, Major," Clinton said. "I sincerely hope you're right, because if you are —well, Arnold could surely do us a substantial favor. And if it were the right one, perhaps it might result in the war's end."

"He confirms the intelligence we've just received about the French fleet, Sir Henry. He seems to think we can defeat the French if we act swiftly."

"Good, for I've already won General Perfection's acquiescence in sending the fleet to Newport. They'll sail within the week."

"What about Arnold, sir?" Magnus asked. "He wants a generalship as well as a large sum of cash. And he wants it whether his plan to deliver us a major command succeeds or not."

Clinton thought a moment. "I would very much like to have Arnold over here, if only to rob the other side of him," he said. "But let's see what he can offer us before we agree to anything. If our man truly is Arnold, at present he can offer us only Philadelphia, and we hardly need that. Have Andre send him a message that we are only interested in winning an important military objective. He'll understand what it is we want. By the way—do you agree that Captain Andre has done a splendid job with this assignment?"

Magnus had no choice but to agree. Andre had indeed done his job well, and it was obvious that Clinton thought so. "Yes, sir," Magnus said, "first-rate."

"Good, Major. Then you can tell the captain that he is no longer a captain. One of my aides was unfortunately struck down by a rebel sniper at Charleston, and so there's an opening on my staff for another major. I am therefore promoting him, effective immediately."

Magnus was stunned. Working as Andre's superior had not been entirely unbearable, but working with him on an equal rank was another matter. He tried to hide his dismay as he saluted his superior, turned and left.

News of Clinton's intelligence coup spread quickly through his staff—mainly because the commander did not regard secrecy as vitally important to the fleet's success in defeating the French.

Upon hearing the news, Schuyler rode to Fish Kill and dispatched the son of a rebel sympathizer to bring John Langley Hunter to him.

It was late in the day before Hunter arrived. When Schuyler informed him of Clinton's plans to surprise the French fleet near Newport, all the spy could do was shake his head. At last he said, "God! There's not a thing we can do about it. There's no telling where the French might be right now, so we can't send a privateer to warn them. And if we send a ship to Newport, the British'll chase it away before it can deliver a warning."

"And if the French are routed, we may lose their help, not only for now, but for good. Isn't there something we can do?"

"I don't know what," Hunter said glumly. "When did you say they're sailing? In a week? Maybe we can go out and scuttle all of their ships so they can't leave New York harbor," he said, giving a sarcastic laugh.

Schuyler, however, did not laugh at all. "Say, I think you've hit on something. Suppose we could make Clinton change his mind about sending the fleet?"

"A fat chance of that, Schuyler. What would make him do that?"

Now Schuyler laughed, as the idea which had taken him moments before became a full-blown plan. "What if Clinton got the idea that the intelligence he'd received from France was false, that Washington had arranged it so as to get the British fleet out of New York, and that the French fleet was not headed for Newport but was going to co-operate with Washington in a siege of New York!"

John Langley Hunter's eyes had opened wide as Schuyler outlined his plan, the look on his face progressing from surprise to awe to delight. "You may be young, boy, but you surely aren't dumb. How'd you ever think up something like that?"

"Remember telling how good General George was at deceiving the British? Well, it just struck me that this was the greatest time to do such a thing. Think Washington can pull it off?"

"If he can't, nobody can," John Langley replied. "I'll get right back to White Plains and see what he wants to do. If I need your help, I'll get a message to you through Stationer."

"Whatever's to be done will have to be done in a hurry, for once the ships have sailed, it won't be possible to bring them back."

"Don't worry," Hunter said, "General George is an expert at getting things done in a hurry. If he had to, I suspect he could even get a ship built overnight—or cross the Atlantic in a week."

Schuyler found the time passing all too quickly as he awaited developments. He was surprised at how nervous and edgy he was at the thought that what happened at Newport could change the outcome of the rebellion. His lukewarm feeling for the rebels' cause seemed to have changed into something much stronger. He cared. He wanted the rebels to win. He felt a oneness with Hunter, with Washington and with the rebels that he had not felt with the Torries.

There were other new emotions too, less positive ones. While his work on Magnus's staff had lacked the excitement Magnus had promised, there was a never-ending tension underlying it, a tension which produced fear. It was always there, the haunting thought that he was about to be unmasked.

"Well, brother, I am shocked to learn that you have become a spy for the rebels. What have you to say for yourself before I have you hanged?"

The words were a nightmare he prayed he would never experience. Still, he knew the risks and was ready to face the consequences if he had to. Would Magnus hang him? He had no doubt that his brother would.

The days passed in a blur and soon it was the fifth of July and Graves's ships were out in the harbor, upping anchor and getting ready to sail.

Schuyler was alone in his brother's office, looking out into the harbor as the British sails were unfurled. Magnus was not in and Schuyler had no idea where he had gone. And didn't care.

Why hadn't he heard from John Langley? Had Washington been unable to deceive the British? Were they simply throwing the French to the wolves? To the seagoing British wolves?

As the ships began moving slowly out of the harbor, Schuyler half-turned at a sound behind him to see that Magnus had just returned, in his hand a folded packet of papers. His brow was furrowed as he opened and spread a large map on his desk. He studied it for many moments while Schuyler looked on in puzzlement.

"Brother," Magnus said at last, "I need your thoughts. Would you come here and look at this?"

"I was just watching the fleet sail out of the bay," Schuyler said. "A magnificent sight, indeed."

Magnus paid him no attention. He continued to study the map, a baffled expression on his face. He looked up only when Schuyler arrived at his desk and stared down at the map.

"Look at this map, Schuyler," Magnus said, "and tell me what it suggests to you."

Schuyler's spirits took a large jump upward at what he saw. It was a map showing Clinton's fortification in New York, Long Island and Staten Island. Each major redoubt had an arrow pointing to it and was marked by a different letter of the alphabet. In the Hudson were twenty oblong circles lined up in battle formation against New York's fortifications—ready to send cannonballs skyward to rain death and destruction on Manhattan Island!

"It looks like a plan for an assault on New York," Schuyler said guardedly. In his mind now was the certain knowledge that Washington had acted to head off the British threat to the French fleet. The only question was whether the map had arrived in time and whether Magnus and Clinton would believe it was what it purported to be.

"Exactly what it is, Schuyler," Magnus replied, his eyes still on the map. "And if it's no trick, it indicates that the rebels will have the assistance of twenty ships in the attack. French ships, no doubt. The same French ships which are supposed to be on their way to Newport, which our fleet is supposed to find and engage."

"Is it a trick, Magnus?" Schuyler said. "Or were the reports from Paris telling us that the French fleet's objective was Newport the ones which were contrived by the rebels? What a brilliant plan, if it was! Here we are, with all our ships gone to seek out the French fleet, and they come sailing boldly into New York harbor to bombard us and help Washington force us off Manhattan Island!"

Magnus slumped back into his chair and closed his eyes. "I wish I knew, Schuyler. I feel I should rush out of here and try to convince Clinton we're in danger, that's he got to recall the ships before they're too far gone. Yet what's there before me on the desk could just as easily be the trick—though I've the strongest feeling it isn't."

"Of course, you must choose," Schuyler said carefully.

Magnus stood abruptly and stared down at the map on his desk. "If this were bogus," he muttered, "and we were intended to see it, the bastards would've left some other documentation—something that made it perfect." With that, Magnus raced out the door, and Schuyler was certain he knew where he was headed.

Elated, Schuyler wished he could witness the scene on the widow's walk of Clinton's headquarters. The general would be up there watching the sea caravan, while listening to Magnus. Would his brother convince Sir Henry?

Only five minutes elapsed before Magnus returned to his office, with Sir Henry in tow, and the two went straight to Magnus's desk and the map spread out on it.

Schuyler's flesh tingled as he watched Clinton inspect the map. None of them knew it, but the map on Magnus DeWitt's desk was the second one Washington had drawn. The first map had been returned to Washington by the commander of one of his patrols, which had captured the Tory spy who carried it.

"Well," said Clinton, "this surely gives one pause. The question is, is it genuine?"

"I believe it is, Sir Henry," Magnus said. "I can't prove it, but it smells just right to me—impressive, but not too much so. If I were planting such a map, I'd be tempted to provide further documentation to assure the other side of its authenticity— a letter or some such thing. This map is all by itself, and that's the way it ought to be, if it's genuine."

Clinton went back to studying the map for a time, then straightened and nodded. "Very good, Magnus," he said, "I'll most certainly take the matter under immediate advisement."

The commander folded up the map and stuffed it into his uniform pocket, then started for the door. Magnus stopped him with a question. "If you please, sir, I must remind you that we've only a few hours in which to stop the fleet. Shall I alert the dragoons so we can take action immediately if you decide to recall the fleet?"

"Of course, Major. And I shall reach a decision shortly, I assure you."

"You really believe the map is real?" Schuyler asked Magnus when the general had departed.

"I wish I didn't," Magnus said, "for I'm afraid Sir Henry has gone to check with his General Perfection and will come back with a decision to allow matters to stand as they are. Washington is a clever man—perhaps even more so than I thought. If I'm right about the map, then somehow the rebel general arranged for false intelligence to be sent us from France about the French fleet's destination. He managed to convince his own general staff of the same fact, while at the same time readying plans for an assault on New York! The man's magnificent! He even convinced Gustavus, who's a formidable general indeed."

"Gustavus? Who's that?"

"Perhaps one day I'll be able introduce him, brother. For the moment, suffice it to say that he's an American officer who wishes to again serve the King."

"Really? But you've made me curious! Can you tell me more?"

Magnus shook his head. "Far too much hangs on the success of this man's defection. Perhaps the entire rebellion will be decided by it—who knows?"

"One man's desertion can hardly mean that much!" Schuyler exclaimed. "Unless, of course, it's the good General Washington who seeks to come over."

"Would that it were, Schuyler," Magnus replied. "But I can assure you that our man is little short of Washington."

Magnus would say no more and the two brothers lapsed into silence as they awaited word from Clinton. Each one hoped for a turnback of the ships, though for an entirely different reason.

More than an hour passed before Clinton sent his orderly to bring Magnus to his office upstairs. When Magnus returned, he was furious and bitterly disappointed. Major Andre, he told Schuyler, had advised Clinton that he had information indicating the map was phony, that it had been drawn up by Washington only to keep the British from ambushing the French fleet.

"Can you believe that, Schuyler?" Magnus asked. "I've been in Sir Henry's service for four years, yet the fool believes Andre rather than me. And Andre is wrong! Completely wrong!"

"Did Andre have proof?" Schuyler struggled vainly to find words which might help Magnus go back to Clinton and put the lie to Andre.

"Andre claims one of our double agents overheard Washington chortling over how he was going to slip one over on us. But that only convinced me that Andre was making it up in order to inflate his importance, for Washington is not a braggart. He would hardly be likely to display himself in that manner, even if he had mounted an operation that had put an end to the war."

"Clinton would risk New York on the basis of Andre's fairy tale?"

"He says he hasn't made up his mind, but I fear he soon will. And he will favor the status quo, for otherwise he'll be forced to take too much action. And Sir Henry despises action when he can avoid it."

"It seems to me that New York is worth considerably more to the British cause than Newport, Magnus. We could lose the war by losing New York to Washington and the French. Only if the reports that the French are heading for Newport are correct can we be safe with the fleet away from New York."

"And Washington is such a trickster that there's no way we can depend on that, Schuyler," Magnus said. "You make telling points. Perhaps I could seek Clinton out now, when he no longer has the asinine Andre with him. Perhaps I can still bring him to his senses."

"It's worth a try, Magnus."

It was an hour before Magnus returned, an hour in which Schuyler became increasingly despairing. The look on Magnus's face cheered him immediately.

"Sir Henry has come around, though I'm not certain it's in time. Messengers are already on their way to signal the fleet to return. Let's hope that it isn't already too late. If Graves's sails have had favorable winds, the last of his ships may already have disappeared from view. I must thank you, Schuyler, however, for your support. You've helped your country greatly."

Schuyler swallowed hard. If Magnus knew where his real interests lay . . . He squelched the thought and settled back to await word that the fleet had returned.

7

NEITHER MAGNUS DEWITT nor his brother turned out to be heroes for their involvement in the recall of the British fleet. By the end of August, it was apparent that Washington would not attack New York as his map had suggested.

The French fleet and General Rochambeau had indeed arrived in Newport and had taken over the former British fortifications in and around the city. Andre still insisted that Washington had never intended to attack New York and pointed to the presence of the French in Newport as positive proof of his allegations. Magnus, however, advised his commander that it was only because of his wise decision to recall the fleet that New York was not now under siege. The French had no doubt sighted the British fleet in New York and avoided a battle

by heading north for Newport. Clinton was inclined to favor the last theory, if only to save face.

Clinton was in such good spirits over the results
of his first two years as head of British forces in
America that he was disinclined to dwell on minor
defeats. Reports from Cornwallis in the South
were glowing and Benedict Arnold had just been
placed in command at West Point. The last was
good news indeed, for it placed the turncoat American general in charge of the best possible British
target in the north.

Magnus DeWitt, however, had mixed emotions
over the news of Arnold's command. The news itself pleased him. But Clinton was so impressed
with Andre's conduct of the "Gustavus" affair that
he had ordered Andre to report directly to him.
Magnus was furious over being bypassed by his
longtime superior. He decided what he needed
was an intelligence coup—like the breaking up of
a Long Island spy ring he now knew was running
messages by speedy whaleboat across Long Island
Sound to Washington's forces in New Haven. Or
the uncovering of definite proof that Tory women
were working for the rebels by getting British officers to talk too freely at social events. Magnus had
recently confirmed what he had long suspected,
that Washington was indeed using local women
who pretended to be Loyalists. One of the women
had confessed and he had instructed her to attempt
to secure evidence against the other women serving the rebel cause. In order to imprison the ladies,
he would need iron-clad evidence, but he was determined to get it.

Now he chuckled softly at the memory of Joanna's thinly disguised attempt to hurt Schuyler

by suggesting that his occasional escort, the lovely Clarissa Beauford, was "probably one of those spies you're always raving about." Magnus had asked Joanna why she should make such a statement, but all she could say was that Mrs. Beauford "covers up her southern accent and tries to sound British— and not only pays court to your brother, but also to that handsome Major Andre!"

"Well," Magnus had said, "what of that? Most ladies enjoy flirting with more than one man at a time." He hadn't thought it prudent to mention Joanna's simultaneous affairs with his father and brother.

"They're both in the spy business, like you. Anybody who's interested in both of them like that is bound to be a spy herself!"

Although he could not fault Joanna's reasoning in one way, he had thought her notion fanciful. Then, in early September, he had received several reports from his New York spies that Clarissa had been seen "talking earnestly" to George Stationer, and his doubts became serious enough so that he decided to investigate her background. He had just learned from another source that Stationer was making far too many "business" trips to the New England states and was probably in league with Washington.

While Magnus was having Mrs. Beauford checked out, John Andre was intent on rekindling his romance with the lady.

Clarissa was genuinely surprised to find Andre at her door. After all, she had made it clear to him that she regretted their earlier intimacy and did not intend to make the same mistake a second time.

Andre, however, was at his charming best as he stood in the foyer of Clarissa's house, striving to gain entry. His career opportunities had been greatly enhanced by the Arnold negotiations, and he knew his happiness would be complete if he could win the stunning Clarissa for his own. That he had not done so already, after their passion-filled session only a few months ago, was both puzzling and disconcerting to him. If there was one area of his life in which he had always encountered easy success, it was with the ladies.

"My dearest lady," he told Clarissa, clasping her right hand between his, "I've done all that I can think of to prove my great affection for you, yet you shun me. Please, tell me what I may say or do to gain your good graces. Soon I am to make a trip which will assure me a high position in the King's army, and then I will be in a position I have long desired—I will be able to marry."

Andre's supposed desire for marriage was of little consequence to Clarissa, but his trip interested her greatly. "You're going away?" she said, trying to maintain a casual manner. "When? Why?"

Andre was pleased with the lady's sudden interest and debated only briefly the wisdom of discussing his trip to meet "Gustavus." He was entirely taken with Clarissa and determined to win her, whatever the cost.

"I can't tell you when I'm going," Andre said, then dropped his voice to a near whisper and bent closer to her ear. "But I will be meeting the rebel officer of whom I spoke before, the one who will defect to the King's army."

"Oh!" Clarissa breathed, sensing the excitement

in Andre's voice. If only he would say the man's name.

Andre liked the sparkle his announcement had put in Clarissa's eyes and decided to go just a little farther. After all, what possible harm would she do, especially to a possible husband? "We will meet in enemy territory," he told her, "across the Hudson, where I could be killed. So please, dear lady, do not betray me."

"Killed? Oh, John, why don't you meet him here, in New York? Or at least on this side of the river and in friendly territory."

"Would that I could. It would be far safer for both of us. But he can't leave the territory he commands and I must therefore go to him to finalize our arrangements."

"Poor John!" Clarissa exclaimed. "My thoughts will go with you. You must pay me a visit as soon as you return and tell me about your trials. I wish to hear everything."

"I would prefer to take your heart with me rather than your thoughts, Clarissa." His eyes dropped to the floor beneath his highly polished black boots. "It's a dangerous mission, through heavily armed rebel territory."

"Don't talk like that," Clarissa said, reaching over to touch his face. "You'll be all right."

Andre seized the chance to kiss her and she allowed him the liberty, knowing that to deny it might arouse his suspicion. "I could die completely happy," Andre said, taking Clarissa in his arms, "if only I could make love to you once more."

Clarissa tried to break his embrace, but without success. "Now you *are* being silly, John. You go meet this whatever his name is . . ." She paused momentarily, hoping he would fill in the name, but he did not. "And come back and visit me," she concluded. "Then we shall see about making love."

But Andre continued to try to convince her that she ought to allow him in her bedchamber, if only because he had to risk his life.

When at last he gave up and left, she immediately hurried across town toward Stationer's establishment. Inside, she scarcely noticed Magnus's Tory informer, a tall man in banker's garb, who made a show of inspecting Stationer's hardware as he eyed the beautiful woman talking softly to the proprietor.

Stationer promised Clarissa that he himself would take her information to Washington tomorrow.

Schuyler, whose reputation as 723 was growing with Washington, was conferring with John Langley Hunter in the barn at Fish Kill when Stationer arrived with Clarissa's piece of news. Hearing it, Hunter all but chortled. "Now we'll get the bastard!" he said. "All we have to do is watch the river. Andre won't chance travelling by land in our territory, so I'd say he'll use the British picket ship, the *Vulture*. All we have to do is follow it and see where it puts in. That'll be where they'll meet."

"We won't be getting Clarissa in trouble by doing this, will we, John Langley?"

"Don't see how, Schuyler. We won't be capturing Andre or questioning him, only tagging along behind him so we can see who he's meeting. When we see that, we'll know everything. And you know what, Schuyler? I believe I know who I'm going to see. If it isn't General Benedict Arnold, I shall be truly shocked."

Schuyler's eyes opened wide at the name Hunter had just tossed at him. "You can't mean that. Arnold's a hero! Injured in battle, commander of Philadelphia, greatly respected by both sides. Why he was just recently placed—"

"In charge of West Point," Hunter interrupted. "Who better than the commander of nearby West Point to suggest meeting Andre along the river banks?"

"I find it impossible to believe that Arnold's the man."

"Treason is always difficult to believe. Schuyler, it would help us a great deal if we had a bit more information on when Andre will be leaving, so I'm counting on you to try to keep your eyes on him. I'll be camped near the *Vulture*'s mooring."

"If I learn nothing more?"

"I'll be here to watch Andre board the boat. When the *Vulture* moves out, I'll be on a whaleboat right behind her." Hunter's jaunty mood faltered a moment later when a new thought entered his mind and he asked about Matthew Bell.

"He's been on no lists of prisoners as yet, John Langley, but I'm told a new batch will be coming in from Charleston soon. I'll watch for his name."

"Even though I haven't heard from him, I'm still hoping he may have escaped before the surrender. Lincoln had to know that Bell's name is high up on the British spy lists. Your brother would dearly love having Matthew as his guest in New York, Schuyler."

Schuyler laughed. "As Matthew enjoyed toying with Magnus in the Golden Hawk Tavern," he said. "What will you do if I learn that Matthew is a British prisoner?"

"I don't know, Schuyler, but . . . well, I'll think of something. I'll have to."

Schuyler returned from his meeting with Hunter with an idea in mind that might eventually help John Langley and Matthew Bell. While Magnus was hard at work trying to get solid evidence on Washington's lady spies and Hunter awaited Major Andre at the Hudson River, Schuyler made it his business to learn more about the infamous British prison ships on which thousands of rebel soldiers and spies were kept. He even arranged a visit to the *Jersey*, an old hulk of a ship moored in the harbor north of Staten Island between the coasts of Long Island and New Jersey.

Schuyler was escorted to the hulk by Joshua Loring, who remained the Commissary of Prisons even though his wife no longer served as mistress to the departed British commander in chief, Sir William Howe. Loring was delighted to take Schuyler to the ship, knowing the youth was brother to Clinton's adjutant.

On his personal longboat, Loring asked Schuyler how Sir Henry was faring in acquiring "the comforts his position demands." Well aware of Loring's reputed gift of his own wife to Sir William, Schuyler merely smiled at the question. Sir Henry already had a mistress who seemed to please him, though she was plump and not nearly as attractive as the blonde, blue-eyed Mrs. Loring. He was tempted to ask if Loring was already tired of sleeping with his wife again, but decided it would serve no purpose.

The day was hot for September and the sun was high overhead when Schuyler climbed on board and was introduced to the ship's commander, Captain Amos Butler. Though the hold was covered by a double-doored hatch, an incredibly foul smell could be discerned coming from it and through the open port holes. Schuyler asked Butler about it.

Butler laughed harshly. "It's the prisoners," he said. "There are about eight hundred and some are always dying, don't ya know. Each morning we clean out the dead and bury them in the deep. But by noon, especially on hot days such as today, there are always a few more to contend with. The heat gets 'em. Be glad you're not a rebel prisoner, Lieutenant," he declared.

A contemptible sort, Schuyler decided after his discussion with the captain, who seemed far more concerned about the smell of the dead than the fact of their deaths.

Schuyler was nearly overcome by the smell that assailed him when he asked to see the hold. Butler's men threw open the hatches and backed away. Schuyer gasped, then forced himself to go inside and descend the ladder. What he saw was squalor such as he had never known existed. There was little light in the bowels of the ship in spite of the port holes, and the prisoners were filthy and nearly naked, their clothing little more than tatters of cloth. They were chained together in columns, each having only enough chain to be able to climb into a hammock slung from the deck pillars or to sit on a wooden bench.

What shocked him most, however, was that there were a few women among the prisoners. The moment he went back up on deck, he asked Captain Butler, "You have women down there?"

The captain glanced at Mr. Loring, who stood nearby smoking a long cigar, then responded, "Aye, there are a few. They were spies for the rebels."

"Why aren't they segregated? Surely they don't belong in the same putrid quarters as the men."

"We do segregate 'em for a while, Lieutenant. Keep them in the crew's quarters, we do. In chains, of course. That's when they first come aboard. Once the crew has its fill of 'em, we toss them below with the rest of the prisoners."

Schuyler looked at the captain uncomprehendingly. Could he mean what he appeared to mean? "Fill of them?" he repeated. "Are you saying that you . . ."

"They're little better than whores, most of them, Lieutenant, so don't waste your sympathy. Anyway, while they're up here with us, they eat better and have a helluva lot more comforts than when we toss 'em below. Smell better, too 'cause we make 'em bathe."

Butler's matter-of-fact tone outraged Schuyler and he had to fight to retain his calm exterior. In his mind he still saw the women he had seen in the hold—thin, emaciated women who wore little more than scraps of cloth across their loins and nothing on top. They were so scrawny and dirty that it was difficult to distinguish them from the men.

"What about their food, Captain? Aren't they fed regularly? They look as if they're all starving."

"We feed 'em once a day, whether they need it or not," said Butler. "They eat well enough."

"Perhaps," Schuyler replied, "but it's surprising

you don't have a rebellion among the prisoners, the way they're treated."

"Them blokes ain't in any shape to rebel, Lieutenant," Butler declared. "First, they're wearing chains on both wrists and ankles. And second, they're weak as kittens. That's one of the reasons we don't feed 'em more often—cuts down on the number of guards we need for them. We make do with twenty men plus myself."

"Seems to me you're risking a rebel attack, if that's all the crew you've got. Your twenty would be no match for a privateer."

Butler shook his head. "We got orders from Mr. Loring here to scuttle the boat—open the petcocks and flood the hold—if we're attacked by a force we can't hope to fight. Then there's the pickets. All we got to do is drop our flag, cut the rope if need be, and we'll have our gunboats here inside five minutes. They drop over here to see us now and then, but not on any schedule so's you can know when they're coming. And we got lookouts fore and aft twenty-four hours a day. No rebel privateer can get close enough to us to take us."

Schuyler felt guilty as he and Mr. Loring took their leave of the ship, but knew he could do little to ease the sad plight of the rebel prisoners, short of attacking the ship in order to set them free. And that seemed a difficult task, if not an impossible one.

During the trip back to the wharf, he asked Loring about the use—or abuse—of women prisoners. Loring immediately rose to the defense of the practice.

"It's an important benefit, Lieutenant," he declared. "It makes an otherwise drab and dirty duty one which some crewmen covet, and even bid for. Without it, we'd have an unhappy crew of guards aboard the hulks and that could well lead to a sell-out."

"A sell-out?"

"To the rebels, of course, for most of the prisoners out there are former rebel soldiers and militiamen. The crew could easily deliver a hulk to an attacking force and that's something we can scarcely allow. Therefore, we keep them happy with good pay and women to warm their beds. Our biggest problem is finding enough women to keep them satisfied, for there are twenty-one men on the crew and rarely more than three or four women on board who are desirable. We cannot, of course, send respectable women to the *Jersey* or one of the other hulks, but we can and do send any other of the sex who run afoul of the law, including indentured bond servants who've run away, and street walkers."

Loring, Schuyler decided, was every bit as despicable as the *Jersey*'s captain. But he was wise as well, for he told Schuyler that the only visitors allowed on the ship were those he personally approved and accompanied, transporting them in his own longboat which was well known to the captain and crew. No other boat was allowed near the ship.

Although he wasn't at all sure an attack on the *Jersey* would be fruitful should Matthew Bell wind up aboard the ship, Schuyler spent the evening faithfully recording every detail he had learned about the prison hulk. He included the approximate number and condition of the prisoners, how many guards were aboard, where their quarters were, and the captain's instructions in the event they were stormed.

Schuyler prayed it would not be necessary for him to turn his notes on the prison ship over to Hunter. He hated to think of Matthew Bell—or anyone else, for that matter—being confined to the hold of the *Jersey*.

Did Clinton know of the inhuman conditions on the ships? Could anyone in authority know of them without taking measures to correct them? Yet Loring approved, and it was therefore inconceivable that his superior did not.

Schuyler's estimation of the British overlords of America had reached an all-time low. His conviction that the rebels ought to win this revolution was more firm than it had ever been.

8

O N THE EIGHTEENTH of September Clarissa
Beauford was paid still another visit by Major
John Andre, who renewed his plea for her
favors. She granted him a few, but would not allow
him in her bed. Nevertheless, she learned he was
to leave on his trip the following afternoon.

As soon as Andre left, she went to Stationer's
store, but he was away, so she paid Schuyler a
visit instead. It was the first time she had seen
him since the night she had given herself to Andre.

Schuyler was surprised and pleased to see her.
"Come in," he told her. His expression said much
more, pronouncing his delight with an eloquence
words could scarcely have achieved.

"Well, that is good news," he said after she had
told him the news of Andre. "Your brother will

want to know about this immediately. It will help him a great deal."

"Will you have someone follow Andre? To make certain of where he goes?"

"I'll follow him myself, Clarissa, to see that he plans on traveling across the river by boat. Once I'm certain of that, I can meet John Langley, and remain with him while he observes the meeting between the traitor and Andre."

Her information delivered, Clarissa turned to leave, only to be checked by Schuyler's hand upon her arm. She looked up and met his eyes.

"You've done well, Clarissa. I'm sure John Langley will be proud of you. I know that I am. Your country owes you a great debt." He hesitated now, seeking the right words. "I . . . I was wrong before, Clarissa," he managed. "Wrong to be angry about what you . . . what happened with Andre. Please forgive me. I know now that you were doing what you had to. These are extraordinary times, in which we must do extraordinary things. Things we often do not wish to do."

Her eyes warmed at his words. "John Langley said you would be a fine addition to our cause," she murmured, "but he had no idea how fine." Then she was against him, his mouth pressed to hers, her body flattening against him as he encircled her with his arms. They were both left breathless and excited.

"Would that I could make love to you now, darling," Schuyler whispered, "for I want you, need you, desperately. But I must go to your brother to inform him, then return to watch for Andre's embarkation tomorrow."

He kissed her tenderly before allowing her to

leave. "Be careful," she said softly, "and come back soon."

Schuyler found Hunter camped near the river, not far from where the *Vulture* lay at anchor. Hunter had a boat nearby and its skipper assured him he would have no difficulty in keeping the larger *Vulture* in sight once it got underway. Schuyler followed Andre long enough to make certain he was headed for the *Vulture*, then went to meet Hunter.

"I'm going with you while you track Andre to the traitor," Schuyler said.

"You can't, Schuyler," Hunter said. "It would be too dangerous."

"You fear I will hang, John Langley? I've been risking such a fate ever since I began aiding you and your cause."

"Our cause," Hunter responded.

"Perhaps," Schuyler said. "In any case, I believe I've the right to go with you."

In the end, Schuyler won his point and was present when Major Andre boarded the *Vulture* at Dobbs Ferry and was taken to an anchorage near Teller's Point. When the British picket ship nosed out into the Hudson, a whaleboat owned and skippered by a New York fisherman who was a rebel sympathizer was not far behind. Schuyler and John Langley were its only passengers.

Hunter figured that the meeting between Andre and the traitor would either take place on the *Vulture* or at a secluded spot along the shore, so they kept close watch from a vantage point on the river bank after the picket had anchored. When Andre did not leave at once for the meeting,

Hunter said he thought the traitor would come out by boat later in the evening, maybe as late as midnight. But he was wrong. No one showed up at the *Vulture* that night or even the next day, and Andre made no move to leave the ship to keep an appointment. On the second night of their vigil, however, things began to happen.

Late in the afternoon a large barge came down the river and put in at King's Crossing. Hunter's eyes lit up as he recognized it. "By God," he exclaimed, "that's Arnold's barge. He's taken Beverly Robinson's house up the river and commutes to his command at West Point in the barge."

The two men could not be certain Arnold was aboard the barge, so John Langley paid a visit to it and learned from the guards on duty that it was indeed Arnold's barge and that the general was aboard. He would be spending the night at the home of Joshua Smith a mile or so to the south. Smith, though purportedly a Patriot, was the brother of Tory William Smith, Chief Justice and propagandist of New York.

Told what Arnold's intentions were, Schuyler asked, "Do you think they'll meet in Smith's home?"

Hunter shook his head. "I doubt it. Is Andre a fool? Meeting Arnold on ground owned by the rebels would be as good as confessing he was a spy."

"Andre's certainly no fool," Schuyler returned, "but neither is Arnold, whom I doubt would venture out of rebel territory for this meeting."

Soon Hunter and Schuyler stood on the shore south of Teller's Point, their senses alert for the sounds of a boat moving toward them, and John

Langley's attention focused upon the *Vulture* in the dim light of a quarter moon. It was shortly before midnight when a boat approached the *Vulture* and discharged a passenger. Then it was re-boarded by the same man, along with another who wore a long blue coat. Hunter handed his spyglass to Schuyler. "Take a look, lad, and see if you recognize Andre."

The man in the blue coat looked like Andre, but Schuyler had to admit that he couldn't be sure.

Hunter took the glass back and brought it to bear on the boat, which now contained four dark figures, two of them rowing almost silently, their oars muffled with sheepskins. "Well, we'll soon know, for they're heading this way," he said.

The boat was only fifty yards away when Schuyler and John Langley heard horses almost directly to their rear. They edged into the woods at water's edge and listened closely as the horses passed a short distance away, then halted. Moments later the rowers shipped their oars and the boat nosed into shore barely fifty yards away. Schuyler and Hunter glanced at each other, then began moving silently through the trees and up the sloping ground at river's edge. They paused every few seconds to listen for voices, but heard none until they had reached a high point downwind from the place where they estimated the boat had come ashore.

Schuyler held his breath when he recognized the first voice he heard as Andre's. "You are Gustavus? General Benedict Arnold Gustavus?"

"Were I not, Major, you would be in deep trouble!" said a second voice. Hunter nodded, indicating that he knew Arnold's voice.

"I'm glad you have a sense of humor," Andre said, "but let's get down to business. You command West Point and can deliver it to us?"

"Of course. But first we must agree on the price. You're authorized to speak for Sir Henry Clinton, I take it?"

"I stand in his place, sir."

"Good. West Point is vital to British interests, and I need to restore my personal fortune. I must have ten thousand pounds, win or lose. Ten thousand pounds and a major-generalship."

There was a moment of silence before Andre responded. "I'm empowered to offer only six thousand pounds in the event of your failure to deliver West Point as promised, or in the event the number of men, stores and arms are more than twenty percent below the numbers stipulated earlier."

Now the two men began to haggle. "He's the scum of America," Hunter declared in a low voice. Schuyler was too shocked to say anything as he listened to Arnold and Andre bargain over the sell-out of West Point.

Hunter began making notes when Arnold and Andre worked out the proposed details of Arnold's treachery—including the approximate date of West Point's delivery and how Arnold would deploy his forces in order to assure that they could be taken prisoner with little difficulty. When it seemed that they had covered everything, Hunter motioned for a quiet withdrawal and they managed it without difficulty. The sky began to lighten as they reached their Patriot boatman, and his whaleboat shoved off for the re-crossing of the river.

By the time the sun appeared over the Eastern shore, they were across and separating, Schuyler heading south to New York and Hunter north-east toward Connecticut, where Washington was meeting with Rochambeau.

Two days later both Hunter and Schuyler were surprised to learn that Andre had been taken prisoner by three rebel mercenaries near Tarrytown, territory that was not considered dangerous to British soldiers, whether uniformed or not. Andre had worn civilian clothes and in his boot beneath his socks were found important papers detailing West Point's ordnance and other information vital to an invader—written in the hand of Major-General Benedict Arnold, the post's commander.

The news did not, however, reach Hunter in time for him to keep Arnold from fleeing for his life, and flee the traitor did. Straight to the British forces in New York.

Both Arnold and news of Andre's capture reached New York while Magnus and Joanna were visiting DeWitt Manor. Magnus's reaction upon his return to New York was one of both pleasure and pain. He was not unhappy, of course, that an important American hero had defected to the British and not as unhappy as Clinton about Andre's capture. But his superior's quite evident pain over the loss of Andre pained Magnus almost as much. Not until it became apparent that the rebels would treat Andre as a spy and probably hang him did Magnus feel complete sympathy for the major. At that point, Magnus again wished that he had been able to talk Clinton out of hanging Scott Laidlow.

When the details of Andre's capture became clear, General Clinton called Magnus in and raged at him as if Magnus had himself played a part in Andre's downfall. Why had the rebels fired upon the *Vulture?* Clinton asked Magnus, and why had the captain of the ship withdrawn and forced "poor Andre" to try to return home on horseback and without escort? Why had the men who captured Andre stopped him in the first place, dressed as he was in civilian clothes? And why had they made him strip, even removing his boots and stockings? Had Andre somehow been betrayed? Clinton was outraged that he had Arnold but not West Point, and especially that his favorite Andre was a rebel prisoner and might well be hanged. He commanded Magnus to get at the truth immediately.

While Magnus investigated the circumstances of Andre's capture, Schuyler received important instructions from Washington. The general wanted Benedict Arnold captured and returned to West Point "at all costs."

What Washington proposed was only a little more daring than John Langley's entry into New York with the orders. When Schuyler got the message, by way of Stationer, that John Langley was in New York, he went immediately to meet the Virginian, who was staying with a "Tory" doctor whose rebel feelings had never been exposed.

For seven days Clinton tried to keep Washington from hanging Andre, first by personal appeal, then by threats of retaliation against "any of your army who fall within my power," the latter in a note Sir Henry had Arnold write. Washington's response to his British counterpart came the day before Andre was found guilty by a court-martial and sentenced to hang at Tappan. The American general wrote Clinton that Andre would be put to death, regardless of his pleas or threats. The rebel officer who carried Washington's note told Clinton privately, however, that Andre could be saved simply by sending Arnold back.

Clinton responded by having Magnus arrest a large number of rebel spies, among them George Stationer, whose activities had only recently been discovered. But the arrests had no effect on Washington's resolve to hang the man responsible for Arnold's defection. He wouldn't be swayed unless the British agreed to return the traitor.

Magnus sent a dozen questions to Andre by way of Andre's servant, who was permitted by the rebels to attend Andre in Tappan where he awaited his death. Magnus received the answers to his questions on the third of October, a day after Andre was hanged. The answers were shocking, for they told him that the only person to whom Andre had confided about his trip was Clarissa Beauford.

That night, while Schuyler was plotting with John Langley Hunter to recapture Benedict Arnold, Magnus paid Clarissa Beauford a visit.

9

SCHUYLER DeWITT and John Langley Hunter
met twice to plan their attempt to retake Benedict Arnold. The first meeting was immediately
after Hunter's arrival in New York, the second after
Schuyler had learned Arnold's location and something of his schedule, both of which were kept
very much a secret by the British because of the
possibility of an attempt on the turncoat's life.

When the two men met on the first of October,
Schuyler had several pieces of disturbing news.
John Langley was silent through the news that
Clinton had shunned Washington's quiet efforts to
swap Andre for Arnold. "Nobody figured he'd go
for that anyway," was Hunter's pronouncement.

Schuyler's second piece of intelligence was more
ominous. His brother had taken Stationer into cus-

tody as a spy, along with eighteen others. Some of them were legitimately rebel spies, but there were others who were not and who were in fact completely unknown to rebel military authorities.

"Stationer?" Hunter repeated slowly. "That is bad news! He's been invaluable to our cause ever since we lost New York."

"Be glad Magnus now disapproves of torture, John Langley," Schuyler said soberly, "or perhaps we would both be in for it. The last piece of news is the worst. It's about Matthew."

Hunter stared at Schuyler, his eyes suddenly hard. "He's a prisoner?" he asked. "In New York?"

Schuyler shifted uneasily under Hunter's gaze. "He's aboard the prison ship *Jersey* anchored in the harbor."

Hunter shook his head, his dismay showing. "I'm not surprised, though I had hoped . . . How long has he been there?"

"I can't be certain. His name is listed as 'Bellknap' and he apparently arrived aboard a frigate about two weeks ago. At least we know he's alive."

"I'd almost rather be dead. If I were in chains aboard one of those British hulks, Matthew would come to my aid even if he were sure he would die in the effort."

Schuyler nodded. "I knew you'd feel that way, John Langley," he said, "and so I paid the *Jersey* a visit several weeks ago to learn what I could about its escape potential. What I learned didn't encourage me. The prospects of a prisoner escaping are nil and the chances of freeing one prisoner or a hundred are remote indeed."

Schuyler related what he had learned about the

ship, its layout and the precautions taken to prevent its takeover from another ship. "The only way you might successfully attack the *Jersey* would be to board the hulk as I did, as a visitor, and take Butler and his crew prisoners. It would have to be done very quietly, for any member of the crew could summon help merely by cutting down the *Jersey's* flag."

"Could you and I get aboard as visitors?" Hunter asked.

"I've thought of that and I'd say it's just possible —primarily because this Loring fellow is so greedy. He's the same one who traded his wife for the favors given him by Sir William Howe. If I told him you were somebody who could do him some good, he might let the two of us aboard the hulk. The trouble is, even if we get aboard and subdue the crew, how would we—" Schuyler suddenly broke off and a wide grin appeared on his face.

"I've got it!" he exclaimed. "We'll up anchor, rig a sail and head for the beach. Captain Butler told me they still had a mainsail, although they had intended to get rid of it and their mast."

"Run her aground?" Hunter said. "Sounds like a good idea to me. Maybe I can arrange to have troops there to fight off any attempt by the British gunboats guarding the bay to pursue and destroy us."

Schuyler frowned as a thought occurred to him. "The only trouble I can see is that once I've helped you with this, there'll be no concealing my role as a rebel spy."

"Don't worry about that, boy," John Langley said. "I'll make certain there'll be no one surviving to mention your name. From what you tell me, the captain is a blackguard and warrants no consideration. And neither does the crew, if it feasts on helpless women. As for Loring, his greed will do him in."

"What about Arnold? Right now he's more important to Washington than anyone."

"Aye, we must take the traitor first—and soon. Let's lay our plans for Monday next. That will give me the time I need to make sure our boat will be on hand on the north shore of Long Island to carry him away. Once that's done, we can act to save Matthew. Aboard a prison ship, each day is an eternity."

"A good thing Arnold has no command, or his habits would have been far more difficult to determine. Magnus says Clinton won't assign him a command for fear of assuring Andre's death. He has even prevented the newspaper from commenting on Arnold's arrival in New York."

"Clinton has already assured Andre's death, first by hanging Scott Laidlow and second with his refusal to return Arnold. A pity we couldn't hang Sir Henry himself."

Schuyler chuckled. "I fear the general wouldn't find that amusing, John Langley," he said. "By the way, Magnus told me that Clinton would gladly return Arnold, were it not for the poor effect it would have on rebel desertions. It seems Arnold hasn't made a good impression on Sir Henry at all."

"Let's hope we can make a good impression on Arnold's *skull* when we take him prisoner," Hunter said, scowling. "And that Matthew won't despair before we can rescue him."

* * *

On the third of October, word came from Tappan that Andre had been hanged the previous day. Though Schuyler had not liked Andre at all, he still found the news sobering and knew Clarissa Beauford would as well, so he went to visit her. He was surprised to find his brother with her.

Clarissa shot him a warning look as Schuyler entered her drawing room. "Well, Schuyler," she said with a nervous laugh, "what a coincidence! Your brother Magnus is here. He has the insane idea that—"

"That you are a spy, madame," Magnus finished for her. He wore no smile as he faced his brother. "A spy whose brother, I might add, is the infamous John Langley Hunter. Did you know that, Schuyler? Hunter—the rebel spy!"

"That's ridiculous, Magnus," Schuyler said. "Clarissa is no more a spy than I am. How can you make such an absurd charge? I know you've been worried that some of our women are spying for the rebels, but I can vouch for Clarissa. She can't be one of them."

"Mrs. Beauford has admitted to me that Major Andre paid her a visit the night before he met with Benedict Arnold. In fact, she was the only person who had knowledge of the meeting, other than Andre, Arnold and myself."

"But I deny that Andre told me that, Major. He didn't come to see me about his business. He came here because . . . well, he was courting me. I wasn't even aware that he was a spy."

"He wasn't a spy," Magnus said. "He was merely conferring with Arnold under a flag of truce. It's unfortunate that circumstances have branded him a spy—and killed him, by the way. The rebels hanged him yesterday, Mrs. Beauford. Did you know that?"

Clarissa's eyes widened in horror. "Yesterday? That's horrible," she gasped.

Schuyler knew Clarissa meant her words, but supposed Magnus would believe she was merely acting. He was right, for now Magnus pointed an accusing finger at the woman and said, "You, dear lady, are the one who should be hanged, for you are most certainly a spy. And a clever one at that. You've even fooled my brother."

Schuyler struggled to come up with a defense for Clarissa which might convince Magnus to leave her alone, but knew with a sinking heart that his brother was sure of his ground and would not be talked out of whatever it was he planned to do.

"Just what are you accusing her of?" Schuyler said. "Specifically, I mean. What is the charge?"

"I accuse her of betraying Major Andre to our enemies, resulting in his capture and death. I accuse her of passing along British military secrets to the rebels through one George Stationer, who posed as a Tory but was actually another rebel spy."

"Stationer?" Schuyler said. "A spy? Please, Magnus, say you're joking. The man is as loyal as I. In all the times I've visited his establishment, I never once received the impression he was anything but a loyal subject of the King."

"Again you were fooled, Schuyler. But we were too, until very recently. He's confessed at great length to me about the spies with whom he consorted against the King—including Mrs. Beauford. There's no question that she's involved in the nest of ladies who have been selling us out to Washington." He turned again to Clarissa, who sat stiffly in a chair, her face white with fear. "Why don't you make a clean breast of it, my dear? Then I could make things easy for you, for I should hate to see such a lovely lady as yourself placed aboard one of the prison ships in the harbor."

"I can't make a clean breast of it, Major, because I am not guilty of anything. Nothing at all! If Stationer is a spy and *if* he told you anything which purports to involve me, and *if* you truly believe him—then you are a fool! I do not deny my brother is John Langley Hunter, but I am not his custodian and what he does can hardly condemn me. We do not share the same views, though we're from the same family."

"Do you deny that you favor the Continentals in the rebellion?"

"I deny your right to even put such a ridiculous question to me, sir! Who I favor means nothing in the matter at hand. What I do or did is the only thing important, and I've done nothing of which I am not proud. If you have proof to support your insane allegation that I am a spy, then show it or leave at once."

"Magnus," Schuyler interjected, "I really believe you ought to check on your facts. There must be a mistake. If Stationer brought Clarissa into the case, it must have been to create a red herring. You certainly can't convince me that she's guilty of anything. The word of a confessed spy is hardly to be trusted. And I know Clarissa well. She cannot be a spy!"

Magnus ignored his brother. "What say you, madame, to the charge that you passed along to the rebels your knowledge that Andre was meeting Arnold across the Hudson near Teller's Point?"

"I had no such knowledge, Major."

Schuyler could not have admired Clarissa more for the manner in which she was handling herself in the face of Magnus's severe interrogation. But he knew she was fighting a losing battle. Magnus would not have confronted her if he did not have the evidence he needed to imprison her. In any case, Magnus could have her imprisoned merely on suspicion of being a spy.

"Here, madame," Magnus said, producing a packet of papers from the pocket of his coat, "is a deathbed statement signed by Major Andre. In it, he testifies to your knowledge of his mission and destination. Together with Stationer's statements, I have more than enough to condemn you."

When she had read through the statement, Magnus cleared his throat. "I can give you one more chance to spare yourself a great deal of pain and discomfort. If you refuse, through a misguided sense of loyalty to a failing cause, then you will be committed to the none-too-tender care of Captain Butler and the prison ship *Jersey*."

"See here, Magnus," Schuyler declared. "You can't do that! The *Jersey* is a sty, her crew a group of pigs. Women prisoners are used like—"

"You've said quite enough," Magnus broke in. "You'd do well to remember that, brother or not, I am your superior. I'm well aware that you have a personal interest in this woman, Schuyler, and that is unfortunate. But she's a spy and will be treated accordingly—*if* she continues to refuse to tell me what she knows. As for you, if you attempt to interfere in any way, I'll be forced to assume that you're her confederate and you'll be sent to the *Jersey* as well."

"You'd do that to your own brother?"

"I would have no choice."

In the end, Schuyler watched helplessly as Clarissa, frozen-faced and without tears, was taken away by his brother to be held overnight in the military jail near Clinton's headquarters and then transferred to the *Jersey*.

Schuyler hastened to see John Langley, but found he was away, apparently attending to the details involved in the Arnold affair. He waited with growing unease for Clarissa's brother to return.

10

SCHUYLER HAD NEVER in his life felt so helpless as while he was awaiting John Langley's return to the residence of the "Tory" doctor. The doctor had only a dim idea of when Hunter would be back. He said, "Morning, anyway."

Morning Schuyler thought, would find Clarissa being rowed out to that hellhole of a prison ship. If Clarissa's earlier sacrifice to Andre had been a terrible price to pay, how much worse were the ordeals which lay in store for her on the *Jersey* . . . Could he and John Langley put their plan into action to free Matthew Bell, and do it right away? They had to, or else Clarissa would suffer intolerably. If they waited, she might well be dead before they could save her.

Schuyler scowled at the thought that he and

John Langley still had to take care of Benedict Arnold. The traitor's capture seemed of little consequence compared to the matter of Clarissa's rescue from the prison ship. She had to come first. He prayed John Langley would agree.

Hunter returned just before sunrise. He was rocked by the news about his sister. "I don't . . . I can't . . ." He shook his head, stunned. "Clarissa—in that devil's paradise?"

"We've got to take that ship tonight," Schuyler declared. "Can you arrange a welcoming committee of Continentals near the beach?"

"Not before tomorrow," he said.

"Can we go it alone? Once the ship's aground, even the weaker of the prisoners can probably fend for themselves. Anyway, they're better off dead than on the *Jersey*."

"Still," John Langley said, "we've got to get Arnold. General George wants him so bad he can taste it. And I can't blame him."

"We can get him, too, John Langley. We'll just reverse the order, that's all. The *Jersey* tonight, Arnold tomorrow. What do you say?"

Hunter stared at Schuyler. "I ought to be saying no, but I can't. So I'm with you. Let's get at it!"

Clarissa still wore the gown she had put on in hope that Schuyler would pay her a visit the night before as she awoke in the jail near Clinton's headquarters in New York. She had slept little. The cot on which she lay was hard and the small room reeked with smells such as she had never before known.

And there were rats. All she saw were their eyes, because there was no light in her cell. The sound of

them scurrying here and there would have driven
her out of her mind had she not managed to force
her thoughts away from her predicament and concentrate instead on Schuyler DeWitt.

Had Schuyler been proud of the way she had
stood up to his brother? She wondered if Stationer
had really talked, had really mentioned her name.
She doubted it, though she couldn't be sure. She
had recognized Andre's handwriting, however, so
there was little doubt that he had accused her. She
couldn't blame him, in view of what had happened
to him.

Her thoughts involuntarily turned to the prison
ship. Could it be as bad as Schuyler said? Would
she be allowed visitors? She had no idea.

At eleven o'clock that morning the British trans-
ported her from the jail to the wharf, thence by
boat to the hulk far out in the bay. Her first glimpse
of the dingy old ship was enough to turn her
stomach inside out with fright.

It was big. Frighteningly big and dark and sin-
ister. By the time she was led up the gangplank she
was terrified. The look of Captain Butler and his
crew did little to ease her mind. Butler was big and
ugly, his eyes leering obscenely as they explored
the low-cut front of her gown.

"Well, we do have a pretty missy here now,
don't we?" he said as her two redcoat escorts left
her standing before him, her arms chained together
behind her back. "And what would be y'er name,
lass?"

Clarissa wanted to balk, but could see no advantage in it. "Clarissa," she said. "And what would
be yours?"

The captain roared with delight. "My, but you're the sassy wench, ain't you?" he declared. "Well, you shall soon learn who I am. Indeed you shall!"

"Butler's your name, right? Yes, I should've known."

"It is, but how did you know?"

Clarissa smiled. "By the fact that you're even uglier than this poor excuse for a ship."

Butler shot her a black look, then grinned. "Taming you is goin' to be more fun than I've had since I was running niggers from Africa a few years ago. Always said a man ain't had a woman 'til he's had one of them black ones, but a spunky white one's even better!"

He reached out, holding her shoulders with one hand while the other darted down inside the front of her gown. He had exposed her breasts before she could realize what he was doing, and he brought tears to her eyes by cruelly squeezing the flesh. She wanted to scream, but she held it in, knowing he expected her to cry out.

But Butler was not dismayed by her refusal to scream. He seemed to enjoy it. He had her taken below to the crew's mess, where she was chained to a sturdy table, her breasts, now bearing bruise marks, remaining out of her bodice. During the course of the next five hours every member of the crew paid a visit to the mess, all of them taunting Clarissa about events soon to take place. They fondled her breasts, then vanished after trying to shock her with more nasty remarks.

It was the supper hour, however, when the plight of Clarissa Hunter Beauford grew harsh indeed. For Captain Butler, whose sexual tastes were at times bizarre, decided that his men could have a look at what they would have after he had finished with Clarissa.

He ordered her gown removed. "But carefully, men, just as the lady would remove it herself, for we wouldn't wish to embarrass her." He reasoned correctly that she would be even more humiliated by having the men groping at her stays than if the gown were simply ripped off. In a vain attempt to frustrate them all, Clarissa set her jaw and silently endured the clammy hands that poked under her garments to find an intimate position. The men's pawings only prolonged the time it took to free her stays.

They had to remove the manacles from her wrists and ankles before they could take off the gown and undergarments, but any thought she had about escaping departed when she found herself held in place by a half-dozen strong arms and hands. A hairy-chested guard lifted her three feet off the floor while another removed the last of her garments a few moments later. The captain ordered her stood up on the table. His eyes gleamed as she was placed there and stood naked and shivering before them.

She had shut her eyes against the sight of the leering men, but could feel their eyes upon her as clearly as if they were actually touching her. She wanted to scream, but didn't because it would do her no good.

"Ah, and ain't she got a set of beauties?" the captain said with a laugh.

"She's a spunky one as well," said another of the men. "She ain't even tryin' to hide herself."

All the men lusted after the white beauty of

Clarissa Beauford, but none any more than their captain, whose desire increased with the presence of the others. His eyes were glued to her as he said, "Now, milady, why don't you do a little dance for us to prove you're a woman?"

The others roared at that, then began to clap in unison. But now a shrill whistle sounded from top-side and the captain frowned, then sent one of his men up to find out why the visitor's signal should be sounded at such an odd time. The man returned moments later with the news that Commissary Loring's boat was approaching and that it carried two men besides Loring and his oarsmen.

Butler cursed, then ordered Clarissa taken to his cabin and lashed down to his bunk. Every man in the room volunteered for the task and their laughter filled the room. Butler pointed to two of his men and they picked up her clothes and lifted her off the table to carry her away.

"And don't abuse her, you bloody bastards, or I'll flog you and throw you below with the prisoners!" the captain called out as the men and their captive disappeared from view.

Butler, angry over the interruption of his fun, went topside to greet his visitors.

Joshua Loring had been less than pleased when Lieutenant DeWitt showed up at his office near Wall Street to arrange an early-evening trip to the *Jersey*. Only when the young officer informed him that it was for his brother, Major Magnus DeWitt of Clinton's staff, did Loring agree to the visit at such an unusual hour.

Loring was therefore quite unhappy when, at

the appointed hour, Major DeWitt did not appear to board his boat. Instead, there was a tall man with an eyepatch whom Lieutenant DeWitt introduced as Major J. L. Hunt, also of Sir Henry's staff. Loring had never heard of Hunt and doubted he could be important. But he couldn't take the chance of offending Major DeWitt's brother, so he shrugged off the change and allowed them to board his boat.

Neither Schuyler nor John Langley wore side-arms, but both had several knives and pistols concealed under their red coats. On Schuyler's first visit to the prison ship, Loring hadn't asked if he carried any weapons. But now, before the boat pushed off, Loring noticed a telltale bulge under Schuyler's uniform coat and reached out to touch it. "I trust this is not a weapon, Lieutenant De-Witt," he said. "I cannot allow—"

Thinking fast, Schuyler reached under his coat to withdraw a gold watch, while pushing aside the handle of the pistol Loring had touched. "If this is a weapon, Mr. Loring, then I do carry one. But as you can see, it's only a watch which helps me to be on time for appointments with my brother and Sir Henry."

Loring looked at the watch, then at the now-flat place beneath Schuyler's coat. "I ought to have you both searched," he said, "for security purposes. Have I your word that you carry no weapons?"

Hunter glared at Loring. "Of course. Now, can we get on with it? I've a very important appointment this evening."

Schuyler breathed easier as Loring ordered his oarsmen to push off. But as the boat knifed through the waters toward the *Jersey*, Schuyler was assailed with doubts about what lay ahead. Could they subdue the crew? Find Clarissa? Free the prisoners and get up sail to head the *Jersey* toward the shore? Worst of all, Schuyler worried that Clarissa had already been handed about by members of the *Jersey*'s crew. He would personally cut the throat of any who had touched her!

Captain Butler was none too cordial in his greeting to the visitors, though he said nothing untoward. John Langley engaged him in conversation, firing crisp, probing questions about the hulk, its ability to ride out a storm, the prisoners and the like. Loring escorted Schuyler down to the hold and helped him throw open the hatch.

"You'll forgive me, Lieutenant, but I would prefer remaining up here," Loring said.

"As you wish," Schuyler murmured. He had counted on the commissary not wishing to contend with the stench of the hold, although Loring's presence below wouldn't have changed his plans a great deal. It would have forced him to kill the man himself and that was not to his liking, but he was prepared to do it.

Darkness had not yet fallen above deck, but the hold, lit by only a few lanterns, was dark and uninviting. Schuyler calmed his nerves by thinking about poor Matthew Bell down there and climbed down the ladder to the first level of prisoners, where he was greeted with curses.

Snatching a lantern from the wall, he entered the level and called out softly, "I'm looking for Matthew Bell and mean him no harm. If he's here, he will recognize me and my name. I am Schuyler DeWitt."

Again there was a chorus of curses, which

drowned out his last words. But then the prisoners quieted and Schuyler heard a weak voice some distance down the row of manacled prisoners. "Schuyler?"

"Is that you, Matthew?" Schuyler called out, louder this time, to make certain he was heard.

"It isn't John Langley," returned the voice, "that's for sure."

The prisoners quieted suddenly aware that this redcoat was not unfriendly, and in moments Schuyler was at Matthew's side. He hardly recognized the man. Matthew's clothes were tattered and torn, his flesh black and grimy, his hair long, matted and filthy, his bones showing plainly through his skin.

"Sonofabitch!" Matthew exclaimed. "It really is you. I'd hug you, but I doubt you'd care to share my lice."

Schuyler shook his head. "You're a bloody mess, Matthew. Would you and your friends care to go for a swim to get rid of your lice?"

"Gladly, but how are you going to manage that?"

"John Langley's with me. He's on deck keeping the captain busy. How many able-bodied men are here? There are only two of us, and there are about twenty guards to eliminate. If we can do it, we're going to sail this bucket right up on the Jersey beach across the bay and ground her. But I need your help."

"Just turn us loose," Matthew said, "we'll do the rest. There's a master key for these irons hanging from the ceiling near the top of the ladder. They keep it there because it makes us mad as hell to see it and know how close freedom is."

Knowing he had little time to waste before Lor-

ing or one of the crew decided to find out what he
was up to, Schuyler raced back to the ladder and
found the key. Moments later he had freed Matthew, then passed the key to the other prisoners.

Matthew could hardly stand up at first, but in a
few moments his blood began to circulate more
freely and he followed Schuyler to the ladder,
cautioning the other prisoners to make as little
noise as they could in freeing themselves.

When the entire level of prisoners was free,
Schuyler quickly explained to them what he proposed to do and asked for volunteers to overpower
Loring and the lookouts. "I'll take Loring," Matthew growled. "This is my second run-in with the
snake. The day I was tossed down here I told him
what I thought of him and he had me lashed forty
strokes with the captain's bullwhip. It pleased him,
but didn't by any means please me."

Schuyler passed knives to Matthew and two
others and watched them creep up the ladder, Matthew leading the way. When they reached the top,
he issued quiet instructions to the others about
freeing the other levels of prisoners and keeping
them quiet until the hulk's crew had been dis-
pensed with.

Then he took two men with him and began
climbing the ladder himself.

Up on deck, Loring was smoking a cigar while
watching the sun set over the Jersey shore across
the water. The Commissary of Prisons never knew
what caused the searing pain in his back before an
inky blackness swept over him and he slumped to
the deck.

John Langley kept Captain Butler talking for

some minutes before stopping abruptly to offer him
the cigar he had obtained earlier from Mr. Loring.
As Butler lit the cigar from a lantern on the fore-
deck, Hunter met his eyes and said casually, "The
real reason I'm here is because of the wench we
just sent you."

"The wench?" Butler repeated, his face suddenly
a mask.

Hunter chuckled. "Don't play dumb with me,
Captain, you know the one. She is probably trussed
up in your very own bed as we speak and you can't
wait to get to her. Am I correct?"

Butler glared at him. "It's no affair of yours,
Major. She's my prisoner and only Mr. Loring can
... What do you want? You don't mean to take her
off the ship, do you? Damn! That isn't fair. She's a
bloody prize, she is!"

The captain stood with his back to the deck, and
couldn't see the stealthy figure in rags emerge from
the hold to creep up behind Loring at the rail.
"Tell you what, Captain," Hunter said quickly,
"I'll allow you keep the wench out here as your
guest for a few days so as not to deprive you of
the pleasure you've been anticipating. But you
must promise to treat her well and not ruin her.
You see, my brigadier has an eye for her and decided ... Well, take me down to see her. I must
be certain she isn't already spoiled."

Butler was confused and uncertain. He glared at
John Langley, shook his head and took a couple of
steps toward the wheelhouse, then turned on his
heel, now facing the deck below. Hunter stepped
between him and the deck to block his view.
"Now, Captain," he said, "I'm in a hurry and I'd

rather my friend and Mr. Loring didn't know my business here."

But Butler was suspicious as well as angry at the thought of losing his prize. He grew more unhappy with each step as he led Hunter down the companionway and past the crew's mess to his own quarters. At the door to his cabin, Butler suddenly stopped and faced Hunter, in his hand the knife he had just yanked out of its sheath on his belt.

"I don't believe your story, Major," he said, "and —" He got no farther, grunting as Hunter drove a six-inch blade squarely into his heart. As the captain died, blood spurting through the gaping wound, Hunter took Butler's knife, shoved it into his belt and opened the cabin door. He dragged the big man's body inside and closed the door, then frowned at the sight of his sister, lying naked on the captain's bed, her arms and legs bound, her mouth gagged with a bandanna.

He quickly cut her loose and held her for a few moments, letting her cry away her fear and relief. He quieted her as quickly as he could, then explained that the rescue depended upon eliminating all of the guards and then sailing the old hunk to shore.

"Did Schuyler tell you I was here?" she asked as she began putting back on the clothes the crew had taken from her.

"None other, and he's with me. You'll see him soon enough. Now stay here and don't open the door to anyone unless you're sure it's Schuyler or me."

As John Langley left the captain's cabin, he almost ran into Schuyler, who held a pistol in one hand, a knife in the other. "We've taken the ship," he declared. "Caught the rest of the crew in their quarters. Those who weren't killed are bound and gagged so they won't give us any trouble."

"What about Loring's boat crew?"

"Dead and in the water. Matthew's a bit weak, but otherwise all right. He did in Mr. Loring himself. Where's Clarissa?"

John Langley grinned. "You should have seen her, boy," he declared. "No, I guess you shouldn't have . . . but you can rest easy. The captain hadn't done his dastardly worst to her yet and won't get the chance now. He's gone to meet his maker."

Schuyler's relief was apparent, but he had no chance to express it, for now a stream of tattered prisoners came below and begand scavenging for food and clothing.

While Hunter went topside to find Matthew Bell, Schuyler went to the captain's cabin, where Clarissa was still struggling into her clothes. When she heard his voice outside, she threw open the door and fell into his arms.

Seeing that Clarissa was unharmed brought a smile to Schuyler's face for the first time since Magnus had arrested her. Several minutes later, however, the smile departed as he went topside and learned from John Langley and Matthew that the sails of the old hulk were badly in need of repair before they could be hauled up the rigging. Worse yet, there was no wind, but that would make little difference if the sails could not be repaired. Schuyler had some experience with sails, having done some sailing with one of the DeWitt Shipping schooners one summer, so he went to look at the sheets while John Langley and Matthew asked for volunteers among the prisoners to make repairs.

The sails were not in as bad condition as he had feared. And several of the former prisoners were experienced sailors, so within a short time the sheets were usable. But still there was no wind.

Meanwhile, John Langley had filled Loring's boat with the weakest of the prisoners and several oarsmen. He instructed them to pull for Powie's Hook, where there was a rebel garrison, and to ask for a platoon of riflemen to man the beach when the *Jersey* reached shore.

Hunter asked the remaining prisoners if they wanted to swim ashore or preferred to wait until the sails could be repaired, so that the ship could be beached.

"What if the British get onto us," one of the prisoners asked, "before we can get this decrepit ship underway?"

"If they attack, we'll fight them to the death," Hunter called out.

"Dyin's a devil of a lot better than bein' taken prisoner," another man said. "Lincoln gave up too easy at Charleston."

Several dozen prisoners dove off the side of the ship and headed for the coast in the wake of Loring's boat. More than six hundred prisoners, some able-bodied enough to swim, some not, remained with the *Jersey*, as all of them prayed for a fresh wind.

More than two hours passed, with no wind. Two British gunboats closed to within shouting distance at different times and the watch officer on one asked for "Harry," apparently a guard aboard the *Jersey*.

Schuyler had put on the clothes of one of the crew, and he responded to the British officer. "Harry's a lucky one," he called out. "We got us a new prisoner and she's a fetching wench indeed! He's down there with the rest of 'em—leering and pawing, while I got stuck with the watch."

There were laughs from the sailors aboard the gunboat as they resumed their slow patrol around the bay. The second gunboat to come by, perhaps an hour later, very nearly caused real trouble. Its commander was apparently an old friend of Captain Butler. Schuyler again mentioned having a new wench aboard to account for Butler's absence, but was taken by surprise when the other captain said, "Well, that's good news! I'll be coming aboard, then. The captain promised me a go at the next wench he got."

"Just a minute, sir," Schuyler called out. "I'll go below and check with him. He's with the girl right now."

"You do that, sailor. Tell him McCuddy's here and—Wait a minute! Tell him I'll be back about midnight, all right? Don't bother him now—wait 'til later. Don't want him mad at me."

Schuyler breathed a bit easier, but knew the gunboat's return in less than two hours would pose a real problem if they were not able to get the *Jersey* moving.

The prisoners were becoming restive as another half-hour passed, then an hour, with still no hint of a fresh wind. Then Schuyler almost jumped for joy when a few rain drops touched his face. And a breeze!

He didn't even have to order the men to raise the sails. They had been standing by the sheets for hours. Men had also been posted at the anchor chain. In less than five minutes, the sails were billowing with wind, the anchor was up and the ship was moving slowly toward the Jersey coast. Schuyler was at the helm, steering the old hulk clear of the rocks which jutted out into the bay while edging her farther and farther in toward shore.

John Langley fetched Clarissa Beauford topside as the storm grew in intensity and the ship began rolling in high waves. Despite the driving rain and their imminent swim in the raging waters of the bay, the prisoners roared their approval as Schuyler steered the ship toward a sandy beach area. "Down the sails!" he called out. "Cut them away if you need to, but get them down. We're going in." He lashed the wheel to hold the ship's course, then hung onto the railing as he awaited impact.

The sails went down quickly, but the ship's momentum and the waves driven ahead of the rain carried it far in toward shore. It beached with a swiftness that was frightening to them all. For long moments it appeared she would flop over on her side, and her occupants clung to whatever was nearest to keep from being swept overboard.

Then, as she righted herself, her main mast toppled over and only her guy ropes kept it from touching the water. "Into the surf!" Schuyler roared as the waves began to batter the beached ship.

Schuyler, John Langley, Matthew and some of the sturdier former prisoners helped the weaker of the prisoners get over the side and into the water. Clarissa refused to go over without Schuyler and so they went together, with Hunter and Bell beside them.

Barely a hundred and fifty yards lay between the wallowing ship and the land, but the storm made the waves so high and frequent that even the sturdiest of prisoners had difficulty swimming in. To make matters worse, within a few minutes of their departure, Schuyler glanced back toward the ship to see the shadowy forms of several British gunboats arriving on the scene.

"Run for it, men," he called out. "We've got company!" He seized Clarissa's arm and all but dragged her through the waist-high water as the gunboats opened fire with small cannon and muskets. Fortunately, the boats could not chance going in closer to land than they were and had to be careful not to be thrown into the side of the beached *Jersey*, so their shots were something less than accurate. But Schuyler and Clarissa passed a number of bloody corpses in the water as they continued their dash for shore.

They were still fifty yards away when a miracle occurred—or so it seemed. Out of the mist-shrouded shoreline appeared a line of soldiers! Schuyler exulted as he saw they held long rifles and were firing one volley after another at the gunboats. That they were accurate was proven by the noticeable slowing of firing from the gunboats. The Loring longboat had reached Powie's Hook and brought Light-Horse Harry Lee and a squad of his crack riflemen to the beach, and it was they who saved the day.

Schuyler and Clarissa reached shore just as John Langley was being embraced warmly by Lee, who was saying, "You've accomplished the impossible. We hadn't thought anyone could successfully attack a British prison ship."

"It wasn't only me, Harry," Hunter said. "If it weren't for Schuyler DeWitt, we'd never have done it. He was—" And that was when a stray shot from one of the gunboats struck Hunter in his right side, knocking the breath out of him. He lost consciousness in seconds and sank to the beach.

Clarissa gasped at the sight of her brother's blood, then followed helplessly as Lee and Schuyler carried him to safety away from the beach. He was bandaged by Lee's company doctor, after the man had removed the musket ball and cleaned the shallow wound.

"He'll need some time to recuperate," the doctor told them. But he assured Clarissa that John Langley would be as good as new within a month.

At Lee's headquarters, Schuyler and Clarissa spent the night together in a small cottage lent them by Lee—after she assured Schuyler that John Langley, resting peacefully, would not disapprove.

Alone together, they talked for a long time, Clarissa needing to speak of her ordeal, Schuyler suffering as he listened. Afterward he embraced her and kissed her with a passion far exceeding what he had felt for Joanna. "No more spying for you, darling," he said. "I won't have it."

Clarissa's reaction surprised him. She sat up straight on the bed and glared down at him. "And what gives you the right to have it or not have it? If I wish to spy, then I will!"

Schuyler shushed her with two fingers against her lips. "I wish you to stop because I love you, Clarissa," he said softly. "I cannot make you stop, I suppose. But I ask you with all my heart to do so, for I can't take the pain I experienced at knowing you were in jeopardy."

She didn't give him any answer until the next morning, but what transpired between them that night left little doubt how she felt.

As for Schuyler, he forgot completely about the plans he and John Langley had made to seize Benedict Arnold and spirit him back to Washington—until Hunter reminded him when they visited him in the camp hospital the next day.

"We blew it!" Hunter said immediately. "I'm in no shape to go back for Arnold. General George'll fire me and I won't blame him."

"Don't worry about it," Schuyler said. "I'll take Arnold alone if I have to."

"You can't, Schuyler," Clarissa protested. "You'll be hurt!"

Hunter rolled his eyes at his sister's display. "He can take care of himself, Clarissa. And anyway, Matthew will go in to help him. Between them, they can do it."

Clarissa continued to protest right up until the moment for Schuyler's departure for New York. But in the end she gave in after he promised to spend weekends with her in Philadelphia, where she would be safe from the Tories.

Clinton was furious over the daring raid that had run the *Jersey* aground, where she subsequently broke up and sank. He threatened to have Mr. Loring dismissed until he learned that Loring was missing and presumed killed by the raiders.

Schuyler had thought long and hard about his brother's probable reaction to the affair. He prayed Magnus would not think him capable of participating in such a reckless mission, even to save his ladylove. He need not have worried, however.

Magnus informed him of the loss of the *Jersey* in so solemn a manner that Schuyler could have laughed. Instead, he played the role that was expected of him.

"Are you trying to tell me . . . good Lord! Clarissa Beauford wasn't on that ship? Tell me she wasn't!" He had risen from his chair as he spoke and now stood towering over his brother, whose eyes were focused on his desk top.

"I'm sorry to say that she was, Schuyler. I can't tell you—"

"How sorry you are? Save your hypocrisy for someone else, Magnus. You put Clarissa on that accursed ship in the first place, knowing it was a hellhole and no place for a lady. Or a man, for that matter!"

"She was a spy, Schuyler. I had no choice. I'm sorry about having to put her there, but quite probably she was saved by her fellow spies and is now with them." Magnus rose from his chair and faced his brother. "How can you be so foolish? The lady was involved with rebel spies up to her pretty neck. You're fortunate that I'm in charge of intelligence and not someone else, or you might now be under suspicion for engineering the *Jersey* fiasco!"

"Perhaps I ought to be, Major," Schuyer said stiffly. "I was more than a little angry with you for placing Clarissa in such jeopardy."

Magnus shook his head. "No," he said, "you're foolish, but freeing the prisoners and running the *Jersey* aground was not an amateur undertaking. I've a feeling my old friend John Langley Hunter was involved somehow. It's the kind of thing he might well plan."

"It sounds as if you rather admire the man," Schuyler said. "Perhaps *you* are a rebel spy."

"Indeed! No, Schuyler, I'm most certainly the loyalist I have always been. As for Hunter, yes, he's an exceptionally capable man. I wish he were on our side rather than Washington's, for we could well use his talents. One can hate an enemy, yet also respect him."

Schuyler met Matthew Bell that night and had to relay some terrible news he had learned just before leaving Clinton's headquarters: Benedict Arnold had been given command of a small force of British soldeirs and assigned to Virginia. Arnold and his brigades had apparently been boarding ships in the harbor while Schuyler and Hunter had been taking the *Jersey*. In any case, Arnold was beyond their reach now.

Matthew did not take the news well, in spite of Schuyler's attempt to calm him. Just before Matthew left New York, he told Schuyler he would get Arnold if he had to chase him all the way to Virginia to do it.

11

IF CLINTON was furious over the loss of the prison
ship *Jersey* and all its prisoners, Washington,
Matthew Bell and John Langley Hunter were
equally enraged by Benedict Arnold's escape to
Virginia. Washington sent Bell down to Virginia
to see what could be done to trap the traitor, but
there seemed little hope as the winter of 1780-'81
began.

In New York, Clinton grew more morose by the
day over his defeats in 1780—Andre's capture and
subsequent hanging, the loss of West Point and
the liberation of eight hundred prisoners from the
Jersey.

Schuyler remained on his brother's staff, though
there was little news to pass along to Washington
in the early months of 1781, and he missed Clarissa

terribly now that she had gone home to Virginia. The last two facts caused him to seriously consider retiring from his military post and his work as a rebel spy.

John Langley Hunter was in Wethersfield, Connecticut, with Matthew Bell's sister, Deborah, who had traveled to New Jersey to nurse him back to health. As soon as he had been well enough to ride in a stage, she had insisted on bringing him back to Wethersfield to recuperate.

Matthew, finding Arnold holed up in Portsmouth, Virginia, for the winter, returned to South Carolina where he aided General Greene in battles against Cornwallis's determined legions at Guilford Courthouse in March of '81 and in another siege two months later.

In early June, Matthew was recalled by Washington, who was plotting a move against New York. Admiral deGrasse's French fleet had at last escaped the English blockade of Brest, France, and arrived in the West Indies, where de Grasse was recruiting mercenaries and had committed himself to aiding Washington's forces against the British in America.

Washington sent Matthew to Connecticut to bring Hunter back, emphasizing how important espionage would be in the coming campaign against New York. As Matthew put it to John Langley, "Washington feels we're but a single major victory away from breaking German George's resolve to pursue this fight, and New York could well be it. If we can drive Clinton out of the New York islands, we can end the whole war."

Deborah Bell sat and listened to the two men, but said nothing until John Langley turned to her and asked her opinion on whether or not he should go back to Washington's service.

"I can't stop you," she said firmly, "but I believe you've done your bit and no one could fault you for not going back."

"Agreed, Deb," Hunter said. "But the damn war's more important than me or any other single individual. And its not over yet, though as Matthew says, maybe it's getting close."

"Can't someone else fight it?"

Hunter shrugged and lit his pipe as he thought things out. He was happier with Deborah than he had ever been. Though they hadn't formalized their marriage with a ceremony, he knew it was only a matter of time before they got around to it.

They ate supper in silence. Then John Langley stood and took the attractive woman in his arms and gave her a warm kiss. "You know I don't want to leave you, don't you, Deborah?"

She sighed and let him kiss her again. "I know," she said. "And I also know that you *will* leave because you feel it's your duty. Well, maybe it is, but I certainly don't have to like it."

"Will you love me less if I go?"

"Not unless you get yourself killed, John Langley."

And that was when Matthew spoke up, a grin on his face. "I'll drink to that!"

The next day John Langley and Matthew headed south.

Clarissa Beauford had retired from the espionage game, her ordeal having left her with an urgent desire to see the war ended and the man she loved at her side. As she told her friend Governor

Jefferson one day in November of 1780, "We've been at odds with the King for more than four years and still he sends ships, soldiers and cannon. Even now when he's at war with France and Spain as well as America. The cost in lives and money must be enormous to England, yet still the war goes on. Is he mad?"

Jefferson nodded slowly. "He may well be just that, Mrs. Beauford, though he is also ill-advised by Germaine and North."

They sat in the sunny drawing room of Clarissa's small mansion, originally built by her husband's family. Jefferson was silent for a time, his eyes wandering aimlessly around the beautiful countryside which could be seen through the window.

"I fear for Virginia, Clarissa," he said at last. "We've been fortunate in being spared the brunt of the war. We've been asked to do no more than produce money crops to buy powder and weapons for Washington's army. Only once have we been sacked by the British."

"You believe things are changing, Governor? That the English will send troops here to pillage and burn? But why? There are no important military objectives here."

"There is one, Clarissa—our money crops, which form the backbone of the revolt. Cornwallis has long counselled his commander to weaken America by hurting us in Virginia. He's been right, but fortunately his superiors haven't seen it. Or have chosen not to believe it. And now Cornwallis holds Georgia and has strong footholds in the Carolinas. I have no doubt that next he'll move against Virginia—and very soon."

"Let's hope you're wrong, Governor," Clarissa had said as they parted.

That night Clarissa wrote a long and stirring letter to Schuyler, telling him of Governor Jefferson's prophecy and begging him to leave the North. "Come to me, my darling, to help me safeguard my farm so that we may have it as a part of our future."

There was now little question in her mind that her future lay with Schuyler, whether in the North or in the South. As for Schuyler, he had sworn his love during a number of delight-filled weekends in Philadelphia with her. Then he had sent her home to Virginia when it appeared that she might be with child. When it turned out that she was not, she had been disappointed, though Schuyler swore he would marry her anyway—"As soon as I've helped bring this damned war to a close."

Would it ever come to a close? It seemed to Clarissa that it would not. Then, a month later, she was filled with trepidation when she heard that Cornwallis was headed for Virginia.

In New York, Magnus DeWitt was shaken by a piece of intelligence from an agent close to Washington's headquarters: It seemed that his brother was working for the rebels. Schuyler, working for the rebels . . . Magnus could hardly believe it. It was impossible—yet the source was unimpeachable.

Schuyler—a spy!

Although it was only a little past noon, Magnus was soon sitting at a table in a tavern near the docks, with a bottle of whiskey before him. He did not stop drinking until the bottle was gone. Then he staggered to his quarters to seek solace with Joanna.

On the same day Magnus learned the truth about him, Schuyler received another letter from Clarissa. She was lonely, lonely and unhappy, although she understood that he could not leave until the job was done. But she also wrote of Arnold's devastation of Richmond in January, of his occupation of Portsmouth, of the failure of the French fleet to defeat a British armada off the Chesapeake capes in March. She sounded fearful, and well she might.

With things as they were, Schuyler knew that Clarissa's farm could not long be safe from attack. And that meant that she was no longer safe.

While his brother was drinking himself into a stupor in a New York tavern, Schuyler was framing a careful message to Washington.

"I have apparently fallen from trust here, for I have been able to learn little of value since early in the winter. Because of my concern for the safety of the woman I love in Virginia, I should like to retire from service in order to protect her. I await your reply."

Less than a week later, Schuyler received a message to meet Matthew Bell at Fish Kill. When he arrived, he shook Matthew's hand warmly, then asked where John Langley Hunter was.

"The general's sent him on a special mission to Virginia," Bell said, "but I can't tell you the details right now. I hear you're worried about Clarissa."

"I am. With the British sacking Virginia, she just isn't safe, so I've asked Washington for his permission to retire. Not that I really need it," he added.

Matthew ignored the last. "You also told the general you were having trouble obtaining important intelligence, Schuyler. Tell me about that."

Schuyler sighed. "Well, Magnus has never been much of a talker, but he's more close-mouthed right now than I've ever known him to be. So I get nothing from him. And Clinton's apparently warned his staff people that he'll throw them aboard a prison ship if they don't seal their lips about his plans."

"I can't help the last, Schuyler," Bell said, "but I can shed some light on the first. Fact is, your brother has learned of your liaison with us, so it's not surprising he isn't saying much."

Schuyler looked at him disbelievingly. "My brother *what*? He knows about me? He couldn't!"

"Our fault, Schuyler, and the general sends his apologies. Seems one of his personal agents turned double—for a large supply of British cash, we're certain. He informed Magnus, though he couldn't have said much about your activities because he couldn't have known of them. Still, the truth is that Magnus knows."

"That settles it, Matthew. Now I have no choice but to leave."

But Matthew was already shaking his head. "The general wants you to stay where you are, Schuyler. He needs you there. And never more than now, no matter what you believe."

"How can I stay? I'll wind up dangling from a hangman's noose like Scott Laidlow and Andre!"

"No, you won't. Your brother has known about you for seven days. If he were going to do anything about you, he'd have done it right away."

"But—"

"*Listen* to me now. The general has considered your situation carefully and is sure you'll be safe if you stay. He believes your brother will try to use you to pass along misinformation to us. It's what any good intelligence chief would do, don't you see? What we have to do is let him use you— at the same time that you're using him."

"He's too smart for that. He'll figure it out and then—"

"Not if we play it smart. Look, Schuyler, the general's in a tight spot now. He's managed to keep up an army and prevent the redcoats from snuffing out the rebellion for five years now, but he has to do something soon if we're to keep our people behind us."

"A major victory?"

"Exactly. And at this very minute, he's working out the details. You'll play an important part in helping him—if you'll risk it."

"What about Clarissa?"

"She's as important to John Langley as she is to you, Schuyler. Don't worry about her. We'll all see to it that she comes to no harm."

Schuyler studied Matthew. If anyone has good reason to quit the war, Matthew had. Yet here he was, still hard at work and risking his life each day. "Very well, Matthew. What do you wish from me?"

"For the moment, nothing more than remaining in place. Listen to what your brother has to say to you. And pay attention to how he says it, for that may be as important as what he says. Chances are you'll hear nothing that they don't wish you to hear, but even that may help us, since we know they're on to you."

"Just what is Washington planning?"

Matthew grinned. "I can't tell you that right now. Ever since Arnold defected, the general has kept his own counsel. Tells nobody a thing until he's got to. But I can tell you that he's sent Wayne to Virginia with reinforcements for Lafayette."

"Will he be attacking New York? Sir Henry is said to believe that Washington must take New York if he's to keep the rebellion alive."

"Said by whom, Schuyler? By Magnus or by someone else? It makes a big difference who's said it."

"I've heard the general say it himself on several occasions, Matthew."

"If Washington decides to take him on in New York, let's hope we can convince Clinton of the opposite. The general and I have a feeling you can be of great help in bringing it off."

"I'll try my best, Matthew."

"That's all we ask. Good luck."

During the ensuing weeks Schuyler watched his brother carefully, but saw no indication that Magnus distrusted him or knew him to be a spy. Magnus behaved so very normally that Schuyler wondered if Washington's information could be wrong.

One day in early June, Magnus let drop an interesting, albeit disturbing, piece of intelligence. A message from Washington to Lafayette in Virginia had been intercepted. In it, Washington informed the young Frenchman that he meant to attack New York with the aid of Rochambeau's French garrison at Newport.

"That's deradful news," Schuyler said solemnly, "though it is an intelligence coup for you. Do you think the rebels can win if they attack our stronghold here?"

Magnus frowned. "Do you?" he asked carefully.

"I don't see how," Schuyler said, managing to keep his poise.

"Agreed. It's unlikely Washington has enough soldiers to take New York, even with the French from Newport. We can't be certain, of course, without knowing the real strength of the forces involved."

For the remainder of the day Schuyler wondered whether what Magnus had told him about Washington's message being intercepted was the truth or was a lie designed to deceive the rebels. By any line of reasoning he used, however, it seemed that it must be the truth, since Washington would surely know if he had written to Lafayette of such plans. And if true, Magnus's action seemed even more puzzling—at least if Magnus in fact knew of Schuyler's affiliation with the rebels.

Schuyler sent a message to Washington relating the information and met with Matthew Bell once more in early July. Bell confirmed that the information Magnus had passed along to Schuyler had been accurate.

"If so, my brother can't possibly know about me," Schuyler said. "Your information must be wrong."

Matthew shook his head. "Our information isn't

wrong, Schuyler, although I admit it looks that way to you and with good reason."

"Then why did Magnus volunteer such an important piece of news?"

"The general and I discussed that very point for a good long time, Schuyler. Either Magnus figured we would know the message had been intercepted anyway, and so it wouldn't matter if he gave it to you, or else he wanted to discourage an attack on New York. The second makes some sense only if Magnus believes Clinton can be beaten in New York—or figures Clinton is in no shape to handle an attack."

"Magnus says he doesn't believe the British can be routed from New York and I think he was telling the truth. I'm not sure I don't agree with him, based on what I know." Schuyler paused, then said, "As for Clinton being in shape to handle an attack—I don't know for sure, but Magnus has often said Sir Henry has become more and more uncertain of himself since being appointed commander in chief."

"We think perhaps that's exactly what's motivating Magnus's caution—but again, we can't be sure. There's a third potential, one we don't like at all. It's the chance that Magnus knows we've found out you've been betrayed to him. If so, passing along a legitimate piece of intelligence such as Washington's letter becomes a master stroke on his part."

Schuyler was dizzied by the alternatives and said so. "Don't blame you," Matthew said with a laugh. "So was I when Washington explained it to me. Anyway, we've decided your brother isn't a genius, so we're going ahead and assuming he was probably just trying to discourage an attack on New York."

"Will the attack be on New York?"

"Washington would like it to be, but I think he's decided he doesn't really need to take on Clinton's main force to get what he needs, so he'll probably go after Cornwallis in Virginia."

"Can Washington beat Cornwallis?"

"He can now. We've just received word that de Grasse's French armada is on its way to the Chesapeake. It's big enough to blockade the coast and keep Cornwallis from getting his usual help from the British navy. So all we have to do is keep Clinton from reinforcing Cornwallis by convincing him we're going to attack him in the North."

"And how are we to convince him of that?"

"You'll do it, Schuyler, all by yourself. At the proper moment, you'll provide Magnus with irrefutable proof that Washington will not attack Virginia—and you'll do it by delivering him Washington's plans to attack Cornwallis in Virginia."

Schuyler had to admit that Washington was playing a heady game with Magnus. He hoped his brother would not figure it out in time to thwart the rebels.

Thus it was that early in August, after Cornwallis had been ordered by Clinton to dig in for wintering at Yorktown after a vigorous campaign in Virginia, Schuyler delivered a detailed set of plans to his brother which, ostensibly, had come to Schuyler from a rebel deserter. The plans indicated that Washington would strike at Cornwallis in Virginia, attempting to take the British general and his army out of the war in a single bold stroke.

Whether Magnus DeWitt would believe it was another matter.

12

MAGNUS DEWITT's enthusiasm in executing his
duties dwindled rapidly after he learned of
his brother's perfidy in serving the rebel
forces. After his head cleared following his afternoon of drinking, he agonized over Schuyler's
activities, knowing he must either put an end to
them, or somehow control them.

Since ending Schuyler's spying activities would
no doubt place him on a hangman's scaffolding,
it was not surprising that Magnus chose the second
alternative. He let no one on Sir Henry's staff know
that Schuyler was a spy, but he tried to keep all
vital information away from his brother. The most
difficult part of his task was maintaining the pretense that nothing had changed, when of course

everything had. He watched Schuyler carefully, yet tried to conceal his wariness.

Joanna was his only saving grace during this period, proving herself every bit as warm and comforting as a woman could be. Although he rarely confided in her, Magnus found he had to speak of Schuyler to someone and so chose her as his confidante. She took the news surprisingly well and said the words he wanted to hear, though he was not at all sure she believed them. She did not rail against Schuyler; she insisted, if none too vigorously, that Schuyler had no doubt been deceived.

Magnus wanted to believe that and did, more or less, in spite of the indications that Schuyler was in fact playing a cool, deadly game. For the first time, Magnus wondered if his brother had truly played a part in the beaching of the prison ship *Jersey* and the liberation of its prisoners. He did not want to learn the truth until the war's end, and so he contemplated no further investigation of the affair.

Fortunately, Magnus had little time to worry about the *Jersey* incident, with the rebels apparently readying a siege against New York and Clinton spending more and more time each day in consultation with his phantom commanding officer, General Perfection. Clinton had grown increasingly paranoid since Washington's letter to Lafayette had been intercepted.

Because of Washington's known expertise in trickery, Magnus had studied the letter especially carefully before reaching the conclusion that the letter was a genuine statement of Washington's intentions. Clinton had held a staff meeting after Magnus presented his conclusions about the letter, and the commander had proceeded to prove conclusively that his sense of reality was slipping badly. He suggested that Washington was placing them in "an untenable position" by considering the attack, and he immediately sent couriers to London, demanding reinforcements in both soldiers and ships, and ordered Cornwallis to send back three thousand of his best southern troops.

Two things prompted Magnus to pass along to Schuyler the news about Washington's letter. First, he hoped Washington might have second thoughts about attacking New York if he knew the British were aware of his intentions. He knew it was a slim hope, for Washington would not cancel a well-thought-out attack merely because his enemy could see it coming.

The second reason was that he wanted to prevent the rebels from realizing that he knew Schuyler was serving their interests. By giving them a legitimate piece of intelligence now, he could perhaps plant a fake piece later which would serve the British cause. If the rebels already knew he had discovered Schuyler's treachery, giving his brother the news of Washington's letter would thoroughly confuse them—a thought that pleased Magnus greatly, though he doubted the rebels could know that he had uncovered Schuyler.

Sir Henry breathed a little easier when Hessian reinforcements arrived from Europe in mid-August. They were immediately deployed to meet the threat of Washington's attack, a threat which seemed to grow in intensity with each passing

week. Magnus's spies had observed that the rebels
had added units from Rochambeau's French garrison at Newport, collected boats on the Jersey
shores near New York Bay and established supply
depots at Elizabeth and New Brunswick. There
could be little doubt as to the meaning of the
actions. But Magnus was uneasy about what was
going on. As the rebels continued their ostentatious
preparations for an assault on New York, Magnus
wondered if it was all a ploy to convince Clinton
that Washington would indeed attack New York.

Just when Magnus was about to confront his
commander with his suspicions, however, Schuyler turned up with a perplexing document: Washington's plans to crush the British in the South,
beginning with Yorktown! And it was unquestion-
ably in Washington's handwriting.

Magnus wanted to believe the documents. Yet
he could not, simply because it had been Schuyler
who delivered them, claiming they came in by a
deserter who had left immediately in order to
escape being identified. Schuyler—a rebel spy.
Schuyler, whose British affiliation would be invaluable in passing along fictional plans to Clinton.
Like the ones in front of Magnus at present.

Magnus studied the documents for several days,
trying to find something that would establish their
authenticity without regard to the identity of their
deliverer. But he was stymied by the suggestion
that the French would have forty battleships ready
to blockade Yorktown and cut off any British escape by the rivers nearby. All of Magnus's information indicated that de Grasse and de Barras
combined could have only about thirty, so the

number stated might well have been designed to frighten the intended recipient of the documents. Him—Magnus DeWitt.

Magnus wanted to show the plans to Sir Henry and let him make the decision as to whether or not they were genuine, but he knew that the general was in a severely agitated state and could not be counted on to make the best decision. He wondered if his own judgment was any better at present, with his brother so deeply involved.

Magnus stewed over the documents for more than a week, then received a piece of news which pleased and relieved him greatly. Admiral Hood had arrived from the West Indies, bringing fourteen ships-of-the-line to New York to reinforce Admiral Graves, and he informed Sir Henry he had paid a visit to the Chesapeake in an effort to find de Grasse's French armada, which had left the Indies shortly before he arrived there. The Chesapeake, Hood said, was empty. Magnus was not completely convinced yet that the rebels meant to attack New York, but at least he now had no other evidence to the contrary.

After consultation with Hood and Graves, Clinton dispatched them to Newport to try to prevent de Barras from sailing to join de Grasse's fleet. He also sent his speediest frigate to the Indies to seek further naval reinforcements.

On the second of September, as Magnus was finishing up a report to Clinton on the bogus rebel plans to attack Yorktown, a Tory irregular arrived from Delaware with devastating news. He had seen a "millyun" Continental and French troops marching toward Head of Elk at the north end of the Chesapeake—and General Washington rode at the head of the rebels!

After assuring himself that the man spoke the truth, Magnus raced for Clinton's office like a man possessed. He had somehow been tricked again.

Clinton went to pieces at the news, but managed to compose himself enough to send word to Graves to head for the Chesapeake and drive off the French.

Schuyler picked up the news almost as quickly as Clinton's courier rushed out of the general's office. Schuyler got off a message to Matthew Bell, who was now across the river in Perth Amboy. Matthew sent a horseman galloping toward the Chesapeake, and two days later the man reached the bay in time to warn de Grasse. A day later, the French engaged Graves in sea battle and narrowly defeated him, driving the British back to New York and leaving Washington's forces free to besiege Yorktown without British interference.

Meanwhile, Magnus decided he had to confront his brother with the truth. He took Schuyler to dinner in a quiet restaurant some distance from Clinton's headquarters on the twelfth of September. They had half-downed their claret when Magnus fixed steely eyes on his brother and lifted his glass.

"I toast your new-found allegiance," Magnus said.

Schuyler frowned. "I don't understand, Magnus. What allegiance?"

"Why, to Washington and his rebel rabble, of course," Magnus said. "Don't try to pretend that you don't know I'm well aware of your rebel connections."

Schuyler sighed, lifted his own glass and drained it with a single swallow.

Magnus, glass still in hand, regarded his brother with cold eyes and an even colder heart. "So you weren't joking when you told me Mrs. Beauford was no more a spy than you. Both of you were working for the rebels all the time."

Schuyler shrugged, uneasily wondering what Magnus intended to do. Both were in uniform, both wore sidearms.

"You knew Washington was planning to attack Cornwallis in Virginia, didn't you, Schuyler?"

"I brought you his plans. Don't you remember?"

Magnus glared at Schuyler. "You also knew I was onto you, did you not?"

Schuyler smiled thinly. "Of course. Washington's intelligence people learned of it and informed me. Under the circumstances, telling you of Washington's real plans was a rather good ruse, I thought."

Magnus grit his teeth and grew silent. Finally he looked up and gave a single negative shake of his head. "And where will you go now that I've chosen to end our charade?"

Schuyler met his brother's level stare. "I'd thought you'd make an example of me, brother—like Scott Laidlow."

Magnus's expression softened somewhat. "Laidlow's death contained the seeds of your own discontent, didn't it, Schuyler?"

"Most assuredly. Yet I disagreed with some of the King's treatment of the colonies even before that—and said so. It was the way the King's forces have dealt with the people here which convinced me I was wearing the wrong uniform."

"In the end it will do you no good, Schuyler,

for Washington, as capable as he is, cannot beat
the finest fighting men in the world."

"He doesn't need to, Magnus. All he must do is
inspire his people—Americans who wish to have a
voice in their own fate—to continue to resist. And
he's done that rather admirably up to now. Clinton
is wrong to worry about Washington attacking
New York. The rebels will reclaim these islands
without firing a shot!"

The two brothers lapsed into a thoughtful and
uneasy silence as their dinner was served. After
dinner, Magnus produced a piece of writing paper
and handed it to Schuyler.

"My resignation?" Schuyler asked, glancing at it.
"So you're telling me to get out of town—is that it,
brother? Well, I suppose that's fair enough."

"It's a damn sight better than getting hanged,"
Magnus grunted.

"Or watching your only brother hanged," Schuyler countered.

"Agreed. You may tell Washington that I admire
his efforts on the rebels' behalf, even though I
abhor his purposes."

"I don't expect to see him, Magnus. But I'll
certainly deliver your message if I do."

"Where will you go, Schuyler?" Magnus asked,
his manner less brusque. "Home? Our mother
would be glad to see you again. It's been a long
time since you were at DeWitt Manor."

"One day I'll go home again, Magnus, but not
now. Now I'll go to visit Clarissa."

"Ah, yes, the good Madame Beauford. So she
survived the beaching of the *Jersey*. I hadn't the
slightest doubt."

"She survived, no thanks to you."

"And you, of course, had nothing to do with the freeing of the prisoners—or with Mr. Loring's death?"

"Do you wish to know? I'll gladly tell you all the details, including what would have happened to Clarissa had certain people not taken certain actions."

Magnus smiled weakly. "No, Schuyler, I don't wish to know. Now do be on your way, before I regain my senses and remember I'm being disloyal to my King by having mercy on my family."

Schuyler quickly scribbled his signature on the resignation and tossed it over to Magnus. "My good wishes to you, brother," he said. "Please convey the same to Joanna."

"Of course."

"She's well?"

"And remains willing, Schuyler. She has the key to lift my spirits. I've decided I might well deprive her of her freedom permanently by marrying her."

"Joanna always was determined to obtain the DeWitt name, one way or another. If she pleases you and makes you happy, I'm sure you could do worse. Good luck."

The two men rose and Schuyler felt a lump in his throat as he realized he might well be facing his brother for the very last time. When Magnus held out his hand, Schuyler took it and then moved closer to fold his arms around his brother. It was the first time in many years that the two men had embraced.

"Cheers," Magnus said softly, his voice cracking.

"Cheers," Schuyler echoed in a hoarse whisper. He felt his brother's eyes on him all the way out the door. And wished he didn't have to go.

13

SCHUYLER HAD CROSSED the Delaware into Pennsylvania before he was able to shake the sorrow he experienced during his final moments with Magnus.

While he had no regrets at having worked on behalf of the rebels, he was suddenly afflicted with tremendous guilt over his participation in helping to trick his brother. Because of the difference in their age, he and Magnus had never been precisely close, but there had always been a mutual love and respect. And Magnus had always made great efforts to be a good and loyal brother. How great a disappointment must he have been to Magnus! Schuyler wondered if he would ever be able to forget the hurt in his brother's eyes during their final conversation.

As he rode south toward Virginia, his thoughts at last turned to Clarissa and a smile appeared on his face at the thought of her surprise when he showed up at her door. She had no idea he was coming home.

Home? Yes, wherever she was would be his home from now on. In his mind he could see the neat white house to which she had taken him when first they met. She would be standing in the doorway, a happy smile on her face as he approached.

His thoughts were interrupted by the appearance of a dozen armed men on horseback, their rifles pointed at him. They appeared to be militiamen, but Schuyler couldn't be certain, so he halted his horse and awaited their advance.

The leader covered him with a pistol. "Who are you, man, and what are you doing here?" he demanded.

"I mean you no harm," Schuyler said, "and could well ask the same of you." Schuyler knew that the danger of the situation lay in the possibility that these men could be Tory irregulars rather than militiamen. If they were and he identified himself as a Patriot, he could well find himself in deep trouble. Just such a group as this had apparently confused poor John Andre into giving himself away and had eventually cost him his life.

"I'll ask the questions, mister, and you'll be answering," the barrel-chested leader said.

"You'll get no answers until you inform me on whose authority you act in accosting me," Schuyler said evenly.

The man studied Schuyler for a moment, then said, "We're Delaware militiamen. Can't you see that by our uniforms?"

Schuyler grinned at the idea that the clothes they wore were uniforms, for they looked like anything but. "I'm from New York and therefore wouldn't know your uniform," he said. "You act then for the Continental Congress?"

"None other," the leader said. "And now you'll tell me you're a Patriot, am I right? What if I told you we were Tories? Would you then become a Tory? Seize him, men, and we'll search him to find out what colors he carries."

Before the men could carry out their leader's order, Schuyler's pistol was in his hand, pointed at the man's chest. In his saddlebags was his redcoat uniform, and that would be difficult to explain. "You're dead if your men approach me," Schuyler said. "I can produce credentials signed by General Washington to prove who I am, but I won't until I'm sure who you are."

"Shall we kill him?" one of the other men called out from behind Schuyler.

The leader shook his head. "I'm afraid we're at an impasse. We're on our way to Yorktown to join Washington, but we have no papers to prove our identities."

"If what you say is true, you'll know the name Hunter, for he acts for Washington in dealing with militiamen."

"I don't—"

"Say, I know that name," said one of the others. "He's a Virginian, name of John Langley Hunter. He surely does work for Washington."

"As do I," Schuyler said, and reached into his pocket for a paper which introduced him as a "friend of the Revolution" without naming him.

It bore Washington's signature. He handed the paper to the leader.

After looking at the paper, the leader lowered his pistol and put it away, then introduced himself and his men.

Schuyler asked if they had any news of the goings-on in Virginia.

"Only that the French fleet was engaged in battle by the Britishers and came out victorious after a battle lasting four days," said the leader. "It's said the British sailed north again with their banners between their legs!" The men all laughed at their leader's remark and so did Schuyler, pleased that his warning of the British fleet's intentions had reached de Grasse in time.

Schuyler rode with the militiamen until they reached Chesapeake Bay, where they turned west toward Yorktown while he continued south.

When he reached the mouth of the Chesapeake, Schuyler saw a sight that brought goose bumps to his flesh. A huge armada of French ships was rolling lazily at anchor, with boats scurrying to and from the shores. Schuyler counted thirty-one ships-of-the-line and none seemed damaged. It appeared that what the Delaware militiamen had heard was correct—de Grasse had defeated Graves and Hood!

Judging by the numbers he saw before him, the British would have been outnumbered and severely outgunned by the French, hard-pressed to defeat them even if the competent Admiral Hood had commanded. But with Graves in command, there was little question in Schuyler's mind that the battle would have been decided the moment it was apparent that the French had the weight of numbers, for Graves was known to have all the daring of a mouse.

Schuyler was about to ride on when his attention was caught by a longboat which now pushed off from the largest of the French warships, which had to be de Grasse's flagship. In the prow of the boat stood a tall soldier whose probable identity made Schuyler's heart beat a little faster. He had never met General George Washington personally, but knew the man's description from Magnus and other Clinton staff people. Raising his spyglass to his eyes, Schuyler focused on the boat and its occupants and quickly confirmed his guess. It was indeed Washington. And sitting near the general was John Langley Hunter. It took Schuyler but a moment to decide to meet the boat, for John Langley would no doubt have news of his sister. And perhaps he would introduce the man Schuyler had been serving for more than two years.

Before Schuyler could reach the landing, however, he was surrounded by a squad of Continentals, who inquired none too affably where he was going. Schuyler offered no resistance, merely trying to explain his intention to see John Langley Hunter as the boat arrived.

Hunter quickly spotted him, surprise showing on his face. "And how is it that you're here and not back in New York?" he asked, wrapping an arm around Schuyler's shoulder.

"Do you know this man, Colonel Hunter?" asked the major in charge of the squad which still encircled Schuyler.

"Would I embrace him if I didn't, Major?" Hunter retorted with a laugh. "Fact is, this is

Schuyler DeWitt and he has personally done as much as any man to arrange the trap we're about to spring on Lord Cornwallis."

The major's brow furrowed. "DeWitt? Isn't that the British spymaster? Major DeWitt?"

"Major Magnus DeWitt is Schuyler's brother. Schuyler was on Clinton's staff, working with his brother, but for us. Thanks to him, we were able to keep Clinton worried about defending New York while we were aiming for Yorktown."

The major looked at Schuyler with awe in his expression, and an embarrassed Schuyler could have stifled his friend John Langley. But now the tall officer from the boat suddenly appeared, a puzzled look on his face at the sight of Schuyler.

John Langley chuckled. "General Washington, this is someone you'll want to meet. Back in New York he had a number, but here—"

Washington smiled brilliantly. "Schuyler DeWitt? Of course! I'm glad to meet you at last." The general offered his hand and Schuyler accepted it and was impressed by the gentle strength in Washington's grip.

"And I to meet you, sir," Schuyler said quietly.

"John Langley has told me much about you and I've admired your work from afar these past years. And appreciated it greatly, I should add. You've been invaluable to me and to our cause. "You'll be amply rewarded when we've ended this war."

"I seek no reward, sir," Schuyler replied. "I've worked for you because I felt you were right in fighting for independence.'

"Nonetheless, you *will* be rewarded, Schuyler. I should think a fitting compensation would be the DeWitt land and business interests, which will no doubt be declared forfeit by the New York legislators because of your brother's and your father's loyalist stance."

Schuyler grinned. "I'm not sure my brother will appreciate that," he said.

"And how is Magnus?" Washington asked warmly. "He's a formidable enemy, and I've long wished he had shared our desire for freedom from the King."

"He's thoroughly unhappy, sir, over your ability to outwit him. But he sends his regards and says to tell you he admires your efforts even if he disagrees with your purpose."

"Yes, that does sound like Magnus. He is well?"

"He's sick over the turn of events, General, but otherwise fine. He allowed me to leave New York in spite of his anger over your Yorktown documents—which did convince him, apparently, that you would strike New York."

"Good. For too long a time he had us confused and we had to rely on intuition in dealing with him. I'm glad he couldn't find enough anger in his heart to do you harm. I'm equally sure he'll never regret his charity."

"I'm eager for the end of this war, General, so that I may again be my brother's good friend."

"Well, perhaps we aren't so very far away from accomplishing that, Schuyler. If all goes well here, the King's advisers will be hard-pressed to continue this conflict. In any event, let's all pray for peace. I've only recently visited my wife after six long years, and she finds me a stranger."

"I hope that John Langley's sister will not find me a stranger, for that's where I'm headed now.'

General Washington again shook Schuyler's

hand. "Go to her, then..We'll meet again, of that I'm certain."

After the general left, Schuyler asked John Langley about Clarissa.

"I visited her not too long ago, Schuyler," Hunter said, "and she begged me to prevail on you to leave New York. She was none too pleased with me when I couldn't do that. I'm certain she won't be too unhappy to see you." He laughed. "Tell her I talked you into coming south, will you? It will restore peace to my troubled family."

"I'll be glad to, John Langley. Have you heard from Deborah Bell? Matthew told me that she's as unhappy with you as Clarissa is with me."

A twinkle appeared in Hunter's eyes. "I fear she's even more so, since I seem to have left her with child."

Schuyler laughed. "You seem not at all displeased, so I'm glad for both of you. Just take care to survive Yorktown so you can return to her."

"If I had a drink in my hand, Schuyler, I would indeed drink to that. Give my love to Clarissa."

A few hours later, Schuyler was shocked when he reached Clarissa's home—or what was left of it. A raiding party of British soldiers had leveled it only a week before Cornwallis was ordered to Yorktown.

To Schuyler's great relief, Clarissa was all right, though presently residing in temporary quarters which had been erected over the stable by her brother and a party of Continental troops. The main house had been burned to the ground by the British.

She cried when she saw Schuyler, and he was so relieved that he could have cried too. For many minutes all they could do was look at each other, kiss and embrace.

Then she told him what had happened. A patrol of Cornwallis's men had paid her a visit and demanded provisions for their army. When Clarissa refused, the provisions had been seized and her property destroyed.

"At least they've done you no personal harm," Schuyler said.

"They might have," Clarissa said, "but for the arrival of a French ship-of-the-line, which had put into port for repairs. They put a party ashore to seek provisions and the French sailors drove off the British before they could burn the stable or do further harm."

Schuyler brought her up to date on what was happening at Yorktown and she asked if the French would stay this time. In the past, she remarked, they had deserted just when they were needed the most.

"De Grasse has promised to stay at least until the middle of October, Clarissa. Let's hope he keeps his word, for Washington's army outnumbers Cornwallis's forces and will surely overwhelm the British here."

"And then? What happens if Washington takes Yorktown? Will he then attack New York and bring this cursed war to an end?"

"Who can tell? It's just possible that Washington won't have to fight in New York again, for a victory here means the British will hold only one small outpost in America and would virtually have to begin a new war. I don't believe England can do that. Not now."

"Oh, Schuyler, I hope you're right, for I'm so tired of this war. I only want to spend my life pleasing you, as you please me."

Their kiss was long and lingering. It ended only when they suddenly became aware that they were entertaining Clarissa's black housekeeper, who had come to straighten up the rooms over the stable.

But Clarissa was in no mood to scold the giggling woman. "I'll straighten up later, Dara," she said.

"Will the mister be stayin'?" the woman asked.

Schuyler replied, a broad smile on his face. "He certainly will, if the lady will have me."

Clarissa kissed him again, heedless of Dara. "The lady will have you, Schuyler. Now and forever!"

14

MATTHEW BELL was not on the scene when Washington took Yorktown on October 19, 1781. Matthew was in New York, stalking Benedict Arnold, who had been withdrawn from Cornwallis's forces just before they dug in at Yorktown. Matthew never caught Arnold, who sailed back to London in December after leading a British force in a bloody massacre and sacking his former home town of New Haven while Yorktown was under siege.

John Langley Hunter, however, was at Washington's side. He was beaming with pride as the British marched out of the fortifications at two o'clock that afternoon, with their colors cased and their band playing a dirge called "The World Turned Upside Down."

Within a month, John Langley rode to New York to where Matthew was camped near White Plains. He had no difficulty persuading Matthew to attend his wedding to Deborah in Wethersfield. Matthew raised an eyebrow when he saw his sister's blooming condition, but made no move for his shotgun.

When they learned that Lord Cornwallis had asked Washington for terms on October 17, Schuyler DeWitt and his bride-to-be had ridden up from Portsmouth. They felt great pride in their country when the British filed out of Yorktown's compounds. Schuyler had later asked Washington for the loan of several prisoners to help in the rebuilding of Clarissa's house. A happy Washington not only granted the request, but detailed a half-dozen prisoners to tear down the Yorktown fortifications to be used for construction materials. Before Christmas of 1781 arrived, a new and more beautiful house had begun to rise from the ashes of Clarissa's old one.

On the day of Yorktown's surrender, Magnus DeWitt was on General Clinton's flagship as it sailed down the Atlantic coast toward the Chesapeake. More than seven thousand soldiers were aboard the twenty-seven ship force—enough to save Yorktown, Clinton was sure. But they were destined to be too late, as Sir Henry learned when they arrived six days later.

The hour of Cornwallis's surrender found both Clinton and his adjutant standing by the rail of the ship, staring toward the American shore miles away. Their eyes met.

"You feel it, too, sir?" Magnus asked.

Clinton nodded. "We're too late. By the time we get there the rebel flag will fly over Yorktown. We can do nothing about it. What's worse is that I fear this loss signals the loss of the entire war."

Magnus said nothing, for there was nothing to say. By itself the loss of so many thousands of fighting men was enormous, but hardly fatal. But after five years of inconclusive battles, five years in which the stubborn rebels lost battles but refused to give up their war, five years in which their brilliant General Washington tricked the British time after time, Yorktown did seem an omen.

Suddenly a thought struck Clinton and he frowned and addressed Magnus again. "Whatever happened to that brother of yours—Schuyler? I don't recall seeing him about recently."

"He's on leave, sir. He's about to marry."

"Well, good for him. A shame he may have to go back to England to settle down."

A wry smile appeared on Magnus's face. If anyone were to be forced to go back to England, it would be himself and Joanna, for a rebel victory was certain to leave him penniless.

But two years later, Magnus learned he was wrong about the war leaving him a pauper.

The last major battle fought by the two enemies had been the Yorktown affair. And on March 4, 1782, the British Parliament had adopted a resolution calling for the end of the war and recognition of the independence of the "revolted colonies." But it was not until September of 1783 that the treaty ending the war was signed in Paris by Benjamin Franklin.

By that time most Tory business interests and real estate holdings had been seized by state governments and redistributed. True to his word, Washington arranged to have the DeWitt interests signed over to Schuyler DeWitt and it was early in October of 1783 that Schuyler and his wife Clarissa journeyed north to DeWitt Manor.

They found Magnus and Joanna DeWitt packing for a sea voyage back to England. Trientje was helping her son and his wife pack, although she had decided to remain in America with her sister in Connecticut.

There was a strained silence in the house when Schuyler and Clarissa walked in. Schuyler broke it by greeting them all, then embracing his mother. He introduced Clarissa to Trientje and left them together while he went in the study with Magnus.

"Well, Magnus," Schuyler said after they had taken the chairs near the fireplace, "you look well."

"I haven't starved," Magnus replied, patting his middle, which had thickened considerably in recent years in spite of his efforts to lose weight. "And you, Schuyler, you couldn't look better. I'm happy for you and your new wife."

"I've missed you, Magnus, and wondered what was to become of you now that the war is over."

"I've an offer to join a firm of solicitors in London," Magnus said. "I'll accept, although I hate the thought of it."

"Why?" Schuyler could see his brother's despondency.

"I suppose because I don't truly wish to leave the colonies . . . America, that is. I do like the territory."

"That *is* an admission, Magnus! You would stay here, even under the rule of the Continental Congress?"

"Yes, even in a free and independent America. It wouldn't be so bad—as long as I didn't have to match wits with John Langley Hunter and George Washington again. Not to mention *you!*"

Schuyler chuckled. "Well, perhaps you'll have to do just that, for I've heard that John Langley is forming a company to ship southern cotton and tobacco to England for General Washington and other southern farmers—in competition with DeWitt Shipping."

Magnus frowned. "What has that to do with me?"

"Nothing, yet everything. I hope that you won't think me presumptuous in believing you would remain here if given a choice. And I am hereby giving you that choice." He handed Magnus a sheaf of papers.

Magnus looked them over and was stunned. "You're turning the DeWitt properties back to my control. They were given to you, yet you give them back to me?"

Schuyler's expression couldn't have shown more affection and hope. "Only half, brother. But enough, I think, to prevent your leaving America. I've never been interested in the shipping company and I prefer Virginia to the North. If you'll agree to run things up here, I can remain with my wife Clarissa and be certain that my interests here will be properly looked after."

Magnus shook his head. "You'd do this for me? In spite of the way things were?"

"I believe you would do no less for me if the situation were reversed, brother. For we *are* brothers. We both love our country, if not in the same way. You could easily have rid yourself of me when you learned of my work for Washington two years ago. Instead, you bid me adieu and let me go to the woman I love. My gratitude was—is—boundless. But I'm not giving you the property because of that. Only because it is right that brothers share." He leaned forward and touched Magnus's hand. "I want you to stay here, Magnus. At DeWitt Manor. I want to have you and Joanna as our guests in our home in Virginia. And I want to bring Clarissa and our children here to see their grandmother, their uncle and their aunt. We're family and always will be."

"I'm overwhelmed, Schuyler. I must tell you how proud our father would be of you. You fought for what you believed, you did it well and honorably." Magnus grinned. "More or less," he added.

"And now," he continued, "you have proven your humanity by your efforts to preserve the DeWitt family interests and the DeWitt family itself. I consider myself fortunate to have such a fine man as a brother."

"War isn't human, Magnus. It's dirty, miserable —wrong. Especially when it pits brother against brother. Let's hope that America may be spared in the future—that our children and grandchildren may live for all time in peace and prosperity. That America at war has become America at peace, forever."

"A noble thought, and one I gladly support. Although I rather doubt war can be avoided forever if your country is to become great."

"Our country, brother," Schuyler corrected.

Magnus grinned. "Indeed," he said. "*Our* country!"

*FIRST IN THE DRAMATIC NEW
FREEDOM FIGHTERS
SERIES:*

Tomahawks
and
Long Rifles

by Jonathan Scofield

*BEGINNING THE SAGA
OF THREE AMERICAN FAMILIES—
AS PASSIONATE AND DIVERSE AS
THE LAND FOR WHICH THEY FIGHT
AND OFTEN DIE ...*

In this blockbuster lead-off novel in the FREEDOM
FIGHTERS series John Langley Hunter, the tall, red-
headed Virginian, fights his first battles with young
Colonel George Washington, loses his child-bride to a
brutal enemy, meets his friend—and rival—Magnus
DeWitt in the climactic battle of the French and Indian
War on the Plains of Abraham—and has a fateful
romantic encounter with the lovely, strong-willed
Deborah Bell of a hardy Connecticut clan.

BE SURE TO READ
TOMAHAWKS AND LONG RIFLES
—ON SALE NOW FROM
DELL/BRYANS

FOURTH IN THE DRAMATIC NEW
FREEDOM FIGHTERS
SERIES:

Guns at Twilight

by Jonathan Scofield

A few short years after the American Rebels had
vanquished the Redcoats and won their hard-earned
freedom from the British monarch, the tables were
turned, and soldiers of the Crown sacked Washington,
and sent President James Madison and his wife Dolly
scurrying across the Potomac.

Youthful Carson DeWitt, despite the royalist machi-
nations of his conniving uncle, Magnus, went to war in
his nation's cause, and despite a romantic scandal that
temporarily lost him his commission, managed to join
his countrymen in a gallant attack against its powerful
enemy—and to find true love in a most unlikely quarter.

DON'T MISS *GUNS AT TWILIGHT* —COMING IN JUNE FROM DELL/BRYANS